"Well, I suppose I should formally introduce myself," she said as she began to unbutton her shirt.

"Especially since the only certain cure for your hypothermia is to share my body heat. But be forewarned, cowboy—I know how to gracefully approach middle age. My thirty-year-old body isn't in as good a shape as yours."

Her shirt hit the floor and was immediately followed by her bra. "Anyway, I'm Charity Wells. I'm a doctor. My specialty is emergency medicine."

She unzipped her jeans and tossed them onto the pile of clothes on the floor. Next she leaned over to slip her heavy kneesocks down her calves. Then she straightened, sucked in a deep breath and let it out slowly as she stepped to the edge of the bed.

"Well, Mr. Burke, ready or not, here I come, and my satin bikini undies are staying on." She gazed down into his handsome face and gently brushed the tumbled locks of hair off his broad forehead. "And, cowboy," she said huskily, "I *will* respect you in the morning."

Dear Reader,

If you're looking for an extra-special reading experience—something rich and memorable, something deeply emotional, something totally romantic—your search is over! For in your hands you hold one of Silhouette's extremely **Special Editions**.

Dedicated to the proposition that *not* all romances are created equal, Silhouette **Special Edition** aims to deliver the best and the brightest in women's fiction—six books each month by such stellar authors as Nora Roberts, Lynda Trent, Tracy Sinclair and Ginna Gray, along with some dazzling new writers destined to become tomorrow's romance stars.

Pick and choose among titles if you must—we hope you'll soon equate all Silhouette **Special Editions** with consistently gratifying romance reading.

And don't forget the two Silhouette *Classics* at your bookseller's each month—reissues of the most beloved Silhouette **Special Editions** and Silhouette *Intimate Moments* of yesteryear.

Today's bestsellers, tomorrow's *Classics*—that's Silhouette **Special Edition**. We hope you'll stay with us in the months to come, because month after month, we intend to become more special than ever.

From all the authors and editors of Silhouette **Special Edition**,
Warmest wishes,

Leslie Kazanjian
Senior Editor

ALLYSON RYAN
Moon and Sun

Silhouette Special Edition

Published by Silhouette Books New York

America's Publisher of Contemporary Romance

With love to

Linda Lucas, whose eager encouragement,
warm friendship and contagious laughter
carried me from page one to the end.

And in memory of

Mister, my best friend
for fourteen years. May your eternity be filled
with playful romps through gentle snowdrifts.

SILHOUETTE BOOKS
300 East 42nd St., New York, N.Y. 10017

ISBN: 0-373-09460-4

First Silhouette Books printing June 1988

Printed in the U.S.A.

Books by Allyson Ryan

Silhouette Special Edition

Love Can Make It Better #398
Moon and Sun #460

ALLYSON RYAN

loves reading, people-watching and traveling.
Starting in Colorado and working her way across the
country, she finally settled in Pennsylvania with her
husband and their four beloved cats. She attributes
seventeen years of marital bliss to her husband's
uncanny ability to remember their anniversary—one
day after the eldest cat's birthday.

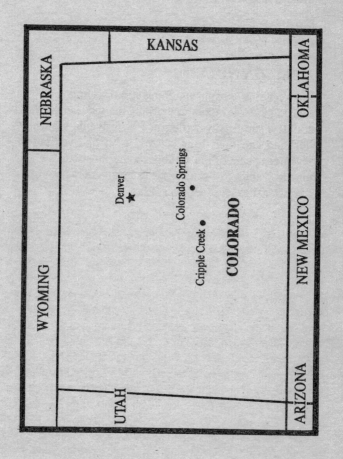

Chapter One

It was ten o'clock at night and ten above zero with a wind-chill factor of twenty below in Colorado's high mountain range. The ice beneath Shane Burke's feet made an ominous cracking noise. Cautiously he tried to move off the surface he'd just stepped onto, but there was another cracking noise. Before he could blink, he was lying full-length in an ice-cold pond.

He leaped to his feet and stumbled out of the water, cursing when he realized his compass now resided somewhere in the shallows of the mountain pond. He glared at the water—a night-black contrast against the white glow of ice and snow—and shivered violently as a bitter wind swept over him.

He moved along the perimeter of the pond, inwardly railing at himself for having assumed it would have been frozen solid. Winter had come late this year, with far too many days having temperatures in the forties and fifties. He should have been more cautious, should have known there was a good chance the ice wouldn't hold him.

He cursed once more as he admitted that as usual his manager, Roger, had been right. He'd been a fool to try to make it to his cabin on the eve of a blizzard, but he had needed solitude—a break from the demanding schedule of his concert tour. However, having his truck break down in the middle of nowhere was pushing solitude a bit too far.

He knew that the first rule of survival was never leave your vehicle in an emergency, but then the prologue to that rule was to always be prepared for an emergency. He'd been so anxious to reach the cabin before the storm hit that he hadn't even thrown a flashlight or a blanket into the truck.

After breaking those rules, he'd proceeded to break another: never leave a main road. Getting lost in the Rocky Mountains in summer was dangerous. Getting lost in them in winter was suicide. Normally he never would have left the road, but he had seen the roof of a cabin when he'd driven through this area last summer. Its presence had stuck in his mind, because he hadn't seen a road leading into it and he'd wondered how the owners reached it.

Instinct had told him the cabin was near, and he'd decided to follow his instincts rather than try to make the torturous five-mile uphill trek to his own cabin. He'd given himself an hour. If he hadn't found the cabin by then, he'd use his compass to get back to the road.

Then he'd gotten tired of wading through snowdrifts that hit him at midcalf and had stepped onto the surface of the icy pond, hoping to give his aching leg muscles a needed rest. Yes, that had definitely been his worst mistake, he decided. He'd not only lost his compass, but he was soaking wet.

Only minutes had passed since his accidental dunking, and already his legs were numb, his feet nonexistent, and his hands a mass of painful, frozen nerve endings. The cloud cover hadn't lifted, so he couldn't use the stars in place of his compass. With a resigned sigh, he admitted the obvious. He was lost, and if he didn't find shelter soon, he'd be dead.

He topped the craggy peak he'd been trying to climb, fell to his knees, and peered into the valley below him, afraid to believe that it was really light he saw on the other side of a stand of towering pines. Certain it was a mirage, he closed his eyes. But when he opened them the light remained, and he sighed in relief. Despite his encounter with the pond, his instincts to leave the road had been right. He had found the cabin.

He pushed himself back to his feet and began his descent, refusing to acknowledge the dizziness in his head as he struggled to walk through each new snowbank that lay in his path. All he had to do was maintain consciousness a few more minutes and he'd be safe.

When he was halfway down the mountain, his legs gave out. He rolled several yards before colliding with a sturdy evergreen tree. He stared dazedly at the thick branches rubbing against his chest, drew in a painful breath, and rolled onto his stomach. Wearily he crawled from beneath the tree and into a small meadow, where he collapsed. The cabin was just on the other side of the trees. He could afford to rest for a minute. Just a minute, he vowed seconds before he lapsed into unconsciousness.

Charity Wells shivered as she cracked open the door, peered into the darkness and whistled. There was no response to the whistle, so she called out, "Come on, Mister! Come on, boy!" Nothing.

"Darn dog," she grumbled, slamming the door closed and reaching for the navy-blue parka that hung on the old-fashioned coatrack. "Here it is, after ten at night, and I have to go out and look for a stupid dog. I should let him freeze," she continued in an irritated monologue. "Senility is setting in fast when he doesn't have enough brains to come in out of the cold. Darn dog," she repeated as she kicked off her slippers and slid her stockinged feet into a pair of rubber galoshes. She lit the fluorescent lantern standing beside the door and carried it onto the porch of her mountain cabin.

Her down parka provided little comfort against the bitter, wailing wind, and she set the lantern down as she stuffed her hands into her pockets and whistled a second time. Still nothing.

She sucked in an impatient breath and immediately regretted it. The air was so cold she could have been inhaling icicles. Her bare hands went numb in the few seconds it took her to secure the parka's fur-lined hood over her hair and thrust them back into her pockets.

Her next pet was definitely going to be a cat, she decided as she leaned her head back and bellowed, "Mister!" Cats used litter boxes and had enough sense to curl up in front of a warm fire on nights like this.

Finally, she was rewarded with a yap and a whine, and she frowned at the small black-and-white party poodle that appeared at the edge of the stand of pines beside the cabin, his long ungroomed hair sporting clumps of frozen snow.

"Get over here, you ungrateful cur," she ordered. "Every time I let you out the door, you decide to play snowman and come back in to melt all over my hardwood floors." Mister yapped and headed back into the trees. "Mister, come here!"

The dog returned and whined before racing back. This time Charity's frown was one of concern. Mister might be lacking in brain matter, but normally he was obedient. Evidently he'd discovered something he wanted her to see.

"This had better be worth it," she said, sliding the lantern over her arm and trudging across the frozen snow. She cursed loudly and vehemently when the surface crust gave way and her foot sank through a snowdrift, burying her leg up to the knee.

"One dead dog coming right up," she announced purposefully as she tugged her leg out of the drift and continued walking in the direction the dog had taken.

Once she entered the darkness of the stand of pines, she hesitated. The wailing wind blotted out all other sound. The small circle of light provided by the lantern made everything around her take on an eerie glow. She giggled nervously and started humming the opening bars of the *Twilight Zone.*

"You're as loony tunes as that dumb dog," she scolded herself, deciding that if she had any common sense, she'd call Mister back and haul him bodily into the cabin.

But lately she hadn't been exercising much common sense. She'd go crazy if she didn't find out what had captured Mister's attention. She decided, however, that his days would be numbered if all this hullabaloo turned out to be nothing more than a rabbit hole.

The dog's shaggy tresses had cut a wide, easy-to-follow trail through the snow, and Charity let out a weary sigh. He'd be covered with the white stuff from head to foot and melting all over the cabin.

Up ahead, the trail veered off to the right. The wind died for a moment, and she could hear Mister whining insistently. She rounded a clump of bramble bushes and froze.

"Oh, my God!" she exclaimed in disbelief.

Mister yapped excitedly, raced toward her, and then raced back to the six-feet-plus body stretched face down on the ground. The seemingly frozen man had white frost for hair, and what she could see of his handsome, ruggedly chiseled face had a blue tinge.

Her years of medical training instantly took over, and Charity raced to his side. She set the lantern on the ground, dropped to her knees and pressed her hand to the side of his neck. She heaved a sigh of relief when she discovered a pulse. It was weak and thready, but he was alive.

She slid her gaze critically down his length. There was no odd twisting of limbs, but that didn't guarantee no broken bones. With her hands she began to explore his long, muscular legs and his equally muscular arms.

There were no breaks evident, so she gingerly rolled him to his back, cursing the fact that he was two-hundred-plus pounds of dead weight. She shuddered at the unintentional pun. It wouldn't have been much longer in this bitterly cold weather before he would have literally been dead weight.

Lifting the lantern toward his face with one hand, she pushed back his frosted eyelid with the other and a brilliant blue eye reacted to the entrance of light, indicating he was not in a coma but very near consciousness.

She placed the lantern back on the ground, cradled his beard-stubbled cheeks between her hands, and began to slap them lightly. "Come on, cowboy, open your eyes for me. You're going to have to wake up." Mister added a yap of encouragement to her determined order. "Open those eyes for me, cowboy. You're way too big for me to carry. I have to have your help to get you out of here. Come on. Open those eyes. Now!"

Her forceful exclamation must have reached him, because there was an instantaneous fluttering of his frozen lashes. Even though Charity had already determined the color of his eyes, she hadn't been prepared for the impact of the pair of stunning sky-blue orbs gazing up at her.

His blue-tinged lips parted, and Charity had to lean close to hear his hoarse whisper. "I guess Mom was wrong. I did go to heaven."

With an amused smile, Charity said, "Sorry, but your angel wings will have to go back into storage. You're still very firmly earthbound." Then she sobered. "Were you in an accident? Are you injured? I have to get you out of here, but before I do, I need to know whether or not it's safe to move you."

"I can't feel anything," he answered.

"That's probably due to exposure," she stated reassuringly. "Once we get your circulation started up again, you'll get your feeling back. Can you tell me what happened? How did you get here?"

"Truck broke down. Started walking," Shane said between painful wheezes. "I fell into a pond. The water was *so* cold."

Charity grew more concerned. When she'd checked for broken bones, she'd noticed that his clothes had felt stiff—as if caked with ice. Now she knew why. She also knew that his body temperature would be dropping dramatically. If she didn't get him back to the cabin, he'd die from hypothermia.

"We have to get you on your feet. Let's sit you up, and we'll work from there."

"Okay."

But as agreeable as he was, sitting him up didn't prove to be easy. His impressively wide chest appeared to carry a good portion of his two-hundred-plus pounds, and he was too weak to provide much assistance. Once she had him raised to a sitting position, she crouched behind him and let him rest his weight against her.

"I'm dizzy," he whispered.

"That's because your blood's starting to circulate again. It'll go away in a minute. Just relax."

"Okay," he answered weakly, and leaned his head back against her.

She checked his pulse once again and was pleased to discover it was already stronger.

"Are you still dizzy?"

"No. I'm sleepy."

"That's the cold working its deadly magic spell," she stated grimly. "Try to sit up by yourself."

He nodded and eased himself away from her. She sat poised, ready to support him again when he swayed unsteadily, but he managed to remain upright.

Charity gnawed on her bottom lip as she tried to figure out a way to get him into a standing position. It would have helped if he'd conveniently collapsed beside a sturdy tree. Her five-feet-five-inch, 106-pound frame wouldn't give him enough leverage, and it certainly didn't provide her with the muscle power to lift him. She was going to have to find another way.

She searched the clearing for a solution and smiled triumphantly when she spied a large broken branch protruding from the depths of the frozen snow. She rose to her feet to retrieve it.

She moved back to his side, frowning at the glassy look in his eyes. His breathing was shallow and labored, and he seemed oblivious to her presence. Squatting down in front of him, she patted his cheek until he blinked and managed to focus on her.

A ghost of a smile played across his lips as he whispered, "You're pretty."

She chuckled. "Thank you. I'd return the compliment, but I'm afraid all I can say is you're a very interesting shade of blue. What I want you to do is hold on to this stick." She poked the stick down into the snow beside him and tested it to make certain it was secure. Then she wrapped his hand around it and instructed, "I'm going to get on your other side. I want you to put your arm around my shoulders. Between me and the stick, you should have enough leverage to push yourself to your feet. Do you understand what I'm saying?"

"Yes."

It took them four tries, but he finally managed to stand upright. Charity almost lost him when he fell heavily against her. Sheer adrenaline gave her enough strength to balance them both, and she gazed up at him worriedly. In the lantern light, she could see that some color had returned to his face, but his breathing was still shallow and his eyes were still glazed. She nearly lost him a second time when she bent slightly to slide the handle of the lantern over her arm.

"Feet numb," he informed her.

"I know," she soothed, praying the numbness was not from frostbite. "But we'll soon have them working again."

Now that his circulation was being restored, he was assaulted with shivers that quaked his entire body. His teeth began to chatter uncontrollably, and Charity gave him a sympathetic smile. "Come on, cowboy, let's get you home and into bed."

Unbelievably, she saw humor brighten his eyes. "Yeah, b-but will you re-respect me in the mor-morning?"

Charity laughed. "You're a real stand-up comic, but I'd suggest you try that line when you can do it on your own two feet."

"I—I'll d-do th-that."

Their progress was slow with his arm draped across her shoulders and the majority of his weight on her. Shivers continued to assail him, causing him to stumble frequently. Charity muttered a prayer of thanks when the end of the trees came into sight. His body might be frozen, but hers was drenched in sweat from the effort of half carrying a man who was more than double her own weight. Mister had raced ahead and stood waiting at the door for their arrival. It seemed to take forever for them to cross the last hundred feet to the porch. Then they were up the stairs and inside with the door closed firmly behind them.

Charity guided the man toward her bed, which was nestled in the far corner of her one-room cabin. She let out a gasp of surprise when he stumbled, tumbling them both down onto the soft mattress. She landed on her back while his long length stretched over her. His dazed blue eyes were staring down into her face as if he was surprised to discover her beneath him, but before Charity could ask him to move, he lapsed back into unconsciousness.

With a long, wavering sigh, Charity tried to push his weight off her. When she couldn't budge him, she wriggled until she was able to ease herself from beneath him.

After she'd regained her feet she automatically reached out to check his pulse. It was strong and steady. He was still shivering, however, and she rolled him onto his back once again.

She let her hands drift over his face, exploring the interesting configuration of planes and hollows. His long, patrician nose, high, prominent cheekbones and square jawline appeared to have escaped frostbite.

Although she was certain the remainder of his vulnerable areas were also unscathed, she still removed his wet leather gloves and examined his long callused fingers before removing his equally sodden boots and socks and studying his toes. Her examination revealed that he had indeed miraculously escaped the affliction.

Assured that there'd be no need for the slow rewarming process required for the treatment of frostbite, she lifted his lean hips enough to remove his wallet. She flipped it open to discover his identity. When she saw his driver's license, she let out an appreciative sigh at the sight of the blond-haired, blue-eyed Adonis who vaguely resembled the rumpled stranger sleeping in her bed.

"It looks like you thaw out pretty nice," she said, tossing his wallet to the top of the nightstand after a quick survey of his vital statistics.

She shrugged out of her parka. Chafing her cold hands together to warm them, she crossed to the coatrack and hung her coat on a hook before turning to scowl at Mister, who was lying in front of the fireplace and defrosting all over her hearth.

"Why couldn't you have brought home a stick, like any decent dog?" she asked. Mister whined and thumped his stubby tail against the floor. "Yeah, take this cavalierly," she told him. "For all we know, this man is an ax murderer." Mister whined again as he rested his head on his paws, looking properly chastised, and Charity gave a resigned shake of her head as she crossed back to the man who was attempting to shiver himself to death in her bed.

"The best thing for you would be a hot shower, but you're not going to cooperate and wake up, are you?" she asked.

The unconscious man's answer was a chattering of teeth as his body curled into a fetal position in search of warmth. His tawny mane of hair was enchantingly disheveled around his strong, rugged features. His long lashes—tipped silver from exposure to the sun—rested against cheeks flushed with feverish color. Charity rested her hand against his forehead. Despite the color in his cheeks, his flesh was almost frigid beneath her touch, and she began to release the buttons on his sheepskin-lined leather coat.

"You know," she told him as she struggled to free one brawny arm from the jacket, "if I'd enjoyed undressing people, I'd have had a whole litter of kids."

His other arm came out somewhat more easily after she'd managed to drag the coat from beneath him, and she went to work on the buttons of his green-and-black-checked wool shirt.

"Don't you know you're supposed to have a little subcutaneous fat to keep you warm?" she asked as she parted his shirt to reveal white thermal underwear molded intimately to a wide muscular chest. The shirt also proved to be difficult to remove, but it soon joined his coat on the floor.

She hesitated when her gaze landed on the large silver buckle at his trim waist. There was something so innately masculine about this man that she was tempted to tuck him under the covers, wet clothes and all.

But the healing side of her nature was much too strong, and she ignored the impulse and reached for the buckle. "According to your driver's license, cowboy, you're almost thirty-six. Didn't anyone ever tell you that when you're fast approaching middle age, you're supposed to start developing a paunch? No self-respecting man keeps himself in shape at your age. You should be ashamed of yourself!"

She released his belt buckle and grimaced when the zipper on his pants rasped harshly as she lowered it. "I sure do hope your wife appreciates what I'm doing. It'll be just my luck that she's already pulled out the life-insurance policy and is planning on how to spend it. Then I'll end up stuck with you forever because she won't want to give up the money."

His jeans hit the floor with a thud. Reluctantly, she eyed the lower half of his long underwear. It fitted as intimately as the upper half, and she tentatively touched both the top and the bottom, hoping against hope that they'd be dry. They weren't.

"How can you still be shivering when it's so darn hot in here?" she complained, running a finger around the collar of her blue flannel shirt, refusing to admit that it wasn't the fire in the fireplace that was creating her discomfort. "You're probably one of these people wasting our fuel supplies by keeping your furnace set at seventy-five degrees."

Her fingers trembled when she pulled the upper portion of his thermal underwear from the elasticized waistband. "If you aren't scarred and war torn beneath this underwear, I'm going to hate you," she warned. "What you're doing to my libido is downright criminal, and I want you to know that my brother is an attorney. It won't cost me a penny to sue you for damages and... Oh, my!" she exclaimed when she tugged the top high enough to get a perfect view of his wide chest, covered in a thick tangle of crisp tawny curls.

She closed her eyes, sucked in a deep breath and firmly informed her fingers that they could not go walking through that forest of hair. They were still arguing with her when she opened her eyes. Unfortunately, his chattering teeth and the gooseflesh that had sprung up when the cooler room air struck his bare chest didn't detract from his masculinity at all.

Her monologue ceased as she once again struggled with his powerful arms, finally freeing them from the sleeves of the thermal underwear and the white T-shirt he wore beneath it. A couple of tugs freed his head, and the upper portion of his underwear joined the growing pile of clothes on the floor.

"I'm a doctor, you know," she stated as she slipped her fingers beneath the elastic at his waist. "Everything you've got, I've seen thousands, maybe even millions, of times before. The male body is just a piece of anatomy to me. Doesn't faze me at all.''

Despite her words of bravado, she closed her eyes as she slid the thermal underwear and what felt suspiciously like a pair of jockey shorts down over his hips. She didn't open them again until she felt her fingers brush against his knees.

"Damn you!" she said irritably. "You could have at least had knobby knees. I've been up in these woods all by myself for a month. When you're suffering from a nervous breakdown, you don't exactly have tons of company hanging around. Do you have any idea how I've longed for a pair of good strong arms around me?'' she asked as the remainder of his underwear hit the floor.

She placed her hands on her hips and tapped the toe of her booted foot impatiently. "Now you're going to just lie there and make me look at you in all your naked, glorious splendor, aren't you?''

Of course he didn't answer, and she reluctantly let her gaze settle on his long, gracefully arched feet, then his finely boned ankles, which flowed into a pair of perfectly shaped calves. His knees, as she'd already noted, were molded to perfection and joined to a pair of sexy muscular thighs covered with the same fine golden hairs dusting the rest of his legs.

Her gaze continued to move upward, but she avoided the sight of his manhood by forcing her eyes to skirt to the outer curve of a narrow hip. There was a gentle, almost imperceptible, dip into his firm waistline that began to flare outward until it widened into that magnificent chest.

Once again her attention was held by the provocative tangle of crisp golden curls, and it was inevitable that her eyes were able to convince her they just had to follow that slim arrow of hair that trailed in a tantalizing path down his taut stomach. It widened again into a thick triangle of hair low on his hips that was a shade darker than the sun-bleached hair on his head.

"Oh, boy," she whispered, raising a hand to wipe away the beads of perspiration forming on her brow.

A convulsive shiver ripped through his body, snapping her out of her sensual fascination. With a recriminating shake of her head, she reached out to roll him once again so she could pull the covers from beneath his weight.

"Uncooperative to the last," she sighed as she struggled to retrieve the quilts and top sheet. Then with one last brief but all-encompassing flick of her eyes over his laudable physique, she settled him beneath the covers.

"Well, I suppose I should formally introduce myself," she said as she began to unbutton her shirt. "Especially since the only certain cure for your hypothermia is to share my body heat. But be forewarned, cowboy—I know how to gracefully approach middle age. My thirty-year-old body isn't in as good a shape as yours."

Her shirt hit the floor and was immediately followed by her bra. "Anyway, I'm Charity Wells. As I said earlier, I'm a doctor. My specialty is emergency medicine."

She gave a rueful shake of her head as she unzipped her jeans. "At least it was until a couple of months ago. I was on duty in the emergency room when the cops brought in a kid flying high on drugs. The next thing I knew, this poor kid had pulled a knife, and would you like to guess who was standing on the other end of it?"

She paused in her undressing and shook her head again. "Yeah, you've got it right. It was me. I'd never been a hostage before, and I can assure you, I don't look forward to ever being one again. It took that kid thirty-two hours to collapse, and after I admitted him, I sat down behind my desk, burst into tears, and didn't stop crying for two weeks. Then, when I tried to walk back into the emergency room, I couldn't do it. Everywhere I looked, I saw that kid and his knife, and I panicked.

"A classic case of burnout, I've been told. Take a vacation, everyone said. So I packed my suitcase, tossed it and Mister into my car and headed up here to think."

She frowned thoughtfully as she lowered the zipper on her jeans. "They say your life flashes before your eyes when you're in imminent danger of meeting your maker, but you know, cowboy, you've got to have a life before it can flash before your eyes."

Her jeans landed on top of the pile of clothes on the floor as she said, "Fortunately for me, I was given more time, and I'm going to finally have a life. I just haven't decided what kind of life I'm going to have. But whatever it is, it has to be better than the one I've been leading the last few years."

She leaned over to slip her heavy knee socks down her calves. Then she straightened, sucked in a deep breath and let it out slowly as she stepped to the edge of the bed.

"Well, Mr. Shane Burke, ready or not, here I come, and my satin bikini undies are staying on." She gazed down into his handsome face and gently brushed the tumbled locks of hair off his broad forehead. "And, cowboy," she said huskily, "I will respect you in the morning."

It was amazing to Charity how, even in an unconscious state, the human body automatically responded to the closeness of another human body. As soon as she crawled between the sheets, the man's strong arms wrapped around her to pull her close.

She shifted, allowing her soft curves to mold to his harder ones in order to help his trembling body warm. With a contented sigh that a child might heave, he nestled his head against her bosom.

His deep, even breathing assured Charity that he'd performed the act as naturally and innocently as a newborn babe, and a smile curved her lips as she gently stroked his hair.

She stared at the ceiling while she went through a list of all the dangers this man could be presenting. He could be a vicious criminal who had performed a hundred sordid deeds, but instinct told her the man wasn't dangerous. His clothes were expensive, as was the slim gold watch that still encircled his wrist. Besides, the Hippocratic oath she'd taken six years ago hadn't made a distinction between good and bad. A life was a life, and she was sworn to do everything in her power to save it.

She yawned as she told herself that she would remain in bed only until he was warm. But minutes later she was as sound asleep as the stranger she held in her arms.

Chapter Two

Mm," Shane murmured in pleasure and fought against waking from the delicious dream. The soft curves of a woman were pressed against him. His hand was drifting over skin that was a magical combination of velvet and satin. He sighed, reveling in his body's response—more a gentle declaration of manhood than a bold arousal.

It had been years since he'd had a dream like this, and he'd *never* had one this deliciously vivid. All his senses were functioning at their peak. He could smell her perfumed fragrance, hear her soft breathing, and feel her heart beating against his chest. There was no way he was going to wake up, he told his stirring consciousness as he let his hand slide back over that wonderful skin.

His eyes snapped open in disbelief when his dream woman purred and slid a silken thigh up the inside of his own hair-roughened one. He blinked exactly three times, but the tumbled mane of shimmering raven hair and the delicately chiseled heart-shaped face sleeping next to him on the pillow didn't go away.

He lowered his gaze and gulped. The covers had slid off her, giving him a perfect view of her slim body, which was clad only in a pair of pink satin bikini panties. He flicked his tongue across his lips as he chastised himself for his blatant voyeurism, but that didn't stop him from allowing himself a slow assessing look.

Her roseate-peaked breasts were small but in perfect proportion to the rest of her small frame. His hand gleamed in dark contrast against the alabaster of her skin as it rested in the feminine curve of her waist, spanning more than half of it. Her hips were softly rounded, and her shapely legs seemed to go on forever.

He tried to recall how he'd gotten into her bed, but his memory was such a hazy blur that he couldn't make any sense out of it. He was, however, sure of one thing. She had saved his life.

She purred again as she snuggled closer, and Shane caught his breath. Her breasts were pressed against his chest, and he could feel the gentle nudging of her nipples. He swallowed hard as he tried to control his body's involuntary response, but the swallow was to no avail.

He frowned as he tried to figure out a way to get out of bed without waking her, but her legs were tangled with his and she was firmly settled on his arm. He almost groaned aloud when he felt her thigh move against his. It was then that he decided enough was enough. He was a man, not a saint, and if he didn't disengage himself from her embrace immediately, he'd end up proving just how much of a man he was. He sat up.

Charity let out a groan of protest when she was tumbled from the cocoon of warmth surrounding her. She rolled to her stomach and pulled the pillow over her head, murmuring, "In a minute, boy," as Mister whined and nudged his cold nose against her arm, declaring his need for a morning walk.

She let out a gasp of surprise when a deep baritone said, "I'll let him out."

All the events of last night came rushing in. She was mortified to realize she'd fallen asleep and was lying in bed almost naked with a definitely naked man. Cautiously she lifted the pillow and gulped when her eyes focused on a familiar golden chest. Color flared into her cheeks when her gaze dropped to his waist. The covers were tangled around his hips, but she knew exactly what they hid. Her blush deepened when he tossed a sheet over her before he reached out to remove the pillow from her head.

"Morning," Shane said, feeling jolted when he found himself gazing into sleepy, exotically tilted green eyes.

"Uh, good morning," Charity answered hoarsely while she nervously pushed her hair away from her eyes and wondered how he could look and sound so casual under the circumstances. However, if he could handle this awkward situation with such decorum, she could, too. "How are you feeling? When I found you last night you were hypothermic, and I had to—"

"Undress me and share your body heat," he finished gallantly when another blush brightened her cheeks. "And in answer to your question, I'm a little sore, but, thanks to you, I'm alive."

Charity frowned as she watched him gingerly touch a large bruise along his rib cage. She hadn't noticed the bruise last night.

"How did you get that?" she asked, levering herself up on her elbows, her embarrassment immediately replaced with medical concern.

Shane's gaze was drawn to her exposed shoulders, and he resisted the urge to touch them as he recalled the texture of her skin. Forcing his attention back on her face, he shrugged. "I fell down the mountain and hit a tree."

"You'd better let me look at it. You may have cracked some ribs."

Before Shane could assure her he was fine, she sat up beside him. Holding the sheet over her breasts with one hand, she expertly examined his ribs with the other.

"Does it hurt when you breathe?"

"No," Shane answered, wondering if he would be able to feel any pain with this exquisitely tiny woman hovering so close.

He watched her long, slender fingers, which were moving over him with practiced ease. Her nails weren't long or lacquered, like those of the women he was used to seeing. He found their simplicity refreshingly attractive and had to fight the urge to squirm as she gently palpated the area around the bruise.

When she leaned toward him so she could see the bruise more closely, her silken hair brushed against his chest and Shane drew in a sharp breath.

Charity glanced up at him, her brow furrowed. "That hurts?"

"Only when I laugh," he responded in an attempt at dry humor, thinking that it definitely hurt, but not in the manner to which she referred. "Anyone watching you would think you were a doctor."

Charity smiled as she continued her examination. "They'd be right. Take another deep breath and let it out slowly."

Shane breathed in and out whenever she instructed, but the woman's closeness was beginning to wear on his nerves. Whenever she moved, the sheet tightened around her, providing him with a provocative outline of her body. When she ordered him to take still another deep breath, he gave a determined shake of his head. She might be a doctor, but she was still a woman, and it was to the woman that he was responding. Didn't she realize what she was doing to him?

He could tell by her concentrated expression that she didn't, and he knew it was time to place some distance between them. "You can stop now. I'm fine. Do you want me to let the dog out?"

The tense edge to his voice made Charity glance up in surprise, and she swallowed when she realized that it wasn't pain reflected in the depths of his eyes. She jerked her hand away from his ribs as if she were burned and scooted nervously toward the edge of the bed. She gulped when his eyes caught and held hers.

For a moment she was frightened, but as he continued to gaze into her eyes, she knew instinctively he wouldn't harm her. He was aroused, but what man wouldn't be if he found himself in bed with an unclothed woman? Why hadn't she had the common sense to get up and get dressed before she'd started examining him?

"You're hardly dressed for a jaunt to the door," she said, her gaze dropping as if to prove her point.

He glanced down at the covers tangled at his waist. "I suppose I'm not. Where are my clothes?"

"They're on the floor, but they're still wet."

"Oh."

She waited for him to turn away so she could get up, but he just continued to sit there, staring at her with an odd expression.

"I need to get up," she said, and when he still didn't turn away, she added, "I need some privacy."

"Of course," Shane said, snapped out of his reverie, in which he was indulging himself in the memory of when he'd first awakened with this woman lying in his arms. Only now, as he stared into her big green eyes, he wasn't so sure he should have decided to be a gentleman. "Sorry."

He dropped back against the pillows and put his arm over his eyes.

Charity quickly climbed out of bed and grabbed her short terry-cloth robe, which rested on a nearby chair. The sooner she put some distance between them the better, she decided as she pulled it on with shaking hands. She refused to ad-

mit that when her fear had fled, it had been replaced with
the warm sparks of desire.

Shane lifted his arm and watched her. Just what had he
gotten himself into this time? he wondered, giving a deri-
sive shake of his head as he took in the gentle lines of her
back, her softly rounded hips, her long legs as she slipped
into the robe and belted it at her waist.

His eyes remained glued to one shapely thigh as she made
her way to the door. He'd always been a leg man, and the
pair she trotted around on would have brought life to a dead
man. What they were doing to him would probably cripple
him for life!

He shifted uncomfortably beneath the covers, placed his
arm back over his eyes and reminded himself that he had
come to the mountains for a few days' rest and recupera-
tion. The reminder didn't ease his desire, but it did give him
enough emotional stamina to ignore it.

Charity let Mister out, too aware of the man behind her
to take much notice of the snow falling outside. She entered the bath, performed a quick morning toilette and
brushed her hair, wondering how long it would take her to
get Shane Burke out of her cabin. An hour at the least—two
at the most—but she'd try to accomplish the task as quickly
as possible. She'd wash and dry his clothes, bundle him into
her car, and drive him into Cripple Creek. She was up here
to think, not to ogle a gorgeous man, and the faster she got
rid of him, the faster she'd get back to her problems.

By the time she walked out of the bath, she'd regained
control of her jumbled nerves, but she didn't risk a glance
toward Shane as she moved toward the pile of clothes beside the bed.

"What does your wife normally feed you for breakfast?" she asked as she retrieved his clothes from the floor
and carried them to the apartment-sized washer and dryer
next to the kitchen sink.

"Since I don't have a wife, nothing."

"You're not married?" she questioned in surprise, automatically glancing over her shoulder to look at him.

The picture he presented made her catch her breath. He was sprawled on the bed, the covers still tangled around his waist and one arm pillowed behind his head, with its tousled golden hair. He looked like a replete lion—very satisfied and very predatory.

"I never found a woman with enough patience to put up with me. By the way, what's your name?"

"Charity. Charity Wells."

"Thank you for saving my life, Dr. Charity Wells."

"You're welcome," she answered, quickly returning her attention to his clothes. He'd offered his gratitude in a husky, sexy whisper that had vibrated through her, causing an alarming surge of feminine awareness.

"I'm Shane Burke."

"I know. I looked at your driver's license. Would you like to take a shower?"

Shane was surprised—and even a little wounded—that his name hadn't elicited more than a neutral response, but then maybe the woman didn't recognize it. Not everyone enjoyed rock music, he reminded himself, and even if they did, they didn't always know the names of the singers. Many people—particularly those Charity's age—knew the names of only the groups they liked.

He started to tell her who he was but stopped. He was fed up with teenage groupies and hangers-on who were hoping some of his fame would rub off on them. It would be nice to spend some time with a woman who knew him only as a man and not as a celebrity.

Yes, he decided, being unrecognized could work to his advantage. For once he could have a normal conversation. He only hoped he hadn't been away from normal conversations for so long that he'd sound like a fool.

"I think I will take a shower. Do you happen to have a razor? I'm afraid a beard does nothing for me."

Charity doubted that. Nothing could detract from the man's masculinity. She laid his clothes aside. "I have some disposable razors. Let me get you one and some clean towels."

"Okay."

She retrieved those items from the small closet next to the bath, refraining from glancing over her shoulder as she listened to the bed creak as he rose from it. When she was certain he'd had enough time to cover himself, she turned to face him.

"Your razor and towels."

He gave her a grateful smile. "Thanks."

"You're welcome."

He walked toward her with an unconscious, swaggering grace that made her curl her bare toes against the floor. The quilt he'd wrapped around his waist didn't do a thing to control her vivid imagination.

"It's snowing outside," she said in an effort to force her attention away from his magnificent body.

"I guess that means the blizzard has moved in."

"Blizzard?"

He nodded as he removed the razor and towels from her hands, delicious little sparks shooting up her arms as their fingers brushed. She was thankful he didn't seem aware of his effect on her as he said, "It's predicted to be the worst blizzard Colorado's had in fifty years. I'm afraid that means I'm going to be stuck here until it's over."

"Stuck here until it's over?"

"I hope you don't mind."

"Mind?"

"I'm the perfect houseguest. You won't even know I'm here."

"Oh, boy," Charity whispered as she watched him cross to the bath, knowing she'd be very aware that he was here. He was so big he would dominate her cabin.

"You'd better let your dog in," he said as he turned in the doorway and winked at her. "It sounds like he's ready to tear the door down."

She nodded dumbly and stood staring at the door he'd closed behind him. When she heard the shower turn on, she shook her head. "Oh, boy," she repeated as she walked to the front door and let Mister back in, verifying the fact that the snow she'd seen drifting down was not a normal storm.

Charity found herself humming along with the musical baritone singing in the shower. "Love Is a Many Splendored Thing" had never been on her list of favorites, but for some reason it had a special ring to it this morning.

She measured soap and dry bleach into the washing machine, separated Shane's jockey shorts and undershirt from his long underwear and eyed them curiously. It had been a long time since she'd handled intimate male apparel, and she had the most ridiculous urge to hug his undergarments to her chest.

"You really have lost your mind, Charity Anne," she said as she stuffed his underwear into the washer and dropped his heavy dark socks on top of his jeans, which lay at her feet.

His wool shirt and leather sheepskin-lined jacket were still on the floor beside the bed. Since they were both definitely dry-clean *only* and still wet, she hung them on a hook next to the fireplace with some of her own damp clothes. The sight of his things nestled intimately among her own garments reminded her of undressing him the night before, and she frowned in confusion at the feminine awareness he aroused in her.

As a doctor, she'd seen a thousand gorgeous naked men, and none of them had affected her in this way. Why had the sight of Shane Burke's unadorned masculine physique stirred her libido as it had never been stirred before?

Before she could find an answer to the question, the shower turned off and the singing ceased. Charity rushed to the washing machine and pulled out the control to start it running. Then she ran to the closet and tugged on a pair of jeans and a navy-blue pullover sweater. One naked person in the room was trouble—two could lead to disaster.

She hurried to make the bed, thereby disposing of any reminder that they'd spent the night together. With a nod of satisfaction at having eliminated any suggestive evidence, she dug through the small freezer next to her refrigerator and found two ham steaks near the bottom.

"Need any help?"

She spun around. Shane was standing in the center of the room; the quilt had been replaced by a pink towel. She forced her gaze away from the damp curls covering his chest and the arrow of hair that traveled in a tantalizing path over his taut stomach and came to an abrupt end where the towel was draped low on his hips.

"You scared me half to death!" she accused him, silently admitting that her irritation was more at her own uncontrollable fascination with his body than at him. Unfortunately, his cleanly shaven face, with his damp head of hair curling riotously around it, was as disturbing as the rest of him.

"I'm sorry. I didn't mean to startle you."

"I'm, uh, just not used to having anyone around."

He nodded in understanding. "How long have you been up here?"

"A month."

"A month? Why?"

"I needed a vacation," she responded. "I think some of my ex-husband's old clothes are around here. They won't be a perfect fit, but they should keep you warm until yours are washed and dried."

"Beggars can't be choosers, and anything beats a pink towel," he said, glancing down at the towel and then up at her, his lips curved in a grin. "It's obvious that blue is my color."

Charity decided she wouldn't touch that line if he paid her to. She walked to the closet. As she dug through the rag box on the floor and uncovered a holey pair of socks, a ragged pair of jeans and an even more ragged sweatshirt, she blessed the fact that she hadn't destroyed everything of Carson's. She handed the clothes to Shane with an apologetic smile.

He accepted them with a nod and walked back into the bathroom to change. She busied herself by retrieving a dozen eggs from the refrigerator and pulling out a skillet.

"Thank you for washing my clothes."

Charity gasped in surprise when Shane's hand brushed against her shoulder, and she turned her head to look at him. Her ex-husband's jeans were too big through the waist and the hips, and his sweatshirt was much too small, but despite the ill-fitting clothes, Shane looked wonderful. Her grip on the handle of the skillet tightened, and she raised it to her chest as she slowly lifted her head until she was staring into his disconcerting blue eyes.

His lips turned up in a smile of contrition, making him look so handsome that he took her breath away. "I startled you again. I'm sorry. Can I help with breakfast? I'm pretty handy in the kitchen."

"No," she answered breathlessly. "I, uh, have everything under control." Except my overactive libido, my pounding heart, my racing pulse, and my very naughty imagination, she added silently. She turned away from him and plopped the two ham steaks into the skillet.

A few minutes later he sniffed the air appreciatively. "It's been a long time since someone's cooked me ham and eggs." When her only response was a nod, he asked, "What's your dog's name?"

Charity glanced down at the dog sitting quietly at his feet and smiled fondly. "Mister. He found you last night when he went out for his bedtime walk and wouldn't come in until I agreed to come see what he'd discovered." Hearing his name, Mister began to pant and thump his tail against the floor. "He loves attention," Charity continued, "so if he becomes a pest, feel free to shoo him off. I'm afraid I've spoiled him unmercifully over the years."

Shane bent down to pat the dog's head. "Thanks, boy. I owe you one." He rose and asked, "Are you sure I can't help?"

"I'm sure."

"I want to thank you again for saving my life," he said.

"You're welcome," she answered with a silent groan. They were already getting into a rut with him thanking her and her you're-welcoming him, but for the life of her she couldn't think of anything else to say.

The washer shut off and he crossed to it, pulled out his underwear and tossed them into the dryer. Charity watched him study the controls and start the dryer. Next he carefully measured out laundry soap and poured it into the washer.

"I always add dry bleach," she offered, pointing the fork she held at the box on the shelf above the washer.

"How much?"

"For that size load, a quarter of a cup."

"Got it. That must be what's wrong with my laundry. Whenever I do it myself, it always looks dingy."

Dingy? A man like this had a word like *dingy* in his vocabulary? "You do your own laundry?"

He shrugged. "Whenever I'm alone. My mother always believed that a man should be able to take care of himself, and she taught me how to cook, clean and do laundry." He gave her a mischievous grin. "I can even sew on a button or darn a pair of socks if I have to. I think she was afraid I'd get married just to get my meals cooked and my clothes washed and mended, so she made sure I could take care of myself."

"She sounds like a smart woman."

"She was," he stated quietly as he glanced away from her and threw his clothes into the washing machine.

When he referred to his mother in the past tense, Charity realized she'd inadvertently stepped into dangerous territory. Not certain how to respond, she returned her attention to the meal.

After Shane had started the washer, he leaned against it, crossed his arms over his chest, and said, "Why are you living up here in the middle of nowhere in the dead of winter?"

"I told you, I needed a vacation," she answered. "Why are you up here?"

"I, uh, needed a vacation."

The blush that rose to his cheeks told Charity he'd just lied, but she decided not to press the issue. After all, he might press back, and she wasn't about to discuss her problems with a stranger.

"How do you like your eggs cooked?"

"Over easy," he replied, finding himself very curious about her. Why would she seek solitude in a remote part of the mountains? He understood his own reasons. He'd built his cabin there because it provided him with the necessary isolation he needed to regain his sanity. Did she, too, need that kind of isolation?

His gaze dropped to her hands, and he was relieved to discover the ring finger of her left hand unadorned. She'd referred to an ex-husband, but he knew that didn't guarantee there wasn't a new husband in the wings.

"How long have you been divorced?" he asked.

She glanced back up to discover him regarding her from behind a screen of tawny lashes. What was he after?

"Long enough. Why?"

"I just find it surprising that you aren't married."

"You do? Why?"

He shrugged. "I just do."

She smiled. "I was surprised that you weren't married."

"Why?"

Her smile widened into a grin. "I just was."

He laughed. "Touché."

Silence fell between them, and Shane glanced around his surroundings as he tried to decide how to pick up the conversation again. The cabin was furnished with an eclectic collection of carefully cared for antiques. Antique lace curtains hung at the windows, and brightly colored rag rugs were spread across a gleaming hardwood floor.

But what really caught his attention was the collection of Navaho arts and crafts that dominated the room. Baskets and pottery filled every available space, and rugs and sand paintings adorned the walls.

"Are you an Indian?" he asked.

"My grandmother was Navaho. This cabin was hers."

"And it's yours now?"

"Yes."

"If I remember my college genetics, that makes you a quarter Navaho, doesn't it?"

"Yes."

He leaned forward, and Charity sucked in a deep breath when his face rested only inches away from hers. He studied her critically for a moment. "The Indian heritage shows."

"It does?" she whispered, feeling an odd tightness in her chest. His warm breath was stirring against her lips, and the clean smells of soap and man were seeping through the odor of frying ham.

"Yes. It shows here," he said as he reached out to gently skim a long finger over her high cheekbone. "And here," he continued, ever so lightly pressing the tip of his finger to the exotic tilt at the corner of one of her eyes. "And finally here," he concluded, running his hand in a feathery stroke down her shoulder-length raven hair.

With each touch, Charity's pulse began to pick up more speed, and her heart was beating in a dangerous cadence by the time he'd finished.

"Oh." The word was more a needed release of breath than a response to his words.

"You are one pretty lady, Dr. Charity Wells," he announced. "How much longer before breakfast is ready?"

Stunned by his sudden shift from the intimate to the mundane, Charity stared at him in disbelief. "Uh, just a few more minutes."

"Good. I'm famished. This freezing-to-death business really builds up an appetite."

Before she could respond, he leaned back against the counter, raised his arms over his head, yawned and stretched. Charity's skeletal structure turned to oatmeal as she watched the muscles in his arms and chest knot and unknot in a rippling motion beneath the too small sweatshirt.

"Oh, boy," she said, deciding she'd been divorced far too long. One more display like that, and she'd be assaulting the man!

"Did you say something?" he asked.

"Just 'Hello, boy.' I was talking to the dog," she improvised quickly. "Why don't you sit down? Breakfast is almost ready."

"Okay."

She dished up breakfast and buttered the toast. Then she turned from the counter and carried everything to the table, settling into a chair across from Shane.

He filled his plate and began to wolf down his food, and Charity decided he really was famished. After he'd finished his eggs and half of his ham steak, he smiled at her as he lifted a piece of toast and took a bite out of it.

"You make good ham and eggs," he said.

"Thank you," she replied.

"You're welcome."

They'd broken out of the rut they'd fallen into, she mused. This time it was her thanking him and him you're-welcoming her. Unaccountably, that made her smile.

"It'll be a few minutes before the coffee's ready," she told him.

"I can wait."

Another silence fell between them as they finished eating, but it was a comfortable, companionable silence that Charity found quite enjoyable.

When the coffee was ready, he waved for her to remain in her chair, rose from his, and got cups from the cupboard. After filling them, he carried them back to the table.

"Milk or sugar?" he asked when he set the cup down beside her empty plate.

"No. Both are fattening," she answered, then lifted the cup and took a long sip of the brew.

He chuckled as he resumed his seat. "I can't even imagine you worrying about fattening. You look like you need to gain a good ten pounds."

Charity shrugged. "I've lost some weight over the last few months, but it'll come back in time. There's no need to develop bad habits just to rush the process."

"If you say so."

After taking another sip of coffee, she said, "Tell me about yourself, Mr. Shane Burke."

"There isn't much to tell."

"Any man who has lived thirty-six years has a lot to tell."

He arched a brow in surprise. "How did you know my age?"

She laughed her first true laugh. It was a throaty, husky sound, and as Shane listened to it, he knew he wouldn't be satisfied until he heard it again.

"I told you I looked at your driver's license," she said.

"So you did." He leaned back in the chair, an amused smile curving his lips. "What do you think you know about me?"

She tilted her head to the side. "I've decided that you're a rancher. I wondered if you had another profession, but I don't think you do."

He decided to join her game, enjoying the experience of being unrecognized. "Why not?"

Her eyes slid over him appraisingly. "Your hands are callused, and your body's in too good a shape. It's the body of a man who indulges in hard work, not one who sits behind a desk. Am I right so far?"

He gave a noncommittal shrug that Charity assumed meant her conclusions were right.

"What kind of ranching do you do?" she asked.

"What kind of ranching do you think I do?"

"Cattle probably, but I bet you breed horses. Arabian horses."

"Really?" Shane chuckled. "That sounds interesting. Do you like horses?"

"I think they're magnificent animals, but I've never been around them."

"Never?" he questioned skeptically.

Her eyes took on a faraway glow. "Well, once when I was very small, my grandmother took me to see some wild horses. I remember watching a stallion racing across the field, tossing his head in the wind. He was unbearably beautiful, and I could sense his freedom. As young as I was, I had already learned to envy that freedom, and I wanted to climb on his back and ride away with him."

"And after an experience like that, you never learned how to ride? Why?"

"I also feared his size and his strength," she answered simply.

"You're afraid of horses?" he asked, incredulous.

"Let's just say I'm in awe of them."

"They're simply animals, Charity, and most of them are as docile and tame as your dog."

Charity reached down to ruffle the hair on Mister's head. He responded by whining and resting his chin on her knee. "Maybe, but you must admit they're a lot bigger."

"Yes, they are."

Charity frowned as she glanced away from his intent gaze. It was as if he were looking through her, delving into her soul, and she didn't like it. She didn't like it at all.

She decided to break the silence by asking, "Would you like some more coffee?"

"I've had my morning quota. Too much caffeine is bad for you."

Her lips twitched at his censure. "I know, but I'm going to have some more anyway."

His gaze was drawn to the natural sway of her hips as she rose from her chair and walked toward the coffeepot, and he shifted uncomfortably on the chair as unwanted desire surged through him. Why was the woman affecting him like this? She was beautiful, but so were three-quarters of the women he met, and he never responded to them like this.

Restless, and deciding he needed something to divert his attention away from her, he rose and walked to the fireplace to examine the sand paintings hanging above it.

He'd spent some time on a Navaho reservation and knew they weren't traditional paintings but pictures made of sands collected from the deserts and mountains of the southwestern United States. At close range, their earth tones of red, brown, black, yellow, green and blue were even more vibrant, and Shane was fascinated by the flowing figures—animals and people. Plants and logs were also dominant in the pictures, as well as the moon and the sun. He felt as drawn to them as he did to the woman who owned them. They also gave him a sense of harmony, a feeling he hadn't experienced for longer than he cared to remember.

His attention was captured by one particularly beautiful sand painting. He'd seen it before and did know its meaning. It displayed the four sacred plants—bean, corn, tobacco and squash—beginning at the top right and going clockwise. In between each plant and the next was the symbol of a frog. With the frogs included, he knew the painting would be used for treating a crippled person or someone suffering from paralysis or arthritis, illnesses believed to be caused by the water people—thus the inclusion of the frogs.

Slowly he turned, sensing that Charity was watching him. She was leaning against the sink, and he moved his gaze over her. The desire he'd felt since he'd awakened intensified. He knew how she felt in his arms. He wondered what it would be like to make love to her.

"The sand paintings are beautiful, aren't they?" she asked.

"They are. Do you know what they mean?"

She looked at them and shook her head. "No, but my grandmother did."

"And she never explained them to you?"

Her smile was sad. "She tried, but in my youth I considered them fanciful. I was certain modern science had more answers than these primitive pictures."

"And now you're not so sure?"

"The older I get, the less sure I am about anything."

"The sand painting is a highly religious ceremony," he stated.

Charity looked at him in surprise. "You know about them?"

He shrugged. "I know a little. I spent two weeks on a Navaho reservation in Arizona a couple of years ago."

"What else do you know?" she asked, walking toward him.

"I know that none of these pictures are accurate. A true sand painting must be destroyed when it's finished or it offends the gods, so the artist changes the colors, such as making a feather red when it should be blue, or leaves out a piece of the picture. Many Navahos believe that even creating a sand painting such as this is a threat. They believe in moderation, and fear that if too many of these pictures are made, the power of the gods will weaken."

"I wonder," she whispered as she came to a stop at his side, staring at the pictures as if by doing so they'd tell her what she wanted to know.

"And just what do you wonder?"

"Nothing," she replied, not willing to confess that she was trying to gain the same peace of mind her grandmother had always been able to find here. Her grandmother had always claimed that the sand paintings talked to her and gave her her answers, but they weren't talking to Charity. "I guess I'm being fanciful."

"We're all allowed to be fanciful once in a while."

"I suppose you're right," she said.

"I have some books on sand paintings. They can probably give you a lot of the answers you're looking for."

"You'd think I'd have read about them before," she said, gazing at the pictures in fascination. "I guess until now they just hadn't meant that much. They were sitting here, waiting for the day when I'd need them, and they're offering me the most challenging puzzle I've yet faced."

"The most challenging puzzle?"

Shane resisted the urge to reach out and touch the curve of her cheek as he waited for her answer. He couldn't get over how ethereal she looked, as if she were only a figment of his imagination. And suddenly he realized that he didn't want to ignore the desire he felt for her. He didn't want to acknowledge that he couldn't bury his face in her thick mane of hair and breathe in her elusive fragrance. He didn't want to acknowledge that he couldn't kiss her, touch her, or lose himself inside her. For a time he wanted to be able to pretend he was a normal man able to lead a normal life. He wanted to be permitted to explore the chemistry stirring between them. And there was chemistry stirring between them. It was as heavy in the room as the snow falling outside.

But before he could reach out and touch her, she answered his question by saying, "I consider the undefined a challenge. A puzzle, so to speak, and I can't rest until I've satisfied myself that I've come as close as possible to finding the answer."

She started to say more, but the coffeepot began to boil on the stove, and she gave Shane an embarrassed smile as if she'd revealed too much of herself and regretted it. "The coffee's heated. Are you sure you don't want some?"

"I'm sure."

"All right, but if you change your mind, feel free to help yourself."

While she poured herself some coffee, he risked another glance around the cabin, wondering if it could give him some answers. His gaze moved over the sofa in front of the fireplace, the maple antique desk and caned chair in the corner, the four-poster bed in another corner, and the oak kitchen table and chairs. The room was spartan yet welcoming. It didn't provide him with any answers, but it did fill him with a sense of contentment—a sense of belonging.

"You're awfully quiet. Bored already?" Charity asked.

He glanced toward her and shook his head. "No. I'm just thinking."

"About what?"

"A lot of things."

Charity clenched her coffee cup when his gaze moved languorously from the top of her head to the tips of her toes, making her stomach quiver and her knees shake. She felt as if her world were exploding around her, and she didn't know how to handle the sensation.

"What kind of doctor are you?" he asked.

"I'm board certified in emergency medicine."

"I'm impressed. That's a demanding profession, but it must be rewarding."

"Sometimes it is and sometimes it isn't."

"But most of the time it is," he guessed.

"Most of the time," she agreed.

"Was your husband a doctor?"

Charity blinked at the unexpected question. She studied him while she tried to decide whether or not she wanted to answer it. Then she chuckled and gave a resigned shake of her head.

"No. My husband was a corporate attorney."

"Another demanding profession."

"Yes, it is."

Shane's intuition allowed him to add two and two together. He came up with a disturbing four he could identify with. He was an entertainer, and she was a doctor. They both had professions that dictated their allegiance to others first and to a personal relationship last. He knew without being told that it was that allegiance that had destroyed her marriage just as it had destroyed what he'd shared with the only woman he'd let into his life.

Diane. How long had it been since he'd even allowed himself to think about her? Five years? Six? It hadn't been long enough, he thought as he stuffed his hands into the pockets of Charity's ex-husband's jeans, feeling uneasy with the past memories she was stirring up.

"Your husband was a fool," he told her. "If I'd ever been lucky enough to catch someone as beautiful as you, I never would have let you go."

Charity blushed at his compliment and ducked her head shyly. "Thank you. You're very kind."

Shane gave a wry shake of his head. Most of the women he met were begging for compliments. She blushed at one— and a true one at that.

"You don't thank a man for telling you the truth," he said.

"Are you sure you don't want some coffee?"

Shane grinned. "Do you always offer coffee when someone gives you a compliment?"

"Of course not," she said with a frown. "Do you?"

"Offer coffee when someone gives me a compliment?"

"Want some coffee," she qualified impatiently.

He chuckled, and even though he didn't want any coffee he said, "Sure."

Charity was muttering to herself when she turned to get him a cup of coffee. Why was he making her so flustered? She was normally cool and controlled when dealing with men. She had to be. The majority of her peers accepted her skill as a doctor, but there were still many who felt medicine was a male bastion and that she was an intruder. Then there were the male patients who were often embarrassed and uncertain about a female doctor treating them. And the men she dated . . . well, she'd been avoiding the dating game during the past year. Most of her dates were sure that as a doctor, she was quite ready, willing and able to leap into bed with them.

But Shane was different. He didn't fit neatly into any of the categories of men she dealt with. She placed the coffee cup on a saucer, but before she could lift it, Shane walked up behind her.

His scent surrounded her. The heat from his body hit her in waves, and she wanted to turn to him and beg him to kiss her. She released her breath slowly. This was crazy. A mature woman did not run around begging a strange man to kiss her.

"Your coffee's ready. Do you take anything in it?" she asked.

"I drink it black."

Charity nodded and turned to hand him the cup.

He accepted it while staring at her, and Charity couldn't tell what he was thinking. It made her extremely uncomfortable. She walked past him, gathered the dirty dishes on the table and carried them to the sink.

She was running water into it when Shane startled her by speaking directly behind her. "Charity?"

"Why do you keep creeping up on me?" she asked impatiently as she turned around.

"I didn't mean to startle you," he soothed, his hand reaching up to cup her cheek. "Really, I didn't. I was just going to offer to do the dishes, but . . ."

"But what?" she whispered, her eyes widening in wonder as his head began to lower.

He didn't answer. Instead, he closed his lips over hers.

Chapter Three

Charity listened to the fire crackle, the dryer whir, and the faucet on the kitchen sink drip. Sound had never been so clear, nor had it ever been in such perfect synchronization with the beating of her heart.

At the first touch of Shane's lips, an internal flame flickered and began to glow more brightly with each passing second until she was sure she was a gleaming beacon of light.

His kiss was gentle, searching, undemanding, but it had been so long since she'd shared a man's kiss that it caused a yearning ache inside that begged for assuagement. Instinctively she parted her lips, feeling frustrated when he ignored her provocative invitation but concentrated instead on tasting and testing each corner of her mouth and the full softness in between.

He cradled her face in his hands, tilting her head upward, and she longed to lean her body against his—to feel his strength against her softness. She lifted her arms in order to wind them around his neck so she could meet its demand. But he released his hold on her face and slid his hands down her arms, capturing them against her sides.

Reluctantly, Shane drew away from the kiss. He hadn't meant to kiss Charity, but when she'd turned toward him, her eyes wide and her lips softly parted, he'd automatically responded. She tasted so sweet he wanted to sweep her up in his arms, carry her to bed and make slow, tender love to her, but he couldn't do that. Charity wasn't from his world—a world that moved too fast and didn't allow time for relationships.

He fought to regain control of his runaway emotions, and for the first time in a long time he found himself wishing for the peaceful, uncomplicated existence other men had. He longed for a wife and a house with a white picket fence. He wanted children, a scruffy dog and a grumpy cat. He wanted . . . He tightened his hands reflexively on Charity's arms. It was foolish to wish for things he could never have.

He'd made a vow years ago that he'd never become involved with a woman as long as he was a part of the rock group Moon and Sun, and the one time he'd broken the rule, with Diane, had nearly destroyed him. Something told him that if he let himself go with Charity, he'd end up breaking that rule again, and he couldn't let himself do that. Only a fool made the same mistake twice, and he was not a fool.

Charity lifted her eyes to his face when he released a soft sigh. He greeted her with a warm smile.

"I'll do the dishes while I wait for the rest of my clothes to dry," he said as he gently pushed her away from the sink. "You just do whatever you normally do at this time of day."

"I usually do the dishes at this time of day," she said in confusion. The man had kissed her—made her ache with longing—and was acting as if nothing had happened! Hadn't their kiss affected him at all?

"Then take a vacation and pamper yourself. Where's the dish soap?"

"Under the sink, but you don't have to do the dishes."

"I know."

She frowned as she watched him retrieve the bottle of liquid detergent and squirt a healthy portion into the water. When the suds were halfway up his arms, she still hadn't figured out what had happened. Her gaze moved past him to the window, and watching the snow pile up at an alarming rate on the sill outside, she felt that the blizzard was an appropriate reflection of her own internal turmoil of the moment.

She finally went to the sofa, deciding that if Shane wanted the unenviable chore of doing the dishes, she wasn't going to argue with him. She settled against the overstuffed cushions and picked up a medical journal from the pile on the floor that she'd brought along to read. But the words in front of her were a blur as she tried to sort her way through the effect Shane was having on her.

She'd been divorced for two years and hadn't been involved with a man. It wasn't from lack of opportunity. It was simply that she didn't believe in making love with a man unless love was involved, and she hadn't met anyone who fell into that category, much less someone willing to put up with her career in medicine.

For as long as she could remember, she'd always wanted to be a doctor. But the competition for admission to medical school was stiff, and although she was intelligent, she certainly wasn't brilliant. She'd had to study hard all through high school and college to ensure that her grades were impeccable. That meant she'd had to give up the dating and parties other girls her age had enjoyed. She'd told herself the fun would come after she'd reached her goal.

It was only after she'd graduated from medical school, done her residency in emergency medicine and had been hired on the staff of one of Denver's finest hospitals that she'd finally felt free enough to relax and indulge herself in a personal life. That was when her brother had introduced her to Carson Montgomery.

Like everything else, Charity had approached her relationship with Carson from a logical standpoint. They had shared the same interests, had the same tastes, and felt the same dedication toward their careers. Not to fall in love with him—the man who had appeared to be her ideal mate—would have been ridiculous.

The first year of their marriage had been good. Then the second year had come, and the problems had started.

Carson had been raised in poverty, worked his way through college and law school, and had an obsessive determination to make it to the top. In order to do that, he had to play business politics, and part of those politics was an active social life with a devoted wife at his side.

Unfortunately, emergency patients didn't stop coming to the hospital just because Carson felt it was important that she accompany him to his boss's wife's charity benefit or to the office Christmas party or a client's pool party or any other number of events. Finally Charity had missed one too many of Carson's important social obligations, and her marriage had ended.

Carson had loved her. She didn't doubt that. But to him, a woman who loved you did everything necessary to ensure you succeeded. He was of the old male school. The school that said you walked one step behind your man, not beside him.

She sighed heavily and shook her head to dismiss the past. Then she glanced toward Shane and frowned. None of her ruminations had explained his attraction, and she was determined to find a logical reason for the wild emotions he sparked within her. It was all very simple, she finally decided. She was lonely and seeking solace from the man. There was nothing wrong with that. People instinctively reached out to one another for support and comfort. It became complicated only if they didn't recognize what was happening. Relieved by her explanation, she no longer felt out of control.

She returned her attention to the journal, deciding that although Mister was a loyal and loving companion, his conversational yaps were not scintillating. It would be nice to have some company until the blizzard passed. And she was an adult. She could handle whatever was sparking between her and Shane Burke. A moment later she was completely absorbed in the article she was reading.

Shane finished the dishes just as the dryer shut off. He gathered his clothes and headed toward the bath.

His thoughts were on the woman in the other room as he stripped off the clothes she'd given him and donned his own. He hadn't had to look at Charity to know she'd been studying him while he did the dishes, and oddly enough, he'd physically felt the easing of her tension. The realization that he was so attuned to her moods was disturbing. Only one other time had he experienced that kind of silent communication with a woman.

Thoughts of Diane resurrected feelings he'd thought were long forgotten, and he closed his eyes to push them away. He was stuck in a cabin with a lady doctor. The blizzard would move on, and when it did, so would he. But he still couldn't help wondering why Charity was here and, more important, why she was making him experience feelings he hadn't had in eleven years.

She wasn't the kind of woman he was used to meeting. She wasn't in the glitzy world of entertainment, nor was she an ardent fan. She was a professional. A doctor. But he was responding to her just as he'd responded to Diane. Another intellect. Another professional. Another woman far above his reach.

But he wasn't involved with Charity Wells and had no intention of becoming involved with her, he reminded himself firmly as he opened his eyes and stepped into his jeans. The woman had saved his life. He was responding to her because he felt grateful and obligated. It was nothing more and nothing less.

When he finally stepped out of the bath, he hesitated. Charity's dark head was still bent over the magazine in her hand, and from what he could see on the cover, she wasn't lost in the world of recipes and homemaking tips. He felt out of his element, and not wanting to disrupt her concentration, he walked over to the small antique desk and sat down on the chair.

His gaze idly roamed around the room. He was certain the fireplace in the corner was her only means of heat, and the soft vibration of a generator from somewhere close outside indicated that was how she supplied her electricity. Compared to his own cabin—which most people would refer to as a vacation home—she was living under destitute circumstances. So why did he feel so much more at home here?

Before he could ponder the question, Charity asked, "Would you like something to read? I've got some mysteries, a horror story and a few spy stories."

"That would be great," Shane answered.

She crossed to the desk, removed half a dozen books from the drawer and laid them on top. Without looking at him, she returned to the sofa and settled down to read another journal.

Shane waited until she was occupied before he perused the books. He selected a spy novel, even though he knew he wouldn't read it. He was too intrigued with Charity to concentrate on much of anything else.

His seating options were limited. He could continue to sit in the chair at the desk, which he knew would soon be uncomfortable. He could join her on the sofa, but wasn't sure he'd be welcome. That left the bed, and with a resolved shrug, he went to it and lay down, piling the pillows behind his head.

Surreptitiously, he watched her flip page after page as she absorbed the material in front of her. Even though he was hungry, he ignored his growling stomach as lunchtime came and went. Charity seemed completely engrossed in the journals she was devouring, the pile she'd read now standing at more than half the height of the unread pile.

But when dinnertime came, Shane knew he could ignore his stomach no longer. He rose to his feet and stretched. Charity immediately looked up at him, and he grimaced inwardly at the wary look in her eyes.

"I'm starving," he announced.

She glanced at the clock on the mantel before sheepishly saying, "I'm sorry. I guess I lost track of time."

"It must have been interesting reading."

"It was. How is your book?"

"It's great," he lied, praying she wouldn't quiz him on the story.

"I'm glad you're enjoying it. Do you like spaghetti?"

"Have you ever met anyone who doesn't?"

She rewarded him with a genuine smile. "No."

"Neither have I. What can I do to help?"

"How are you at making a salad?"

"My mother always claimed I was a great salad maker, but she might have been prejudiced."

"Well, I'll take her word for it, anyway. Help yourself to the vegetables in the refrigerator."

Watching him go to the refrigerator, she released a heavy sigh. All day she'd been aware of his every move, and she felt as jumpy as the proverbial cat on a hot tin roof. The man was electric, and she seemed to be attuned to his energy.

It was loneliness, she reminded herself, but that didn't ease the heat that started simmering in her middle when she watched him bend to search the refrigerator, his jeans taut across his lean hips.

Charity was silent as she prepared spaghetti while Shane made a salad. When he finished, he set it on the table and then retrieved the dog dish from the floor. He fed Mister, rinsed his hands and leaned against the counter.

"Charity, is something wrong?" he finally asked when she continued to ignore him.

"Of course not."

"You're awfully tense."

"I'm just hungry," she said, stirring the tomato sauce.

"I see. Do you have a radio?"

"A radio? Why?"

"I wanted to see if we could get a weather report."

"I don't have a radio. The mountains are too high. You can't pick up the signals."

Shane started to contradict her but stopped himself. Charity's cabin rested in the valley. His sat on top of the mountain. He also had a satellite dish that provided him not only with radio but with television.

"How far are you from the road?" he asked.

"About a mile."

"Do they grade up to the cabin?"

"They will after a storm like this. The sheriff knows I'm here."

"You're terribly isolated up here. Do you have a gun?"

She finally looked at him. "No one bothers me. I don't need a gun."

Shane didn't reply, but his scowl communicated his disapproval succinctly, she thought. He looked just like her brother when he was ready to give her a lecture on staying in the woods alone. Charity turned her attention back to the spaghetti, deciding the only way to avoid the lecture was to maintain her silence.

Shane settled at the table when she poured spaghetti sauce into a bowl. She set the bowl on the table, refusing to meet his eyes, and went back to the stove to get the spaghetti.

After she'd sat down in the chair across from him, she risked a glance at his face. His brows were drawn together in frustration.

She sighed, rested her chin in her palm and said, "All right, Shane. You might as well get whatever it is off your chest."

"I know you're intelligent, so why are you behaving so stupidly?" he growled at her.

"And how am I behaving stupidly?"

His eyes began to glitter dangerously. "Anyone could walk into this cabin, and you have no means to defend yourself!"

"I don't need to defend myself."

The curse he muttered was quite imaginative.

"No one has ever bothered me here, Shane."

The curse he muttered this time was even more imaginative.

"Shane—"

"The days of being a trusting soul are over," he interrupted her angrily. "You should have some protection. If not a gun, then at least a knife. Do you have a knife? And I mean something besides the paring knife and steak knives in the kitchen drawer."

Charity blanched as the glistening silver edge of a knife blade flashed through her mind. "No."

Shane was so frustrated that he didn't notice how pale she'd become. "There are crazy people out there, Charity. You don't know when they're going to knock on your door."

"I doubt too many crazy people are going to come to my cabin in the dead of winter."

"I did, didn't I?" he pointed out.

"Are you saying you're crazy?"

"Are you so sure I'm not?"

She blinked at his comeback. "If you were, I would have known by now."

"And what makes you so sure of that?"

A shiver moved up her spine as he stared at her challengingly. His eyes were so cold they could compete with the temperature outside, and the harsh set of his features made her gulp. Despite his words, she knew he wasn't crazy; however, he was angry.

"Shane—"

"You didn't answer my question."

"You aren't crazy!" she exclaimed impatiently.

"How do you know?"

"You don't look like a crazy man," she offered weakly.

"And what does a crazy man look like? If they were that recognizable, don't you think they'd all be under lock and key?"

"I—"

He leaned both elbows on the table, leaning toward her as if to add emphasis to his words as he interrupted her again. "What about those people who aren't crazy but are just downright vicious and mean? How would you handle them?"

"Just like I handled you," she answered simply. "I'm a doctor, Shane. I'm devoted to saving lives, and I probably couldn't use a weapon against another human being if I had to."

Shane frowned at her admission, realizing that it was most likely true. It only made him more convinced that she shouldn't be up here alone, but he decided to keep his opinion to himself, since it was really none of his business.

Instead, he said, "You'd better eat. You're too skinny to miss meals."

"I'm not skinny," she protested indignantly.

He grinned. "Well, you will be if you don't eat."

But as determined as his order to eat had been, Charity had lost her appetite. She moved her food from one side of the plate to the other, the image of a knife blade refusing to go away.

She'd lived through thirty-two hours of terror, and she couldn't seem to shake off the effects the episode had had on her. She loved her work, but the thought of even walking back into the emergency room sent shivers of fear racing up and down her spine. Should she go into private practice, and if she did, would it offer the same challenge? Be as rewarding?

For the past month, she'd been up here searching for her answers, and she was no closer to finding a solution than she'd been the day she'd arrived. Now she was beginning to wonder if there was an answer.

"There are starving people in Africa, Charity," he said, breaking into her thoughts.

"What?" Charity said, glancing up at Shane in surprise. She'd actually forgotten about him, which was quite a feat, considering how magnetic he was.

"I said there are starving people in Africa," he repeated patiently. "Are you going to eat your spaghetti?"

She glanced guiltily at her plate. "I guess my eyes were bigger than my stomach. I'm not very hungry."

Shane started to tell her she should eat but once again told himself it was none of his business.

"Why don't we put it away? You can heat it up later if you get hungry," he suggested instead.

"That's a good idea."

"I have one every now and then," he said wryly.

She couldn't help but smile when faced with the amusement dancing in his eyes. "Would you like more?"

"I've already had three helpings. If you notice, the bowls are almost empty."

"So they are." She started to rise to her feet but stopped when his hand came down over hers.

"Charity, would you like to talk?"

"No!" she said more vehemently than she'd meant to. "Sorry, but talking to you wouldn't help."

"You're sure?"

"I'm positive. Why don't you go back to your book while I do the dishes?"

"All right," he agreed easily, even though he was more convinced than ever that something was definitely wrong. He also decided that before he left, he'd find out what it was.

Why did he care so much about a woman he didn't even know? he wondered as he piled his dishes together to make it easier for Charity to gather them. Because she was alone and needed someone, an inner voice answered. Was that what was missing from his life? Did he need someone to need him? He'd been restless and unsatisfied for the past three or four years. Music was his life, but it wasn't fulfilling him as it had in the past.

Deciding that it was all much too complicated to even think about, he dismissed it. He'd be here until the blizzard was over—two or three days at the most. Then he'd walk away and never see Charity Wells again.

He rose from the table and once again stretched out on the bed. He held the book and even turned a page now and then, but he wasn't reading. He was staring at Charity's back.

Her shoulders were slumped while she did the dishes, looking for all the world as if she held a tremendous weight on her shoulders. He resisted the urge to go to her. The sparks flying between him and Charity were too volatile. He feared that if he tried to comfort her, that comforting might flare into something much different.

But as he watched her he found himself longing to see her smile and hear her laughter. He wanted to see her green eyes glowing with humor as she engaged him in easy banter. He sat up on the bed when she turned away from the sink and carried a chair to the closet.

"What are you doing?" he asked.

"I'm getting some blankets."

"Why?"

"It's almost bedtime, and I'm going to sleep on the sofa."

Shane eyed the sofa dubiously. The manners he'd learned told him he should offer to sleep on it, but it was so small, he knew he could never manage it. Instead, he said, "It looks awfully uncomfortable to me. I think you should sleep in the bed."

"And just where did you plan on sleeping?" she asked, her eyes automatically taking an inventory of his body. When her imagination began to supply some X-rated scenarios of a night in bed with a conscious Shane Burke, she gave a self-chastising shake of her head.

He smiled rakishly as he answered her question. "In the bed."

It was her turn to arch a brow. "Yeah. As I said, I'm sleeping on the couch."

"Don't you trust me?"

"This has nothing to do with trust. It's a matter of decorum." She opened the closet door and climbed up on the chair.

"You slept with me last night."

Charity almost fell off the chair. The man was standing right next to her, having sneaked up on her yet again. Good heavens, he was the one who should be part Indian!

She looked down into his upturned face and felt as if her knees were dissolving. It had to be a sin to be so handsome, she decided as her tongue flicked out over suddenly parched lips. She shivered when his gaze followed the action.

"Chairs are dangerous. I'll get your blankets," he said as he put his hands around her waist and lifted her to the floor.

She had to put her hands on his chest for balance and was having a difficult time removing them with his hands still around her waist. Their eyes locked, and his blue ones began to darken with sensual promises. He lowered his head slightly, and Charity readied herself for the inevitable kiss.

But Shane surprised her by winking and turning toward the closet. "Where are the blankets?"

He'd done it to her again! Every time he got her motor started, he turned away!

"On the shelf," she answered, trying to keep her voice neutral.

"Mmm." He began pulling blankets down and tossing them at her. Suddenly he stilled. When he turned toward her, there was an old guitar resting in his hands. "Do you play?"

Charity shook her head. "No. That was my grandfather's."

He reverently caressed the battered guitar. Then he removed the pick and ran it over the strings. Charity watched him, mesmerized as he began to tune the instrument. He tilted his head to the side as he played a chord, and then readjusted the strings.

"Do you mind if I play it?"

"No," she whispered, enjoying the look of pure rapture that had settled on his face.

He carried the guitar back to the bed, sat on the edge and began to hum as he strummed a series of chords.

Charity sat on the chair beside her as he began to softly croon the words to an old love song that had always been one of her favorites.

When he was done, he asked, "Like it?"

"I've always thought that song was beautiful. Do you know who wrote it?"

Shane refrained from telling her he had. Instead, he said, "It was written by one of the lead singers of Moon and Sun."

"The rock group?"

"None other. Are you familiar with their work?"

"Not really," she said. "I remember a few of their early songs. They've been around a long time, haven't they?"

"Eighteen years," he answered with pride as he played a new series of chords.

"That's a long time for a rock group to remain popular, isn't it?" Charity questioned thoughtfully.

He continued to strum the guitar as his mind took him through a journey of his career. It had been a long road, but along the way he'd found a happy family. There was Roger, his manager, whom he regarded almost as a father. Then there was Derek, his partner, who was as close as—maybe even closer than—any brother could be. And finally, there was the band. Four rowdy, happy men who shared their families with him. He loved them and loved what he did— couldn't even imagine what it would be like to not be on the stage—but it took hard work to stay on top in the fickle world of music, and despite his good friends, the demands were beginning to wear on him.

He glanced up and discovered Charity regarding him curiously. Feeling uncomfortable beneath her quiet scrutiny, he asked, "Do you have any requests?"

She smiled. "No. Surprise me."

Shane nodded. "Okay."

He closed his eyes and carefully picked out the notes to a song he'd written the week before. Charity would be the first person to hear it, and he wanted to see her reaction. He hummed along with the music for a while, then began to sing the words. As he did, he opened his eyes, watching her face.

It was a ballad of a man whose career had taken over his life. He had everything he'd ever dreamed of having. Fame. Money. Power. But he was desperately lonely and searching for the one thing that fame, money, and power couldn't buy. The love of a good woman.

The room was silent when he sang the last note. Even the wind had quieted as if paying homage to a song so heart-stirring that Charity couldn't find her voice.

She drew in a deep breath and let it out slowly before she asked, "Did he find her?"

Shane shrugged. "Not yet." He played a few more notes on the guitar, wondering what Charity would say if he told her the song was entitled "Self-Portrait." "Would you like to hear something a little more cheerful?"

"You're a professional musician, aren't you?"

He grinned and strummed the guitar. "I thought you said I was a rancher."

"I did, but I was wrong, wasn't I?"

"Were you? What makes you think a rancher can't play a guitar?"

"A lot of people play the guitar, but..."

"But what?" he prompted her.

She gave a self-conscious shrug of her shoulders. "I don't know. I just sense that song was about you. Are you really that unhappy?"

Her insight caused Shane to play a discordant note. Stiffly, he asked, "Do I look unhappy?"

"I'm sorry. I'm treading on ground I have no right to tread on." She rose from the chair and carried the blankets to the sofa.

"Charity?"

"Yes?" she responded, refusing to look at him. He might refute her words, and she was mannerly enough not to contradict him, but nothing he could say would convince her she was wrong. His life was as miserable as hers was at the moment. The difference was, he could do something about it.

"I am a musician, and maybe I am that unhappy. My life is good, but it's demanding. I think I may be getting too old to handle all the demands."

"Then change them," she said, turning to face him. "Your song told me you have every advantage, so take those advantages and make them work for you, instead of against you. Go out and make all those dreams you hint about in that song come true."

"Advice is easily given but much harder to put into practice. If I do what you're telling me to do, I'll be hurting a lot of people. People who depend on me for their livelihoods."

"We're quite a pair, aren't we?" she questioned softly. "A musician with dreams he can't fulfill, and a doctor who—"

She stopped abruptly as she realized how close she'd just come to telling him her story. She turned back to the sofa and began to straighten the blankets.

"A doctor who what?" he asked.

"Needs a good night's sleep," she answered.

"Charity, I wish you'd talk to me. It might help."

"It might, but I'd rather work through this on my own. That way if it turns out wrong, I won't have anyone but myself to blame."

"All right," he said, silently vowing he wouldn't give up. The least he could do to repay her for saving his life was to be a good listening friend. "Do you want the bath first?"

"No. You go ahead. I have to let Mister out."

At the sound of his name, Mister rose from the hearth, stretched and gave a sleepy shake of his head. Without waiting for instructions, he lumbered to the front door.

By the time Charity had let him out, Shane had closed the door of the bath behind him. She paced restlessly through the small cabin, waiting for both man and dog to complete their nightly rituals. Mister returned only moments before Shane walked back into the room.

"It's all yours," he said.

"Thanks. Good night, Shane."

"Good night, Charity. Sleep tight."

"I'll try."

She pulled a long flannel nightgown from the closet and walked toward the bath. Just before she entered it, she glanced back over her shoulder and froze as Shane pulled his underwear over his head.

She was staring in fascination at his bare chest when he asked, "What is it, Charity?"

Since she didn't dare answer him truthfully, she said, "Are you a famous musician?"

"Some people think so. I'm one of the lead singers in Moon and Sun."

Charity's eyes widened in disbelief. "I'd say that's pretty famous." When he only nodded, she didn't know what else to say, so she said, "Good night."

Before he could respond, she closed the door behind her and leaned weakly against it. She had a famous rock star sitting in the other room! She told herself that her loss of strength was due to his identity, but deep inside she knew that was only partly true. The sight of his bare chest had had as much an effect on her as his revelation of who he was. Why was his body so fascinating to her? He might be famous, but he was a man just like any other man. *But oh, what a man!* that little voice inside supplied with a dramatic sigh.

Shane's eyes shot open, and he stared at the ceiling. It took him several seconds to remember he was not in a hotel room but in Charity Wells's cabin.

He frowned as he tried to figure out what had awakened him. The room was silent except for the low wail of the wind outside. Then he heard Charity's soft moan, followed by Mister's quiet whine.

He rolled to his side, his gaze automatically settling on the sofa where Charity slept. She was tossing and turning among the blankets. In the low flicker of firelight, he could see that her brow was furrowed and her lips were moving in silent protest. Mister was standing beside his mistress, and he whined again as he looked at Shane.

"I understand, boy," Shane said as he threw back the covers and crawled from the bed. He made his way to the sofa, where Charity still struggled with the blankets, and he caught one of her hands in his. He was startled to find it ice-cold.

"Charity?" he whispered in concern as he clenched her hand more tightly.

"No!" she protested, attempting to pull away from him.

"Hey, lady, you're having a nightmare." Shane sat down beside her and began to chafe her cold hand between his warm ones.

Her lashes fluttered as if she were fighting against waking from the dream, and then they lifted until she was gazing up at him. For a moment, she looked totally disoriented. Then she blinked at him in sleepy confusion.

"What's wrong?" she asked groggily.

"I told you you'd be uncomfortable, and now that the fire's died down, you're freezing to death," he grumbled as he slid his arms beneath her and lifted her slight weight off the sofa.

"What are you doing?" Charity gasped, fully awake now and much too aware of his bare chest, which was just a breath away from her lips.

"Putting you in bed, where you belong. You're making more noise than that damn blizzard outside."

"But—"

"Keep your buts to yourself," he ordered her as he crossed to the bed and settled her beneath the covers. "You can put some pillows between us if you want, but I'm going to spend the night sleeping, not listening to you moan and groan. Got that?"

Charity nodded as she self-consciously pushed her hair out of her eyes. She gulped and scooted across the bed as Shane crawled in beside her. Having him stick her into bed with him wouldn't have been quite so bad if the man had been wearing more than his jockey shorts!

She gulped again when he lay down, causing the center of the old mattress to dip. She gripped the side of the bed with the same desperation she would have held the door handle of an out-of-control car. Shane shifted, and the dip deepened.

"Charity?" he said with a weary sigh.

"What?" she answered.

"I don't bite."

"I didn't think you did."

He chuckled. "Then why are you trying to defy gravity?"

"I'm not trying to defy gravity."

"Liar."

Before she could answer, he wrapped a hand around her waist and rolled her toward him. When Charity came to a stop, her flannel nightgown was tangled around her legs and she was lying in his arms.

"That's better," he said with a yawn. "Go to sleep, okay?"

"Okay," she agreed hoarsely, wondering if she'd ever be able to sleep again. The crisp golden curls on his chest were brushing against her cheek, and his body was pressed intimately against hers from shoulder to knee.

He lay still beside her, his breathing slow and deep. Charity waited until she thought he was asleep before she cautiously shifted a leg, trying to untangle the nightgown. It didn't move, so she tried moving the other leg. When that didn't work, she slowly lifted her hips.

She jumped when Shane said, "Are you always this restless in bed?"

"My nightgown's caught."

He raised himself up on his elbow and gazed at her, his lips twitching in amusement. "Then uncatch it."

She nodded, but when she tried to pull the nightgown loose, it only became more tangled. Suddenly Shane tossed back his head and laughed.

"I'm glad you're having so much fun at my expense," she muttered.

"You are enjoyable to have around," he responded, his eyes dancing with more laughter. "Let me help you."

"No!"

But her soft exclamation was too late. Shane had thrown back the covers and was regarding her dishabille and the expanse of her bared legs with interest. When his gaze came back to her face, all his mirth was gone.

"I think you'd better do it yourself," he said gruffly.

She nodded and quickly readjusted the nightgown, praying he couldn't see the blush that had stained her cheeks. As soon as she was untangled, Shane tossed the covers back over her and lay down.

But this time, his breathing wasn't slow and deep. It was fast and shallow, and Charity's pulse quickened in response. She jumped again when he reached out and laced his fingers with hers.

"How many sheep have you counted?" he asked.

"Three hundred and ninety-two," she answered.

He chuckled and gave her hand a fond squeeze. "You're about fifty behind me."

"I guess I'll have to count faster."

"Charity?"

"Yes?"

"We slept together last night and nothing happened."

"Last night you were unconscious."

"True."

He brought their clasped hands up to his cheek and rubbed them against it. The rough stubble of his beard felt so sensuous, it made her tremble.

"We have to get some sleep," he said, aware of her response but choosing to ignore it.

"Yeah. Mister gets up early," she replied.

Silence stretched between them. She tried to remove her hand from Shane's, but he tightened his grip and brought it to his chest, where he released it.

He rubbed his cheek against Charity's hair, marveling at how good she felt in his arms. It was as if his arms had been made to hold her, as if his body had been specifically designed to mold to her soft curves.

"Relax," he whispered as he slid his hand beneath her hair and began to massage her neck.

Charity barely managed to swallow the moan that rose to her lips. She'd never known that her neck was an erotic hot spot until Shane had touched it, but she couldn't find the strength to tell him to stop. She stared at her hand, mesmerized by the mat of curls it was nestled against. Of their own accord, her fingers shifted to tentatively touch his nipple, which teasingly peeked out from a whorl of golden hair. Shane's response to her touch was immediate. The pectoral muscles under her fingers jerked, and the nipple puckered into a hard peak. Her fingers splayed out, and her palm came to rest against the magic she'd just created.

"Shane, are you going to make love to me?" she whispered as a tremor of longing raced through her.

His hand curved around her chin, and he tilted her head up so that she was forced to look at him.

"That was not the right question, Charity. The right question is, do you want me to make love to you?"

"Yes." He was enchanted to see that her brows drew together as she uttered the word and a bewildered expression settled on her face. Shane was tempted to take her answer as a literal statement, but as he took note of the confusion in her eyes, he knew he couldn't. He wanted her—had wanted her since he'd first awakened this morning—and knowing she also wanted him only increased his desire. All he'd have to do is kiss her and everything would progress naturally from there. His loins tightened, urging him to close the short distance between his lips and hers, but he held himself back. She was so sweet and gentle, so innocent compared to the women he knew, that he wouldn't be able to stand it if he made love to her tonight and she regretted it in the morning.

He dropped his hand between them and moved it in an intimate caress across her abdomen. "In here, you want me to make love to you." He raised his hand to brush his fingers against her forehead. "But up here, you're not sure, so I can't."

Charity drew in a deep breath as she stared into his handsome face. She wanted him to make love to her. She wanted—no, needed—to feel alive.

She released her breath slowly. She had to be honest with herself, and the truth was she was too insecure with her own femininity to allow herself a night of pleasure. Shane was not only the most masculine man she'd ever seen but a famous singer who probably had women throwing themselves at his feet. A part of her would die if she gave herself to him and couldn't please him.

She could feel the tension in his body and decided it was time to distract them both. The best way to do that was through conversation. "Shane?"

"Uh-huh?"

"What's it like to be a rock star?"

At first he stiffened, wondering what had motivated the question. Was she like all the others? Was the fame an enticement? But when he gazed into her eyes, all he could see was honest curiosity.

He stroked her back as he considered her question. "I'm not sure how to answer that. When I first became one, it was exciting. Sort of like living out a fantasy. There was all the glitz and glamour that comes with fame, but then the fantasy began to fade. It didn't take me long to realize that most of the people who were trying to be my friends wouldn't have glanced at me twice if I hadn't been *the* Shane Burke from Moon and Sun. It was such a shallow world compared to the one I'd been raised in."

He sighed heavily and once again rubbed his cheek against her hair. "After the fantasy faded, it became work. For every hit song we wrote, we were challenged to write another, and another and another. After a while, it becomes a little frightening. You begin to wonder if when you go back to the creative well, it's going to have finally gone dry."

"But it hasn't," Charity stated knowingly.

He tugged gently at a lock of her hair. "Not yet, but by tomorrow, who knows?" He wound her hair around his finger and began to caress it with his thumb. "Anyway, it's a hard way to make a living. In order to stay on top, you have to remain visible. About the only way you can do that is to go on a concert tour. I spend about six months out of every year on the road. I get to the point where I hate hotels, would give my right arm for a home-cooked meal, and yearn for some anonymity. That's when I start threatening to retire and my manager sends me to my cabin for a rest."

"Is that how you ended up here?"

"Yes." He decided he didn't want to talk about himself any longer. It only made his doubts about his way of life more real. "So, tell me what it's like to be a doctor."

"It's not nearly as an exciting a life as yours. Every day I go to the emergency room, see an endless number of patients, fix them up as best I can, and either send them home or admit them. It's not very glamorous."

"It sounds glamorous to me."

"It does?" she questioned in surprise.

"Sure. I envy you your work. You're doing something worthwhile. You're saving lives. All I do is write and sing music."

"But that's worthwhile, too, Shane. Maybe even more worthwhile than what I do."

"Oh, yeah?" He shifted slightly so he could see her face. "How did you come to that conclusion?"

"People come to me to be fixed up. I patch them together and, hopefully, put them back on their feet. Then they go back to their lives, and I don't see them again until they need a new patch job. But you touch their lives every day. You bring them the beauty of music. I heal their bodies, but you keep their spirits going. I envy that."

He gently traced the ridge of her cheek, unable to believe she was real. How could she compare their lives and bring him out on top? To him it was inconceivable, yet those damn green eyes of hers told him she had meant what she'd said.

"When you put it that way, I guess I'm more important than I thought." He smiled and tapped the end of her nose playfully. "I suppose the grass is always greener on the other side of the lyric."

"Yes, I suppose it is," she whispered, wondering what he'd do if she kissed him.

His eyes darkened as if he were reading her mind. For a moment Charity thought he might take the initiative, and when he didn't, she found that her courage to initiate the kiss had fled.

"I think it's time we went to sleep," he said huskily.

"Yes," she murmured.

He pulled her head back down to his shoulder and began to hum an old English lullaby. By the time he'd finished, Charity had drifted off to sleep.

Shane lay quietly beside her, enjoying the weight of her on his arm. When her breathing slowed to the steady rhythm of deep sleep, she shifted so that she was nestled more intimately against him. It was torture for Shane to have her so close and not be able to make love to her, but it was such a delicious torture that he wasn't about to shift away from her.

He let his hand glide over her gently, memorizing each hill and valley of her body, and then he tangled his fingers in the rich strands of her hair. He brought it to his face and rubbed it against his cheek.

He wanted to hold her, to kiss her and to love her. He wanted to absorb the essence of Charity, sensing that she'd somehow heal some of the small wounds in his spirit, and in return he'd let her absorb the essence of him. He'd give her all the beauty he had inside.

What was wrong with that? he asked when a little voice inside spoke up in protest. He wasn't wishing for something he couldn't have; he only wanted to grasp the moment. A beautiful moment he could carry with him through the remainder of his life.

The voice remained doubtful, and he once again ignored it. One beautiful moment in life wasn't too much to ask for, and if he had an opportunity to make love to Charity, he would take advantage of it. He wasn't going to let anything, not even his conscience, take it away from him.

Chapter Four

The first thing Charity noticed when she awoke the next morning was that the room was silent. The second thing she became aware of was that it wasn't Shane she was holding in her arms but a pillow.

She cautiously opened her eyes and was surprised to discover Shane wasn't in bed. Then she realized what the silence meant. There was no wind. She glanced at the window to confirm what she already knew. The sun was out. The blizzard was over.

She immediately sat up, glancing around the room, a sense of uneasiness assaulting her when she discovered it was empty. Automatically, her gaze shifted toward the fireplace and the hook that had held Shane's coat and shirt, and she began to panic. Both garments were gone. He'd left and hadn't even bothered to tell her goodbye!

She threw back the covers and climbed out of bed just as the front door burst open. Shane entered, his arms loaded with firewood.

Charity pressed her hand against her chest in an effort to control the racing of her heart. He hadn't left. But it had been ridiculous to think he had. Even if the blizzard was over, he couldn't leave until the roads were plowed. He'd be stranded here at least until tomorrow.

Tomorrow? she repeated, realizing in that instant just how little time was left. It would take a day for the road crews to clear the roads, and then Shane would leave.

"Good morning, sleepyhead!" he greeted her cheerfully as he dropped the wood into the box beside the fireplace and then knelt to place some logs into the fire. "I've decided that dog of yours is part snowshoe rabbit."

"Oh?" she questioned uneasily, still trying to come to grips with the realization that he'd soon be leaving. "Why?"

Shane glanced toward her and grinned. "He's out there bouncing in and out of snowdrifts with so much energy he makes me tired."

"He's always liked snow," she offered, thinking how handsome the man looked with his cheeks reddened from the cold. She had the urge to go to him and rest her hands against his cheeks to warm them. And when they were warm, she'd draw his head down and—

She caught herself before her imagination could complete the fantasy she was weaving, but she couldn't take her eyes off him. For those few moments when she'd thought he had left, she'd felt crushed. Would she feel the same way when he was really gone? It was too depressing to think about.

"Have you been up long?" she asked as she crawled back into bed and pulled the covers up to her neck in an effort to remove the chill she'd gotten from the cold room.

"Long enough to shower, shave, whip up some pancake batter and gather some wood. Hungry?"

He meant that as a literal and not a rhetorical question, she firmly informed herself as her eyes drifted over him, taking in every nook and cranny of his body as he pulled off his coat and hung it on the rack.

"I think I could manage a few pancakes," she replied. "Are you cooking?"

He laughed. "I love a woman who gets her priorities in order, and, yes, I'm cooking. If you're nice to me, I just might even serve you breakfast in bed."

Shane felt his heart skip a beat when she gave him a small, almost shy, smile and confessed, "I haven't eaten breakfast in bed since I was ten years old and had the measles."

She looked about ten years old right now, he decided as his eyes drifted over her tousled hair and her face, which still appeared soft from sleep. She also looked all woman—warm and welcoming. He yearned to strip off his clothes, crawl into bed with her, and cuddle while she warmed his body. And then he'd...

He pushed the thought away. It wasn't time for that. Not yet. Maybe not at all, he acknowledged. His time was running out. The storm had ended, the sky was blue, and the snowplows would begin to clear the roads. By this time tomorrow he'd be gone.

"Well," he said huskily, "I think it's been much too long since you've been served breakfast in bed. So while I try to coax that crazy dog of yours into the house, I want you to stay under those blankets. Then I'll cook you pancakes that will melt in your mouth, and serve them in bed. Okay?"

"Okay." She snuggled down under the covers.

Shane crossed to the door and called for Mister. Charity laughed softly when the dog ignored him. He glanced over his shoulder and said, "I thought your dog was obedient."

"He's well-behaved. There's a big difference."

Shane chuckled. "Yes, I suppose there is. So what should I do? Go out and try to drag him in, or let him play?"

"Let him play. He'll come to the door when he's ready, and then we'll spend an hour mopping up the floor."

"Whatever," Shane said as he closed the door and headed for the stove.

Charity watched him place the ancient pancake griddle on the burner. He was humming to himself, and she wondered if he realized just how much music was a part of his everyday life. If he wasn't humming, he was whistling. If he wasn't whistling, he was singing. Some of his songs were familiar; otherwise he kept humming or whistling certain bars over and over, as if searching for the end of the tune. Was that how his songs came to him? From out of the blue as he cooked or did laundry or made a cup of coffee?

She found the thought fascinating and closed her eyes, letting the music move soothingly around her while she tried to make up words. She'd drifted off into a shadowy land that was between sleep and wakefulness, and her eyes flew open in surprise when Shane spoke from above her.

"I told you to snuggle, not go back to sleep!" he exclaimed in mock indignation. "You can't appreciate good pancakes unless you're fully awake."

"I'm awake," she assured him as she slid upward in bed.

Shane placed the tray of food on the foot of the bed, then grabbed the pillows and fluffed them. After making a big show of positioning them behind her back, he set the tray on her lap.

"Aren't you having any?" she asked as she eyed the pancakes, which were grilled to a perfect golden brown and smothered in maple syrup.

"I'll steal a bite of yours while mine finish cooking," he said as he slipped off his boots and sat down beside her. "Good?" he questioned after she'd taken a bite.

"Delicious. Of course, food always tastes better when it's cooked by someone else's hand," she added impishly as she speared a bite of pancake with her fork.

He chuckled, caught her hand and brought her fork to his mouth, stealing the bite of pancake hooked to it. Their eyes caught, locked, and something flared between them. It was warm; it was alive; and it was more than desire.

Charity felt shaken, and she could only stare at him. Shane smiled wryly and said, "They are good, aren't they?"

"The best," she whispered. "Want another bite?"

"If you can spare one."

"You can always make me another pancake, right?"

"Of course."

She found it funny, but her hand was steady as she cut off another bite of the pancake and lifted it for him to take into his mouth. She would have expected it to be shaking, but it appeared that all the tremors were internal.

He opened his mouth, and she placed the fork inside. But when she started to remove it, he caught the tines with his teeth. He held it for a moment as he gazed deeply into her eyes, and then he released it, immediately pushing himself to his feet and returning to the stove.

Charity regarded him curiously, wondering what was running through his mind. His eyes had gone through myriad changes in that short moment, but it had happened so rapidly, she hadn't been able to interpret a single emotion.

Shane drew in a deep breath, flipped the pancakes on the griddle, and stared at them unseeingly. There was a fire raging through him that was so hot, he'd be surprised if it didn't consume him.

In that brief moment when he'd taken the pancake from Charity's fork and looked into her eyes, he'd been given a glimpse into her soul. The innocence and vulnerability he'd seen reflected there had given rise within him to a protectiveness that was primitive in its intensity.

He'd never experienced such a feeling toward a woman, and to have it hit him with such force was terrifying. He wanted her, wanted to make love to her, but he feared what would happen if he did. Something deep inside told him that if he made love to her he'd feel responsible for her, and after thirty-six years of being single, he wasn't sure he was capable of living up to that kind of responsibility.

The type of life he led had no place for a career woman like Charity. He needed a woman who was flexible and willing to travel six months out of every year. A woman who wouldn't complain about changing one nondescript hotel room for another every day—sometimes twice a day. He needed...

He closed his eyes and drew in an impatient breath. He was doing it again. Wishing for something he couldn't have. He'd watched his singing partner, Derek, go through three disastrous marriages, and after his own disastrous affair with Diane, Shane had sworn that as long as he remained a part of Moon and Sun he'd never again become so attached to a woman.

But maybe he was making more out of his feelings toward Charity than he should. He wanted her more than he'd ever wanted another woman, and he knew she wanted him. Was it just a case of physical attraction precipitated by their confinement? If they made love, would the fire cool, or would it grow hotter? There was only one way to find out, but was he ready to face the consequences if the fire didn't cool?

His hands opened and closed convulsively around the handle of the oven door as he tried to latch on to his emotions, which were spinning in a hundred different directions. He was still trying to sort them out when a loud sound reverberated through the room.

He spun around in startled surprise and couldn't help the grin that sprang to his lips when Charity burst into pure, uninhibited laughter as she took in his confused expression.

"Mister wants in," she told him, laughing again as the front door rattled on its hinges. "I think he's had enough of his romp in the snow."

"I guess I'd better let him in before he breaks the door down," Shane said.

"Shane, wait. I should tell you..." Charity began as he walked across the room and curved his hand around the doorknob, but he jerked the door open before she could issue her warning.

Mister came through the door, nothing more than a streak of white. He raced around Shane half a dozen times before stopping long enough to shake, sending snow showering over Shane from head to foot.

"Oh, you think that's funny, do you?" Shane exclaimed with pretended anger as Charity began to roar with laughter. He'd have sent the dog back out and gone through the entire episode a hundred times if he'd been assured that she'd continue to laugh.

Shane stepped through the door, grabbed a handful of snow, and came back inside, advancing ominously toward the bed.

"Shane, you wouldn't!" Charity exclaimed as she scooted toward the far side of the bed, bringing her hand to her mouth to stop the giggles surfacing.

"I wouldn't?" he asked as he continued his approach while molding the snow into a compact ball. "Why wouldn't I?"

"Because... because..." She couldn't finish as the giggles burst forth, and she grabbed a pillow and held it in front of her like a shield.

Shane chuckled as he knelt on the edge of the bed. "Come here, Charity, and take your punishment with a stiff upper lip."

"No way," she laughed, scooting even closer to the edge of the bed. When her back came up against the wall, she knew she was trapped. Her gaze dropped to the snowball in his hand. "You wouldn't really do that to me, would you? After all, I tried to warn you, but you were too fast. You—"

She let out a gasp of surprise when Shane grabbed her wrist and gave it a tug that sent her sprawling on the bed. He was thrown off balance when the dip in the center widened, and he came down over her, but the anticipated cold of the snowball Charity prepared herself for never came.

She shifted her head until she was gazing into his eyes. He looked stunned. It was the same look he'd had on his face that first night when she'd half carried him into the cabin and they'd fallen to the mattress.

"Shane?" she whispered hesitantly.

"Tell me to go away," he pleaded hoarsely. "If you don't..."

He didn't have to finish the sentence. She knew exactly what he was saying. She also knew he was giving her a choice. Every ounce of woman in her rose to the surface, and as she stared at him, she realized she'd been a fool to worry about whether or not she could please him. When the chemistry was this strong, nothing but pleasure could be derived from their union.

She slid her hands over his wide chest, tested the muscles in his arms, let them travel over his strong shoulders, until they finally rose to wind around his neck. The fingers she buried in his silken hair were still tingling from the shock of hard, responsive muscle beneath her exploring touch.

"Get rid of that snowball, and kiss me," she ordered, vaguely wondering if that throaty, sexy voice could really belong to her.

"Lady, you've got a deal," he said, tossing the snowball over the foot of the bed and eagerly settling his lips on hers.

I shouldn't be doing this! Charity exclaimed inwardly, but that didn't stop her body's voluntary compliance when he slid his hand under her and pressed the small of her back, arching her against him.

She clung to his lips, drinking thirstily of his life-giving force. She couldn't protest when he slipped his callused hands beneath the hem of her nightgown, moving over every line, every curve, every indentation of her body and causing desire to sweep over her in undulating waves.

With a groan, Shane molded her to him, and Charity gasped at the strength of his arousal, which burned against her despite the clothing separating them.

"I've wanted to do this from the moment I opened my eyes yesterday morning," he rasped as he shifted and pulled her even more intimately against him. "I want to kiss you until you can't breathe; then I want to make love to you until you can't move. I want to touch you, have you touch me. I want—''

"Don't tell me—show me!" Charity gasped as his words vibrated through her, causing a volcanic eruption of longing.

"Easy, sweetheart," Shane crooned as she dug her fingers into his shoulders. "Let's take it slow and easy."

"Slow and easy?" she repeated disbelievingly.

He chuckled and continued to caress her under her nightgown. Some distant part of her brain informed her that he meant his touch to be soothing, but it was as if he were covering her with fire, and she caught his head and pulled it down to seal his lips with a frantic kiss.

She groaned in protest when he ended the kiss and began to ease himself away from her. "I'll be back," he whispered. "My pancakes are burning."

"Oh" was all she was able to manage as a reply.

She watched him walk toward the stove and then closed her eyes, forcing herself to face the questions rising to the surface. Was this what she wanted? By tomorrow he'd be gone, and she'd be left there alone. Would it be easier to watch him go if she let him make love to her?

No, she admitted, but she also knew she was going to go through with it. All her life she'd walked the conservative path, never performing one impetuous act. She was determined to make changes in her life, and even though she'd always considered it wrong to make love to a man when love wasn't involved, she knew she was going to give in to her desire for Shane Burke. He was offering her the chance to experience something special—something she might never find again.

"Change your mind?" Shane asked as he stood at the side of the bed and gazed down into her face.

Her eyes were closed, and her brow was furrowed. He knew he'd taken a chance when he'd walked away from her, but besides the fact that he couldn't have let the cabin burn down, he'd known he had to give her an opportunity to change her mind. An opportunity to say no.

She opened her eyes and whispered, "No."

Shane felt his heart hesitate, his stomach lurch and his knees weaken as she spoke the very word that had been present in his mind. He was still reeling from what he thought was her denial, and it took a moment for the rest of her words to sink in.

When they did, he swallowed hard and said, "Would you repeat that?"

"Make love to me."

He was so relieved he couldn't answer. He could only nod. His fingers were trembling as he began to unbutton his shirt, and Charity licked her lips as he tossed it to the floor and pulled his underwear over his head.

Her fingers itched to explore his chest, to intimately acquaint themselves with every golden hair on it, but she didn't reach for him. She lay still, watching as he undid the zipper on his pants and let them drop to the floor. While he removed his socks and the remainder of his underwear, she sat up on the bed, pulled her nightgown over her head and tossed it onto the floor heedlessly.

Shane drew in a long breath and let it out slowly as his eyes traced the slender but curvaceous lines of her body. "I liked the pink panties, but the royal blue are something else," he told her as his gaze settled on the scrap of lace encircling her hips. "How many colors do you have?"

"I don't know. Would you like me to check?"

"Later," he answered as he placed a knee on the bed and reached for her. "Are you sure about this?"

"Yes."

"There'll be no regrets?"

"No." And at the moment she knew it was the truth.

Shane searched her eyes to reassure himself that this was what she wanted. Finally he was convinced it was, and even though he wasn't convinced it was right for him, he knew he wasn't going to pull away. He'd promised himself one beautiful moment, and by damn, he was going to take it.

He kissed her deeply as he gently lowered her to the bed and lay beside her. The fire inside him became an inferno when her legs tangled with his, as smooth and fine as gossamer.

"You're so tiny," he whispered as he began to explore her with his large hands. "I feel like I'm going to crush you."

She smiled and pressed a reassuring kiss to his lips as she began an exploration of her own.

He shivered as she moved her fingers over him, homing in on every erogenous zone he had. "I've never made love to a doctor. I have a feeling it's going to be quite an experience. After all, what you know about anatomy will put my own techniques to shame."

The small echo of doubt in his voice made the remainder of Charity's hesitancy flee. He might be the most virile man she'd ever known, but he was right. She had a knowledge of anatomy that would make her his equal, and she set about proving it.

Shane groaned and shifted restlessly beneath her hands and lips, but he didn't fight her, didn't try to take control. He sensed it was important for her to be the active partner. Why had her husband ever let her go? he kept asking himself as his body became even more tense and his longing increased to a level he'd never known before. Finally, he could take no more, and he rolled, pulling her under him.

She cried out in exquisite pleasure as his lips captured a sensitive nipple and drew it into his mouth. He moved his lips and hands over her in a finely orchestrated pattern designed to drive her to madness, and he brought her to the peak of completion but drew away before she could leap over its edge. Then he brought her there again and again, and still again.

She clung to him, begging him to bring it to an end, though she contrarily wanted the pleasure to continue forever. When he stripped her panties from her hips and moved his lips to her most secret places, she cried out in wonder. He barely held her back from the edge.

Shane whispered her name when he finally decided it was time to know her as only a man can know a woman. She parted her thighs in invitation, and her green eyes were dilated with wonder as he thrust into her.

Shane hadn't been prepared for the feelings that becoming a part of her would bring, and he could barely hold back enough to let her adjust to him. He drew in several deep breaths as he waited for her to relax. She was so tiny, so very, very tiny. He couldn't bear to hurt her, yet the hot velvet sheath he'd entered was encouraging him onward and he knew his patience wouldn't last long.

When she wrapped her arms around his neck and arched toward him, Shane let out a sigh of relief. He began to move inside her with a gentle rocking motion, changing his rhythm only when she demanded it. At last, all control left him and he concentrated on bringing them to the finale. And then they were at the end, singing the closing note, and collapsing as its echo surrounded them.

Shane rolled, pulling Charity with him and enclosing her in his arms. It was a long time before their breathing slowed and their hearts stopped racing. He pressed his lips against her damp forehead before tenderly brushing her hair back from her brow.

"Beautiful music," he murmured. "We make beautiful music."

"The best," she whispered tiredly, resting her head against his shoulder.

Shane moved his hands over her, stroking her back and her hip, encouraging her to relax. When she was pliable under his caresses, he asked the one question that had continued to perplex him. "Charity, why are you up here?"

Charity didn't know if it was because she was so relaxed—so satisfied—or if he had just managed to finally erode the barrier she'd unnecessarily erected between them.

All she knew was that it no longer mattered if he heard the truth.

She yawned, snuggled closer and said, "I was held hostage in the emergency room for thirty-two hours. Afterward I had some kind of nervous breakdown."

"Hostage?" Shane repeated in concern. "What kind of hostage?"

"A sixteen-year-old kid went crazy on drugs. When the cops brought him in, he pulled a knife on me." She felt Shane's hand tighten around her buttock, but she ignored it. "It took him thirty-two hours to collapse. During that thirty-two hours I was at knife point."

The lack of emotion in her voice told Shane how terrifying the experience had been. He'd once had the same reaction when some fans had broken through the line of guards and assaulted him and Derek. When he'd asked a psychiatrist he'd met at a party why he felt as if it had happened to someone else, the man had explained that people tended to put up emotional barriers to a fear of such intensity. They could handle it more easily if they felt it hadn't happened to them.

Shane drew in his breath and held it. The thought of Charity at the other end of a knife petrified him. "He didn't hurt you?"

"No," she answered with a sleepy yawn. "I remained calm throughout the entire incident, but when it was over, I fell apart."

"You said this lasted thirty-two hours. Why didn't the cops subdue him?"

"I wouldn't let them. He didn't know what he was doing, and I knew it was only a matter of time before he collapsed. Besides, he was so irrational and frightened, he was quite capable of violence." For the first time she showed some emotion. She shivered, and Shane automatically drew her closer as she said, "I didn't want them to take a chance. If they made a mistake, I was the one who was going to get hurt."

"You said you had some kind of breakdown?"

"I'm afraid," she answered, shuddering again. "I'm absolutely terrified about going back to the emergency room. I keep wondering whether I can handle it if it happens again."

"The chances of something like that happening again must be pretty slim."

Her laugh was shaky. "I'm not so sure. Denver is a big city."

He still thought the chances were slim, but he didn't say so. "What are your options?"

"Private practice."

"But...? I sense a big *but* in there."

"It isn't the same challenge. I love my work. I feel...important. Do you know what I'm saying?"

"No, but I think I can understand. Several people have asked me why I haven't retired. Thirty-six is a little old for a rock star."

"And what's your answer?"

"I love the applause," he answered honestly. "Some musicians want more. They want to write musical scores for movies and screenplays. I've never had that desire. I want to do exactly what I'm doing."

"That's not what your song says," she reminded him. "You want more. You just haven't figured out a way to get it."

He sighed as he nodded in acknowledgment. "I suppose I'd like to have the best of both worlds."

"If you keep looking, maybe you'll get it."

"Maybe you can help me get it," he murmured as he pressed a tender kiss to her lips.

When the meaning of his words sank in, Charity drew away from him slightly. "Shane, don't make more out of this than what it is."

He stiffened and his brow furrowed with a frown. "Just what do you think this is?"

"Exactly what it is. A one-night stand."

"Damn it, Charity, this is not a one-night stand!" he exploded angrily.

"Then what is it?" she asked. "Shane, I'm attracted to you. I'd be crazy to deny that, but we live in separate worlds by entirely different sets of rules. What could we possibly have in common?"

Shane hated it, but he had to admit she was right. But there was no way to determine whether or not they had anything in common without spending some time together, and he was using up the only full week of rest and relaxation Roger reluctantly gave him in the middle of a concert tour. When he left Charity's cabin, the one thing he wouldn't have to spare was time.

He glanced down at her face. Her eyes were filled with concern, and she nervously caught her bottom lip between her teeth as his gaze met hers. She was the most wonderful thing that had happened to him in a long time, but she was right.

"I still say this isn't a one-night stand," he insisted.

"Maybe it's an encounter," Charity offered, sensing his need for reassurance.

"Maybe," he agreed, relaxing slightly. *Encounter* didn't sound quite so bad. He mellowed even more as she began to stroke his chest.

"Shane?"

"Yes?"

"How many times do you think we can make love before you have to go?"

He chuckled. "You're the doctor. Why don't you tell me?"

"I can't. Every man is different."

"Then I suggest we see just how different I am," he murmured huskily, shifting his hips toward her to prove that he was ready to start the music again.

Chapter Five

On Friday morning Charity sighed as they stood on her front porch and watched the snowplow creeping up the road.

Where had time gone? she wondered. Why hadn't they had more of it? The blizzard had moved away too fast.

Shane tightened his arm around her and pressed a kiss to the top of her head. "Are you all right?"

Charity glanced up at him and smiled as a gust of wind ruffled the blond hair on his forehead. She reached up to smooth it into place. "Of course."

His eyes were dark with concern. "You're sure?"

"Of course."

"No regrets?"

She brushed her fingers along his cheek and jawline as if memorizing their contour. "Our... encounter was something I'll always remember."

Her words echoed his own feelings, and impulsively he asked, "May I call you when I'm back in Denver?"

The little voice inside her cried a vehement *No!* But Charity said, "Yes."

"Our last concert for the season is scheduled there in three months. I'll make sure you have a ticket."

"I'd like that."

He paused then said, "Charity?"

"Yes?"

"When are you going home?"

"I don't know. I'm still looking for my answers."

"Will you make me a promise?"

She shrugged uneasily. "I suppose that depends on what the promise is."

"Promise me that you'll go home if you haven't found your answers by the end of the month. It worries me that you're here by yourself with no protection."

"I have Mister."

Shane looked at the dog sitting beside them on the porch and shook his head ruefully. "Forgive me, Charity, but Mister doesn't look like he could scare off a rabbit, let alone a full-grown criminal."

She chuckled. "You're right, and he's so friendly, he'd probably invite a burglar in and show him where everything is."

"Then you'll go home if you haven't found your answers?"

"I'll think about it."

Shane didn't like her response, but he knew he couldn't demand more. He'd made love to her, become a part of her, and knew he'd never be able to forget her. He wanted to make demands, but what right did he have to make them when he'd be walking away any moment and wouldn't see her again for at least three months?

"Where do you go from here?" she asked.

"To Cripple Creek, where I'll call my manager and tell him I'm safe. I have a concert in Chicago on Sunday, so I'll have to get down the mountain and onto a plane."

That was the day after tomorrow. She wanted to ask him to delay his departure until morning, but pride kept her from doing so.

As if reading her mind, Shane said, "Three months will pass fast, and I'll have a few days after the concert in Denver to spend with you."

A few days, she repeated inwardly. If she became involved with him, that's all he'd ever be able to give her. No more than a few stolen days out of a schedule that was as unrelenting as her own.

Why in the world had she let herself become involved with a rock star? But even as she asked the question, she knew she'd never trade the time she'd shared with him. They had been the most exciting—and most satisfying—days and nights of her life. Even if she never saw him again, Shane Burke had given her something she'd never had: the knowledge that she was a woman—capable of giving a man as much pleasure as he could ever want.

As the snowplow came closer, Shane said, "I'm going to ask him for a ride."

"I could give you a ride into Cripple Creek."

He shook his head. "I think it's best if we say goodbye here."

He was right and she knew it, even if she didn't want to admit it. "You'll call?"

"You know I will, but you'll have to be at home to receive my calls."

She released a long breath and nodded. "I'll be home by the end of the month."

"With or without your answers?"

"Yes."

His arm tightened around her shoulders. "I'll call you at the end of the month.... Charity?"

"What?"

He frowned in concentration as he stared down into her face. "Choose what's best for you. Don't let yourself get trapped into a situation you're not happy in. Once you're in that kind of situation, it's impossible to break out of it, because when people begin to depend on you, you become responsible for them. Take your time to find your answers. Promise me you'll do that."

She wondered if that's how he felt about himself. Trapped in a situation that made him unhappy. She wanted to ask but didn't. There just wasn't time. "I won't make any hasty decisions."

"I'm glad." He pulled her into his arms and kissed her deeply. The roar of the snowplow got louder, and Shane reluctantly released her. He glanced toward the plow, then back at her. He didn't want to go, and he could stay until tomorrow, he realized. All he'd have to do was ask the man on the plow to make a collect call for him. But even as he considered the possibility, he dismissed it. He wasn't sure he'd ever be able to leave if he spent any more time in Charity's arms. "It's time for me to go."

Tears welled into her eyes, but she blinked them back. "Goodbye."

"You never say goodbye. It's too permanent. You always say *au revoir*," he told her.

"Until we meet again," she said.

"Yes, until we meet again." He caressed her cheek before turning to race toward the snowplow, which had turned and was heading back down the road.

Mister whined and rested his head against Charity's leg as Shane climbed into the cab, leaned out and waved at her. She watched until the plow had driven away. Only then did she let the tears begin to fall.

Why was she crying? she asked herself as she impatiently wiped at her tears. She'd known from the beginning that he was only passing through, that he'd never stay. But the loving had been so good, she'd wanted him to stay with her.

But Shane had responsibilities just like she did. And it was time that she made up her mind about how she was going to handle them.

She walked back into the cabin with Mister on her heels. She absently ruffled the fur on his head as she dropped onto the sofa and stared at the sand paintings.

Her grandmother had always been able to find her answers here, so why couldn't she? She gazed at the pictures, willing them to tell her their secrets.

As the hours passed, she wearily laid her head against the overstuffed cushions. Mister rested his head on her foot. She tried to focus on her problems—the decisions she had to make—but all she could think about was Shane. And it was Shane who was still foremost in her mind when there was a knock on the front door.

Charity bolted upright and stared at the door in disbelief. Her gaze shifted to the clock on the mantel when the knock sounded again. It had been five hours. Had Shane returned?

He must have returned. Who else could it be? Her heart began to thump erratically, and she raced to the door. But before she threw it open, Shane's words came back to her: *You don't know who could come knocking at your door in the dead of winter.*

She called out, "Who is it?"

"Your brother, Jim."

Charity had been sure it was Shane and was disappointed. She forced a welcoming smile and opened the door.

Jim's eyes had dark circles of fatigue beneath them, his black hair was tangled, and his clothes were rumpled from the long drive he'd just made. He looked as disheveled as she felt.

"I've been worried sick about you, and I've come to take you home," he announced with a determined lift of his chin.

With a sob, Charity fell into his arms and began to cry all the tears she'd been holding inside. When she was finished, Jim was drenched and they were both shivering from the cold outside.

"It looks like I've arrived just in the nick of time," he told her.

She sniffed and pulled him into the cabin. "Would you like some coffee?"

"Do bears like honey?" he asked as he closed the door.

He pulled off his parka, hung it on the coatrack and tucked his chambray shirt into his jeans. Then he settled himself on the sofa as he watched her put the coffeepot on the stove.

"You're not any better," he said when she finally turned to face him.

"I am and I'm not."

"Would you care to translate that?"

"Not really. Why are you here?"

"I told you. I've come to take you home. There was a blizzard up here, in case you didn't notice, and you don't have a telephone or a shortwave radio. If you had an emergency, what would you do?"

Immediately her mind turned to Shane. He'd been an emergency, and she'd done what had to be done. Crawled into bed with him. But that wasn't something she could tell her older brother.

She studied Jim's face. He was two years her senior, but he appeared younger than Charity. He also looked like a proud Navaho brave, with his lean, sharp features and coal-black eyes. He should have inherited the cabin, she thought. He was the one who belonged here. The one the sand paintings would talk to.

"How's Chris?" she asked, deciding that talking about his wife was preferable to a lecture on staying in the woods alone.

"Worried sick about you, like I am. She said I wasn't to leave here unless you were with me, so if you have any sympathy for me and my marriage, you'll agree to come home. There's another storm moving in, but if we go within the hour, we'll miss it."

Charity started to say no but stopped. After a month at the cabin she was no closer to finding her answers than she'd been the day she'd arrived.

Her answers simply couldn't be found there, she finally acknowledged, and with the memory of Shane hovering over her, she'd only become more depressed. She needed to get away from the cabin. It was time she faced her world head-on.

"Give me forty-five minutes," she told her brother. "Then we'll leave."

He looked skeptical at her easy capitulation, but she knew he wasn't about to question it.

"Would you like to talk about it?"

Shane shook his head and looked away from his singing partner, Derek Halston. They were the antithesis of each other. Shane was blond and tan; Derek was dark and pale. Shane was tall and muscular; Derek, although as tall, appeared smaller because he was so slim. Shane was gregarious and easygoing; Derek was withdrawn and moody. But despite their contrasts in looks and personality, they'd been together for eighteen years, and Derek was the nearest that Shane had ever come to having a brother. But how could he explain Charity to his friend?

"It looks like love to me," Derek said as he stretched his long legs beneath the airplane seat in front of him.

"Love?" Shane repeated with a rueful laugh. "You're kidding!"

Derek shook his head, his face a picture of offended pride. "You of all people should know that the last thing I'd ever kid about is love—if you remember correctly, I send out three alimony checks a month. What happened up in those mountains?"

"Nothing," Shane answered, glancing out the window and listening to the four band members laugh and joke in the seats around them. He wondered how much longer it would be before they landed in New York. Did he dare try to call Charity tonight?

Three weeks had passed since he'd left her, and every day he'd reached for the telephone not once but several times, only to stop himself. She'd touched him in ways he wasn't sure he wanted to—or even could, for that matter—handle. Besides, he persuaded himself, trying to reach her would have been a waste of time. She'd said she wouldn't be home until the end of the month, and he still had a week to go. But maybe he should try to call her. The worst thing that could happen would be that she didn't answer.

Absently he fingered the business card in his pocket that held her home address and telephone number. Except when he'd showered, he'd never let it leave his person. She'd told him it was an unlisted number and if he lost it he might not be able to reach her, since she'd taken a leave of absence from the hospital.

He smiled ruefully at the window, which gave him a view of fluffy clouds and nothing more. It wouldn't have mattered if he had lost the card. Her number had been indelibly imprinted in his mind from the moment he'd first read it.

Finally, the plane landed at Kennedy. Roger waved him and Derek out, remaining behind with the band to ensure that all the instruments were unloaded properly.

As usual, the airport was crowded with fans, and Shane shivered when a group of security guards surrounded him and Derek. He'd never grown accustomed to the madness, probably never would. How could people claim to love him so much yet want to tear the clothes from his back?

He was being jostled through the corridors, following the path the guards created. He let his gaze wander around him, taking in the faces of screaming girls and boys barely old enough to drive, if they were indeed that old. Then his heart lurched as he saw the back of a small woman with shoulder-length raven hair.

"Charity?" he whispered, and pulled away impatiently from the security guard, who grasped his arm to keep him within the tight circle.

It had to be Charity. The raven hair shimmered the same way, and the woman's body was so small, so terribly slender.

"Mr. Burke," the guard stated impatiently, "you can't—"

"The hell I can't," Shane muttered as he moved toward the woman.

When he reached her, he touched her shoulder, ready to grab her and pull her into his arms. He was hit with a wave of shock when the woman turned toward him, her black eyes cautious and wary.

"Excuse me," Shane said hoarsely. "I . . . I thought you were someone else."

She smiled as she took in his black leather pants and white bolero shirt, which was open more than halfway down the front. "I wish I were."

Shane turned away from her without responding.

"It's love, all right," Derek said as he took Shane's arm and began to lead him down the corridor. "Damn, I never believed it would happen to you after that fiasco with Diane. What's her name?"

"It's not love!" Shane exclaimed impatiently. "You don't fall in love with a woman in two days!"

"Then how long does it take?" Derek asked, his lips twitching with suppressed laughter.

"I have no idea, but it takes longer than two days," Shane snapped as he pulled his arm away from Derek's hand. "In two days the only thing you have is . . . infatuation."

"Uh-huh. Well, my infatuated friend, I suggest you stop wandering away from our guards. If you don't, we're both liable to end up torn to pieces. It's a good thing Roger's handling the band and the instruments. If he'd seen you pull that stunt back there, he would've had your hide. When are you calling her?"

"Calling who?"

"Ms. Infatuation. Who else?"

"Tomorrow."

* * *

Charity awoke early, stared at her alarm clock, and wondered if this would be the day Shane would finally call. She'd expected him to call every day for the past week and had spent each waking moment in anticipation, only to be disappointed. She'd told him she'd return by the end of the month, and there were only a few days left. So why hadn't he tried to call?

Where was he? What was he doing? She'd asked him his schedule before he left the cabin, but he'd shrugged and said, "I always know the beginning and the end, but other than that, I never know more than what's directly ahead of me. If I try to keep track of more, it becomes too complicated."

She had told him she understood, even though she really didn't. She couldn't always know her exact schedule, but she at least had an idea of what each day ahead of her held. If she didn't, it drove her crazy.

It was just one more thing they had going against them, she realized as she crawled out of bed when Mister pawed at the sliding glass doors and whined.

When had she started making a list of the good and bad of their relationship? she wondered, letting the dog out. Good heavens, it wasn't even a relationship! she reminded herself as she pushed her hand impatiently through her hair. They had had an encounter—an unexpected meeting—and an encounter did not a relationship make.

She wandered into the bath, performed her morning toilette and let Mister back in. He followed her to the kitchen, where she fed him and began to fix herself some breakfast.

Tomorrow she'd begin a new routine, she realized as she settled down at the kitchen table and began to nibble on toast smothered with strawberry jam. Tomorrow she'd begin working temporarily at the clinic down the road, filling in for a doctor who was undergoing back surgery. It would be her first venture into private practice, a chance to find out if she liked it.

She'd visited the emergency room once to gather some of her personal belongings. She'd been glad that she'd applied for a leave of absence, because by the time she'd walked out, she'd been drenched in sweat. Everywhere she'd looked she'd seen that kid with the knife, and she couldn't have functioned under a crisis situation if she'd had to.

But private practice? She just couldn't envision herself in an office with a never-ending parade of patients, many of whom had nothing more wrong with them than the need to talk.

Emergency medicine offered a challenge she'd never find in an office. Of course, even in the emergency room she'd had a few patients who wandered in, looking for nothing more than someone to listen to them, yet there were the trauma victims, the heart attacks. People desperately in need of her attention in order to survive.

She dropped her toast on her plate, frowning at the African violets blooming in the kitchen window. Was she so egotistical that she had to be challenged with a life-or-death situation in order to derive satisfaction from medicine? Was she trying to elevate herself to some kind of godhood?

The questions worried her. She'd never considered herself egotistical, nor had she ever felt that she was playing god, but medicine should fulfill her whether she was in the emergency room or in an office. Making people well was what was important. And what was the difference between treating a patient with a head cold and a patient with a serious head wound? Both were ill. Both needed help. However, Charity knew she'd choose to treat the head wound before the cold.

Imminent danger was her challenge. She was egotistical. She did enjoy playing god. She wanted to defy the fates and snatch back a life before it could be taken away. She was...sick, she decided. Sick and in need of help.

Her knees shook as she rose to her feet and crossed to the telephone. She flipped through her phone book until she found the number she wanted. Then she dialed, knowing she'd get an answering service. When she did, she said, "This is Dr. Charity Wells. I need to speak to Dr. Rutherford right away. Is it possible to reach her?"

"If you'll give me your number, I'll have her call you right back," the man on the other end stated.

Charity recited her telephone number, hung up and dropped weakly back into the chair she'd just vacated. Self-insight was devastating, she decided. So devastating that it took a professional to help. Mary Rutherford was one of the best psychiatrists in the country, and a friend. Charity needed both right now, she realized as tears began to course down her cheeks. She definitely needed both.

Shane cursed when he got a busy signal for the fifth time. His nerves were stretched to their limit, and his tension wasn't eased with the knowledge that Charity was home. He wanted to talk to her. To know she was all right.

"Still trying?" Derek asked as he wandered into the living room that separated their suites.

"Yeah," Shane answered. "Where's our schedule for the remainder of the month?"

"Roger has it."

"Why don't we have a copy of it?"

Derek arched a brow at Shane's irritated tone of voice. "In eighteen years, neither of us has ever wanted it. We live for the moment, remember? All those mundane chores like schedules are Roger's province."

"I want a copy of the schedule," Shane stated as he reached for the telephone and asked the operator for Roger's room. When there was no answer, he cursed and slammed down the phone. "Where the hell is he?"

"Probably doing whatever managers do at this time of day. Calm down, Shane. If you want a copy of the schedule, Roger will give it to you."

Shane nodded, rose to his feet and began to pace restlessly around the room.

Derek collapsed on a nearby sofa and rested his feet on the glass coffee table in front of it. "I think you need to talk," he said quietly. "Whoever this woman is, she's driving you crazy. You haven't been the same since you came back from the mountains. What happened up there?"

"She saved my life," Shane answered as he stopped at the penthouse window that looked out over the streets of New York.

"Saved your life? How?"

Shane ignored the question. He didn't want to spend time telling Derek the story. He wanted to talk to Charity. Now.

They were scheduled to fly out of New York late this afternoon. Then they'd be in Miami. They'd give a concert the day after tomorrow, and then they'd head for New Orleans. From there, his future was a blank. Roger held it all in his hands. Why couldn't he reach Roger? He wanted to be able to tell Charity where he was going. He wanted . . . to be with her, he realized.

He pivoted on his feet and strode purposefully toward his bedroom.

"Shane, what are you doing?" Derek questioned worriedly from the doorway as Shane opened his suitcase and began to stuff clothing into it.

"I'm going to Denver. How about calling the airport and booking me on the next flight out?"

"Are you crazy? Roger will hit the ceiling. Will you be back in time for the Miami concert?"

"I'll make Miami. Are you going to make that call?"

"Is she worth that much to you?"

Shane hesitated in his packing and gave a confused shake of his head. "I don't know, and until I see her again, I probably won't. Does that make sense?"

"It's the only thing you've said in the past three weeks that does make sense."

Charity sniffed and swiped at her nose for what seemed the thousandth time that day. Mary Rutherford had called her back, and they'd talked for more than an hour. Mary had assured her she wasn't egotistical nor trying to play god. She merely had the type of personality that functioned well in the crisis environment of an emergency room. And thank God there were people with that kind of personality! the psychiatrist had exclaimed.

When Mister nudged his empty dog dish with his nose, Charity frowned at the clock. It was already early evening, and Shane hadn't called. That only made her more depressed.

It had been twenty-three days since he'd left her cabin, and he'd probably forgotten she even existed, she decided as she filled Mister's bowl and gave him fresh water. Why would Shane remember her when he had thousands of young sexy girls throwing their nubile bodies at him everywhere he went?

She wandered into the living room and dropped down on the sofa as she tried to imagine what his life was like. She let her memory recall the bits and pieces she'd read and heard about rock stars over the years. They led glamorous lives, many of them changing wives and girlfriends as often as they changed their clothes. There were groupies to contend with, and even rumors of drugs.

The thought startled her. Drugs? Imagining Shane involved with drugs was impossible. But still— No, she decided with a firm shake of her head. He took too good care of his body to ever let himself destroy it with a poison like that. She could imagine him with other women, but she couldn't imagine him involved in the drug scene.

She also couldn't imagine where he was. The silence in the house was unnerving. She picked up the remote control for the television set and pushed the On button. She flipped through sixteen channels, and not one of them had a program that sparked her interest.

She turned off the TV and went over to the stereo system. Lying beside the tape deck were three tapes, all with their wrappers still on. All were of the group Moon and Sun. Did she dare listen to them?

She decided that listening to Shane sing couldn't be any worse than thinking about him, so she opened the top one, which declared itself to be *Greatest Hits, Volume 1*, and inserted it into the tape deck. Soon Shane's voice was echoing around her. Shivers of recognition raced up and down her spine, and tears filled her eyes as he crooned the words to the old love song he'd sung at her cabin.

She lifted the plastic holder that had held the tape and touched a finger to Shane's image, which was printed on the paper inside. Had he really been at her cabin, or had he just been a vision brought on by loneliness?

The warmth that flooded her body assured her he had been there. He had been real. He had made love to her. And then he'd gone away.

Where was he? What was he doing? she asked herself for at least the hundredth time in less than an hour. If she only knew his schedule, she'd be more relaxed. She could imagine where he was at any one moment. She— Her thoughts were interrupted by the ringing of the doorbell.

She walked to the door, grabbing the envelope that held the paperboy's money off the small table in the foyer. She pulled the door open and extended the envelope, her mouth gaping and her eyes widening when she realized it wasn't the paperboy but Shane standing on the other side. Had the sound of his voice conjured him up? Was he real?

"Shane?" she whispered uncertainly.

He nodded, unable to move as he stared at her hungrily. She was even more beautiful than he remembered, and he wanted to pull her into his arms and never let her go. But she wasn't moving toward him, and he shifted from one foot to the other as he glanced down at the envelope in her hand.

"I think that's supposed to read 'paperboy,' but it looks more like 'pepperbox.' Is it true that doctors have to pass a course in bad penmanship before they can get their medical degree?" he asked in an effort to cover his indecision.

"It's not a course," Charity automatically answered, still unable to believe he stood right in front of her and wondering why she wasn't throwing herself into his arms. But he hadn't opened them, and she wasn't certain how to respond. "It's just that you have to take so many lecture notes that the words start to run together. It's a habit that's hard to break. I . . . Shane, what are you doing here?"

"I brought you my books on sand paintings," he answered as he tapped the texts he had tucked under his arm. "But I'm only lending them to you. I do want them back."

"Of course you want them back." He'd brought her his books on sand paintings? she wondered in confusion. Was that the only reason he was here?

He leaned against the door frame and grinned. "There's a condition that goes along with borrowing them."

"What condition?" she asked breathlessly, trying to decide if the man really had become more handsome or if her memory wasn't as accurate as it should have been.

"You have to give me a kiss for every word you read," he replied huskily.

"A kiss for every word?" she echoed.

"A kiss for every word."

"If I kiss you now, will that count for one of my words?"

"I'm feeling expansive. I'll let it count for two. But," he warned her as he set the books down on top of his suitcase and opened his arms, "it'd better be worth two words."

"I'll try to make it a three-word kiss just for good measure," she said, and fell into his embrace.

Chapter Six

Charity's kiss had definitely been a three-word kiss, Shane decided as he forced himself to ease away from her. Actually it had been more like a ten-word kiss. He wanted to crush her slender body to him and make love to her right where they stood. He also wanted to talk. Before he made love to her, he had to know what she'd been doing for the past three weeks. Had she found her answers? Were they the right ones? Had she missed him?

He hadn't meant to let that last question creep in. He'd been ignoring it, but now that it had surfaced, he wanted to know the answer.

Charity gazed up into his face and wondered how she'd survived twenty-three days without hearing from him. She wanted to wrap her arms around his neck, pull his head back down and kiss him until he lost all control. She also wanted to hear his voice. She wanted him to tell her every detail of his days since she'd last seen him. How was his concert tour going? Was he all right? Had he missed her?

Now, where had that question come from? If he'd missed her, wouldn't he have tried to call? But she'd told him she'd be staying at the cabin until the end of the month, so he wouldn't have had any reason to call, she reminded herself.

"I usually get paid for a performance," Shane murmured as he gently touched a finger to first her cheek, then the tip of her nose, and finally her lips, wanting to reassure himself she was real.

"What?" Charity questioned in confusion.

He smiled. "Don't look now, but your neighbors are beginning to congregate in their yards at an alarming rate. Don't you ever have any company of the male persuasion?"

"My neighbors?" she repeated, risking a glance over her shoulder. She grinned. "Even Mrs. Barnett is standing out there. If she approaches you, tell her you're my new interior decorator. If she finds out I'm harboring a rock star, she'll probably tar and feather me."

"Which one's Mrs. Barnett?" Shane asked as he studied the neighbors who had come out into their yards, trying to look busy instead of curious, which, considering the winter temperature, only made their efforts more conspicuous.

"She's the one in the pink sweat suit with curlers in her hair."

He chuckled and let his hand slide down Charity's back. "Is she the neighborhood gossip?"

"Among other things. You aren't even concerned, are you?"

"No. I haven't lived in a neighborhood since I was eighteen years old. I've missed it. Right down to the gossipy Mrs. Barnett, but since you're going to have to continue living here, how about if we go inside?"

"I thought you'd never ask," she answered. "Where are you going to be staying?"

Shane hesitated as he picked up his suitcase. Had he expected too much? He cleared his throat uncomfortably.

"I'd, uh, hoped to stay here. If I won't be intruding, of course."

"You won't be," Charity immediately assured him. "I just thought that since you're so famous..."

Shane carried his suitcase inside and closed the door behind him. "Since I'm so famous, what?"

"Don't you need special...protection?" she said hesitantly as he removed his coat and extended it toward her. She hung it in the entry closet.

"Only from women intent upon ravishing me, and that couldn't possibly happen here, could it?" he teased.

"I'm not joking, Shane," she said as she closed the closet door and leaned against it.

She looked so serious, so sober, and so very concerned that a new wave of desire shot through Shane. How long had it been since a woman had been concerned about him? Too long. Much too long.

"Derek is the only one who knows where I am, so I'm safe."

"You're sure?"

"I'm positive."

Charity let out a sigh of relief. "Good. Would you like some coffee? I've just put on a fresh pot."

Shane's lips twitched as he recalled that when she wasn't sure about herself or her circumstances, she offered coffee. It was an endearing quality he'd missed.

"I'd love a cup of coffee."

She nodded and turned to lead the way to the kitchen.

Still not certain what his "guest" status entailed, Shane left his suitcase behind. He didn't want to make any false moves. He wanted to make love to her, but, oddly enough, being with her was more important. If she decided to ensconce him in a guest bedroom, he'd accept that. As long as she didn't ask him to leave.

"Mister!" Shane exclaimed when they walked into the kitchen and the dog raced toward him.

Charity smiled as she watched Shane kneel on the floor and roughhouse with the dog. "I think Mister likes you."

"Well, I'm glad, because I definitely like him. But what did you do to him? He looks like a half-naked rat!"

"I had him groomed."

"Groomed?" Shane eyed the dog's traditional poodle cut dubiously. "Shaved is more like it. Huh, boy?" he questioned Mister as he rolled the dog around on the floor some more. "He doesn't even look like Mister, but at least you didn't do something ridiculous like having bows stuck all over him."

"He pulls them off," Charity said as she poured coffee into two mugs. "How's your concert tour going?"

"It's going," he answered as he rose to his feet and accepted the mug she extended toward him. "And how are you?"

"I'm fine," she replied, leading the way toward the enclosed sun porch off the kitchen that served as a dining area.

Shane followed, his gaze shifting to take in his surroundings. Charity's home was expensively furnished, yet warm and inviting. But it wasn't as comfortable nor as welcoming as her cabin had been, and he couldn't dismiss the slight uneasiness the admission caused.

They'd made love together. Beautiful love. More beautiful than he'd ever experienced, but was this the same woman? He let his eyes drift over her slim figure which was clad in a red sweater and black slacks. She looked the same, talked the same, and walked the same. But there was something different. Something he couldn't quite put his finger on.

All his doubts fled when they walked onto the sun porch. It was as if they'd entered an exotic jungle, and mixed among the large selection of plants were handwoven Navaho baskets and handmade pottery. She was the same woman. Only here, she was a little more civilized.

Charity sat down at the white wrought-iron table and let her eyes drift over Shane. He looked magnificent in the yellow sweater, which molded to his chest, and the brown slacks, which were impeccably tailored. He was thinner, though, she decided, and he looked weary.

"You're tired," she said.

He nodded as he absently sipped at the coffee. "It's been a rough few weeks."

"Where have you been?"

"Do you want the towns or the states?"

"Which is easier?"

"The states. I've been in Illinois, Ohio, Massachusetts, Pennsylvania, and New York."

"And how many concerts have you given?"

"Eighteen."

"Eighteen!" Charity gasped. No wonder he was tired. "You've only been gone twenty-three days and you've given eighteen concerts?"

"In the old days I would have been gone twenty-three days and have given thirty or forty concerts. Fame does have its advantages."

"How can you do it?"

He shrugged. "Singing is my career." He sipped at his coffee again, then asked, "When did you come home?"

She gave him a wry smile. "The day you left."

"The day I left?" Shane repeated in disbelief.

"Yes. Five hours after you'd gone, my brother showed up, determined to drag me home. I decided that my answers weren't at the cabin, so I left with him."

It took Shane a few minutes to absorb the fact that she'd been here ever since he'd left her. He'd spent the last twenty-three days avoiding the phone, forcing himself to wait, and all he'd gained was a lot of long, lonely days that he hadn't had to live through. He should have followed his instincts and tried to call.

But would talking to her during all that time have soothed his nerves or only made him more agitated—more determined to see her? He had a feeling that the latter was the answer, and he wasn't sure he liked it. In two days Charity had made more of an impact on his emotions than any woman he'd ever met. He tried to tell himself it was because she'd saved his life, but there was a little doubting voice inside he couldn't quite ignore. There was more than gratitude involved here. There was . . . infatuation. He wondered if he was too old to be infatuated.

"And have you found any answers here?" he asked.

"No, but I'm going to try a temporary venture into private practice. There's a clinic down the road that needs a doctor for three months while a member of their staff is recuperating from back surgery. It'll give me a chance to see if I like private practice."

"That sounds like an ideal opportunity. You won't be forced to make any commitments, and if you don't like it, you'll be able to walk away with no regrets."

"Exactly," Charity said.

"When do you start at the clinic?"

"First thing in the morning."

"In the morning?" Shane questioned, then tried to hide his disappointment when she nodded. He was scheduled to fly out of Denver tomorrow afternoon and had planned on spending every minute till then with Charity.

He started to ask if she couldn't delay starting at the clinic for another day but changed his mind. Doctors couldn't just call in and cancel appointments. He had enough knowledge of medicine to realize that.

The thought only made him more poignantly aware of how ill-fated any relationship between them would be. She couldn't be available whenever he had the opportunity to come see her, and there was no way he could adjust his schedule to be with her when she was available. If he had any common sense he'd walk out the door right now, board the next plane to Miami, and never come back. If he had any common sense, that was. Where Charity was involved, he was convinced he didn't.

"How long can you stay?" she asked him.

"I'll be leaving in the morning."

"For where?"

"Miami. And after that, New Orleans. From there I'm not sure, but once I am, I'll let you know."

She nodded, attempting to hide her disappointment that he had to leave so quickly and consoling herself with the fact that he hadn't had to come. He could have simply called.

"Would you like a tour of the house?" she asked.

"I'd love to see it. Lead the way."

Shane was impressed with Charity's home. It wasn't a large house, but it gave the impression of space by the use of glass tables, a minimum of furniture, and strategically placed mirrors. Off-white walls were brightened with colorful paintings, and each room was a combination of browns and pastels.

She led him through the living room, kitchen, dining room and two guest bedrooms. When she finally arrived at the master bedroom, Shane smiled as her cheeks colored noticeably.

"And this is my room," she told him, ducking her head shyly as she pushed open the door.

Shane let out a low whistle when he stepped inside. This room was Charity, he realized as his eyes took in the dramatic display of colors. Once again her Indian heritage surfaced. Navaho rugs were scattered across the floor. A Navaho-patterned bedspread covered the bed. Portraits of Indians covered the walls, and pottery filled every available space.

He could have been back at the cabin. The only things missing were the sand paintings, he realized.

"I gather you like the room," Charity said.

"I love it. It's you."

She smiled. "I'm not sure about that, but I do feel at home in here."

"So why didn't you decorate the rest of the house the same way?"

"Too much of something destroys its impact. Besides, I don't always like sharing my heritage. It's personal," she confessed. "I'm not ashamed that I'm part Navaho. I'm proud of it. But..."

"But some people might react with bigotry, and you don't want to be placed in a position where you have to defend your heritage," he said, exhibiting an insight that Charity found startling.

"In a manner of speaking. I'm basically a pacifist. I try to avoid conflicts of any kind. I'm also very involved with my Navaho roots at this point in my life. If someone questioned them or placed me in an uncomfortable position, I'd overreact. I've been doing that a lot lately," she admitted.

"In what way?"

"A lot of ways. Ways I can't really explain. I'm just not being me."

"Or maybe you are being you and that's where the conflict is entering," Shane stated. "Have you ever let yourself just be you?"

She stared at him assessingly before countering with "Have you?"

He chuckled. "That's a question too deep to even consider at the moment."

He crossed to the sliding glass doors that led out to the backyard. Right now the trees that loomed against the sky were no more than barren skeletons, as were the rosebushes and various other plants. But he could imagine what it would look like in spring when the trees flourished with new leaves and the roses began to bloom. It made him yearn for the innocence of youth. The days when he'd lived and played in a yard very similar to this. Except one of those barren trees had had a rickety tree house that had been his unconquerable domain.

He liked Charity's home, he decided, and he agreed with her decision to keep the Navaho part of her life separate. It allowed her to maintain a certain amount of anonymity. A part of herself to bask in. He'd lost that anonymity eighteen years ago and had learned to regret it.

"You're being awfully quiet," Charity remarked.

Shane smiled down at her as she stepped to his side, and he draped an arm around her shoulders to draw her close. "I'm being envious," he explained.

"Envious?"

"Yes. Whether or not you realize it, you have it all. At least you have the most important part of life that a man or woman can have."

"And what's that?" she inquired.

"Stability. A place to call home. I don't have that, and it's the only part of my career I really hate."

"So why don't you buy yourself a home?"

"Because I'd be buying a house," he answered as he leaned his head against hers and gazed longingly out at the backyard. "In order to have a home, you have to live in it. You have to mark it with all the things that make you as you. I'm never around long enough to do that. If I'm not on the road, I'm making special appearances or recording or doing a thousand other things that promote Moon and Sun."

"Then maybe you should reassess some of those obligations. Decide which ones are responsibilities and which aren't. Give yourself some time to make a home."

"Maybe I should. The only problem is . . ."

"Is what?" Charity prompted him.

"It wouldn't keep the loneliness away," he answered.

Before she could respond he shifted so that she was facing him. Cradling her face between his hands, he tilted her head upward so he could gaze into her eyes. He was going to kiss her, Charity realized, and held her breath in anticipation.

Shane stroked her cheeks with his thumbs and let his eyes absorb every detail of her beautiful heart-shaped face. He could write a thousand songs about her and never scratch the surface of what she made him feel. For a moment—just a moment—he let himself wonder if she was good for him. She was putting cracks in his armor. Cracks that he wasn't certain could be repaired. But he knew he wouldn't be able to walk away from her, and he admitted that today's journey was just the beginning of what was going to be a precarious, and most likely disastrous, relationship.

Time was their enemy. It would keep them apart when they should be together, and he could see no way that either of them could put more time into their days. But they could put every moment they had together to good use. They could make every second special and memorable.

He lowered his head and gave a rapturous sigh when her lips parted welcomingly beneath his. For now, this was where he belonged. In the arms of the most exquisite woman he'd ever met.

Charity was stunned by the yearning she felt in his kiss. It was as if he were trying to absorb her—as if it were his only means of assuring himself she was real.

The need he was communicating struck a chord deep inside her. A chord of desperation that she could not ignore. She wrapped her arms around his neck and rose on tiptoe so that she could lean into his strength. He slid his arms down her back so he could pull her more intimately against him. Oddly enough, even though his kiss was filled with a violent passion, his body was not communicating the same need.

Charity felt confused, and she pulled away from the kiss to gaze up at him in concern. "Shane, are you all right?"

"More than all right," he answered as he rubbed his nose against hers playfully. "But I happen to be starving. What are we having for dinner?"

"Dinner? You're worried about dinner?"

"Is there something else I should be more concerned about?" he questioned huskily, nuzzling her nose again.

"Yes," she answered bravely. "You should be concerned about me."

He arched a brow. "Why? Is something wrong with you?"

"You know there is, and I want to know what you're going to do about it."

"All I was waiting for was an invitation," he said as he swung her up into his arms and walked toward the bed.

He lowered her to the spread and lay beside her. He moved his hands over her in gentle exploration that was designed to refamiliarize himself with her soft curves rather than excite her.

Charity smiled and let her own hands move over him, getting to know him again and reveling in the muscle and sinew she encountered. Only when his caresses began to change did she let her own become more intimate, and her smile turned into a grin of satisfaction when he groaned and caught her lips with his.

Once again his kiss was filled with yearning, only this time his body was also responding. Charity rolled over, molding herself to him, and she murmured in protest when he eased himself away from her.

"I can't take your sweater off if you're glued to me," he told her as he sat up and began to tug it over her head.

When he'd removed it, he gazed down at her with eyes that were dark, passionate pools of promise. So gently that she could barely feel his touch, he skimmed his fingers along the top of her bra. Then he released the front catch and let out a ragged breath.

"Beautiful. You are the most beautiful woman I've ever met," he said as he caught her breasts in his hands, tested their weight, and then lowered his head.

Charity caught her lower lip between her teeth to keep from crying out as he drew a nipple into his mouth, bringing it into a hard nub. When satisfied with his effect, he moved to her other breast, and while he teased it into the same response, she began to tug at his sweater.

He laughed softly as he sat up, dragged his sweater over his head and threw it to the floor. Then he caught her hands and urged her upward, pulling her against him when she was sitting beside him.

Heat surged through her in pulsing waves as he brushed his bare chest against her breasts in a tantalizing motion.

Then he caught her head in his hand and kissed her so deeply that she was lost in a whirlpool of sensation, hardly aware when he lowered her back to the bed and slid her slacks down over her hips.

When had he removed the rest of his clothes? Charity wondered vaguely when his bare legs tangled with hers. But the question didn't really demand an answer, and even if it had, she was so lost in the pleasure he was creating, she wouldn't have heard it.

As he had at the cabin, he brought her to the edge of oblivion but drew back before she could go over. When she tried to return the favor, he caught her hands and murmured, "Let me make love to you. Just relax and let me do everything."

She couldn't have argued if she had wanted to, and she let him make love to her in a way she'd never been made love to before. By the time he finally came to her, it took no more than his entry to push her to the stars. But when she came shooting back down, he began rocking against her, stopping her downward flight and sending her careering upward again.

They reached the heavens together, sharing an explosion that left them both weak and trembling. Shane rolled to his side, bringing her with him. He was so exhausted he couldn't think, but the fear of crushing her had surfaced. They were still joined as he locked his hands behind her and hugged her close.

"We're better!" he whispered hoarsely. "We're even better than before."

"Yes, we're even better," she agreed. They were as mismatched as any couple could be. Yet when they were in each other's arms, they couldn't have been more matched. But there was more to a relationship than sexual compatibility, and Charity knew she couldn't continue to see Shane without some form of a commitment toward a relationship. The question was, how did she explain that to him? "Shane?"

He didn't answer, and when she shifted so she could look into his face, she smiled indulgently. He'd fallen asleep, and she gently brushed her fingers against the fatigue lines at the corners of his eyes.

Reluctantly, she withdrew from his embrace. After covering him with a blanket, she put on a robe and went into the kitchen to start dinner. She kept all her thoughts and doubts at bay while she made a chicken casserole and slid it into the oven.

Then she went into the living room and curled up on the sofa, staring at a potted ivy as she listened to another of Shane's tapes. The entertainer behind the voice was a man she really didn't know, and she began to worry about that fact. Shane was multidimensional, and she'd only seen one dimension. If she got to know the complete man, would she even like him? She pushed her hand through her hair as if the gesture might clear her head.

For the past three weeks, Shane had rarely left her thoughts, and when he'd shown up unexpectedly today, she'd felt as giddy as a schoolgirl in love. But what was drawing her toward him besides the physical attraction? And there was more involved. She just couldn't put her finger on it.

She recalled him standing in her bedroom and staring out at the backyard with longing while he'd confessed being lonely. Was she only latching on to his loneliness because she shared it? Was she trying to create something out of nothing? Was she so desperate for companionship that any was preferable to none?

They were disturbing questions, and their elusive answers were even more disturbing. Because if she and Shane were being drawn together for no reason other than loneliness, both of them could end up getting hurt.

She sat up in surprise when Shane said, "Do you want me to leave?"

Her gaze drifted over him. He was standing, naked and beautiful, at the entrance to the hallway leading to the bedrooms. Charity couldn't help the rush of feeling the sight of his body created, and she shook her head, not certain if it was a denial to his question or to the effect he continued to have on her.

Shane let his clenched hands relax at his sides when she shook her head. He'd awakened and come looking for her, but she'd looked so serious, so withdrawn, curled up on the sofa that he'd felt a sense of fear. Had he rushed her? Had he misinterpreted her intimation that she'd wanted to make love? As he'd admitted when he'd first arrived, he could handle her not wanting to make love, but he couldn't handle her wanting him to leave.

He pushed a trembling hand through his hair and said, "Would you mind getting my suitcase? I'm afraid I'll really stir up the neighborhood if I walk in front of the windows dressed like this."

"No problem," Charity said as she pushed herself up off the sofa and went to retrieve his suitcase.

When she gave it to him, he said, "Thanks." He hesitated. "Charity, is something wrong?"

"No," she lied, and then blushed when he arched a knowing brow.

"I think we need to talk," he said. "We'll do it as soon as I'm a little more decent. Is it all right if I take a shower?"

"Of course. My house is yours."

"If only that were true," he said, and turned away before she could answer.

Had he sounded bitter? she wondered. Or was it only her imagination?

Shane took his time to shower and dress, trying to decide just what he wanted to say to Charity and how he wanted to say it. He knew she was having doubts. So was he. She'd brought forth longings and feelings he'd thought dead. She'd also been a catalyst to give rise to a major question he'd been ignoring for the past eleven years. There had to be more to life than his career, but how could he find a happy balance?

Eleven years ago, he'd tried to develop a relationship. Thank heavens, he and Diane had never made it to the altar. They'd parted so bitterly that he couldn't even imagine what would have happened if they'd had to drag it through the divorce courts.

His major problem back then had been—and still was, for that matter—time. Of course, with Diane he'd had even less time than now. He'd still been building his career—moving toward the top. And like Charity, Diane had had her own career to consider. Soon their rare times together had become battlegrounds rather than loving grounds. He'd been angry with her because she wouldn't give up everything and come with him; she'd been angry with him because he wouldn't give up everything and stay with her. And now he was coming full circle. For the past eleven years, he hadn't let himself become involved with a woman, and when he finally did find one he wanted to be involved with, he was faced with the same pitfalls he'd faced before.

But that wasn't exactly true, he admitted. Outside of her career, Charity couldn't really be compared to Diane. There was a softness to her, a shyness and gentleness that Diane had never had. There was also a reality to her that he'd lost with his parents. She made him want to become the man he knew he could be, and yet he feared he might have become too jaded and couldn't live up to the image of that man.

He stared at his image in the mirror, combed his fingers through his hair and sighed. The average man lived to be in his early seventies. He was thirty-six. Statistics said he'd lived half his life, yet half of his thirty-six years had been devoted to Moon and Sun. He didn't want to spend the rest of his life alone, nor was he ready to walk off the stage. Not yet. Maybe when he was forty. Forty sounded like a graceful retirement age for a rock star. But then again, some singers hadn't even made it to the top until they were in their forties.

But a decision about retirement was for the future and years down the road. Charity was the present, and he had to deal with her now. Did he dare try to develop a relationship with her? Was it worth the risk? He was older, wiser and more stable in his career. He'd also learned that if a woman's career was essential to her, he couldn't fight that. A woman had a right to her own autonomy—a right to make her own mark on the world—and no man had the right to challenge that, even if it meant giving her up.

Giving her up. The words echoed through his mind. If he let himself become involved with Charity and their relationship reached a point where he was forced to give her up, would he be able to do it? Was he enough of a man to release his hold on her?

He'd have to be, he realized, because the alternative was to walk out the door right this minute and never see her again, and he wasn't ready to do that. When he was with Charity, it felt right. If he turned his back and walked away, he would always wonder what he'd denied himself. He would always feel as if he'd left a chapter in his life unfinished.

He released another sigh and left the room to go in search of her. For better or for worse, he was going to see this through to the end.

Restless and not quite able to figure out Shane's mood, Charity wandered into the laundry room and donned freshly laundered underwear and a gray-and-pink sweat suit. It would soon be March, but in Denver it might as well have been January. Snow still covered the ground, and the weather forecast predicted heavy snowfall for the coming weekend. Winter had come late. It looked as though spring was going to come even later.

She stepped into the kitchen, checked the casserole and then went out to the sun porch. Since Shane was showering, she had time on her hands and decided to water the plants, which weren't really due to be watered until tomorrow. But a day early was better than a day late, she thought as she lifted the small hose and began the tedious process, telling herself that it really was time to get rid of some of the plants.

But each was a gift from a patient, and each told a special story. The red begonia had been a present from Mrs. Harper, who'd been certain that if Charity hadn't been her doctor, her appendix would have ruptured. The two ficus trees, from Mrs. Smith, symbolized the birth of her identical twin boys, who had, of course, been delivered by Charity when the woman had shown up at the hospital in a taxi, ready to give birth. The prickly pear cactus had been an appropriate gift from the surly Mr. Parsons, who had given an irritable grunt when she'd told him his indigestion was not a heart attack but a result of his wife's spicy Mexican cooking.

And the list went on and on. To get rid of one of the plants would be like getting rid of a part of her life. A part she might never be able to replace under her current circumstances. It was a depressing thought, but one she had to face. Her life was shifting, and like a mountain that released its blanket of snow in an avalanche, when it was over she'd be different.

Shane stood at the entrance to the sun porch and watched Charity water each plant, stopping to remove a dried leaf or break off a dead flower. It was such a simple act she was performing, and yet it was one of the most beautiful pictures he'd ever seen. She looked as delicate as the flowers and plants she moved through, and her delicacy was only emphasized by the dramatic backdrop of rugged snow-covered mountain peaks that loomed in the distance.

For a moment he let his gaze leave her and move to the mountains. He'd always loved Colorado, and although he had been born in Virginia, if he had roots, they were here. The mountains beckoned to him, defying him to challenge them. At the same time they whispered promises. To him they were like a mermaid to a sailor. Enticing and potentially deadly. But they had led him to Charity. It was almost as if she was his destiny.

Charity felt Shane's presence, but she waited until she had finished her watering and shut off the hose before turning to look at him. Her lips turned up in a smile. He was dressed in jeans and a white T-shirt with bold black lettering that read No Day Can Pass without Moon and Sun.

"Very thought provoking," she said, thinking he was like a ray of sunshine in her seemingly moonlit world.

"What?" Shane questioned, pulled away from his reverie.

"Your shirt."

He grinned. "A present from an ardent female fan. She handpainted the letters."

Charity would have sworn that she felt a flash of jealousy, but that was ridiculous. She didn't know Shane well enough to be jealous. But she couldn't dismiss the feeling, and she gathered up the dead twigs and leaves and carried them to the wastebasket in the corner.

"Charity?"

"Yes."

"Are you going to tell me what's wrong, or am I going to have to worm it out of you?"

"Nothing's wrong."

Shane frowned at her answer. He was an open man, quick to express his thoughts and his feelings. Evidently, Charity was accustomed to holding everything inside. His first impulse was to challenge her, force her into telling him what she was thinking. But as he'd decided in the bedroom, he was much older and wiser now. He could find out what he wanted with a light touch just as easily as a heavy one.

"Good. That means we can talk about what's wrong with me," he said.

"About what's wrong with you?" she repeated uncertainly.

"Yes." He grabbed one of the chairs sitting beneath the wrought-iron table and turned it around. After he straddled it and leaned his arms across the back, he said, "I want to know what your intentions are."

"My intentions?"

"Yes, your intentions. A man can't be too careful these days. Women tend to wine and dine him, lead him down the garden path, and then when he least expects it, they drop him flat on his... Well, you get the picture."

"I've never served you wine," she said, her lips beginning to twitch. Whatever his mood had been before, it had disappeared, and the old Shane—the one she enjoyed so much—was back.

"You will," he said with a knowing nod. "I'm not going to be led down the garden path."

"Good. Because it's pretty cold in the garden this time of year. You might end up with pneumonia," she quipped.

His gaze once again drifted toward the mountains. When he looked back at her, his mood had changed once again.

"We can't go on like this," he stated quietly. "It isn't right."

Charity was caught off guard by his seriousness and turned back to the plants. She moved a few pots around so their inner leaves were facing the window before she found the courage to face him and say, "And what is right?"

"We need to make some form of commitment." She opened her mouth to respond but stopped when he raised his hand for silence. "I'm not asking for anything but time, but time is a rare commodity for me, and I know it is for you. What's happening between us is special. It might last and it might not, but if we don't make a commitment, I can guarantee it won't last. I don't want to lose what might be the best thing that's ever happened to me, simply because I don't take the time to explore it further."

"The best thing?" she echoed.

"The best. I'm no saint, Charity, but I'm not a rake, either. My hell-raising days were over long ago. I want—no, need—some kind of permanence in my life. Some form of stability. I guess what I'm asking you for is . . ." He grinned suddenly. "How would you like to go steady?"

Confused by his sudden mood changes and not certain which one she should be responding to, Charity decided to add a little levity to the conversation. "Does that mean I get to wear your letter sweater?"

He didn't smile at her joke. "My high-school letter sweater burned up in the fire that killed my parents."

"Oh, Shane, I'm sorry. I didn't know."

He shrugged. "It happened fifteen years ago." He gazed past her to the mountains. "I've gotten over the pain, but I've never gotten over the regret. My parents weren't poor, nor were they well-off. We were an average family with an average income that paid the bills and allowed us a few luxuries. I just wish they'd been around long enough to share in my success. My dad always wanted to go fishing in Scotland, and my mom always wanted to see the Acropolis. I could have eventually given them that."

He shook his head as if to rid himself of the past, and the act must have worked, because when he returned his attention to her, his eyes were once again filled with humor.

"I'll give you my college class ring. You'll have to wrap it up with a ton of string to make it fit, but that's what going steady is all about, right?"

"You graduated from college?"

"Yes."

"When? You started singing when you were eighteen."

"Ah, but I was a bright boy. I knew if singing didn't work out, I needed another profession to fall back on. So I slipped in a few courses here and there, and eight years later, voilà! I had my degree in business administration."

Charity stared at Shane in wonder. He was full of surprises. She could imagine how difficult it had been for him.

He'd been trying to build a career, which meant he'd been touring and recording and going to college at the same time. And if it had taken him eight years to get his degree, he'd continued to work for it even after he'd made it to the top. His degree had meant more to him than he was admitting.

"Why business administration?" she asked. "Why not music?"

"You can make more money," he answered. "So what do you say? Will you go steady with me?"

Charity didn't know why she felt hesitant about giving him an answer. After all, she'd already decided that she couldn't continue seeing him without some form of commitment, and it was evident he felt the same way.

She was wary, she supposed, because she really didn't know the complete man. But he didn't really know her as a complete woman, either. His teasing offer to go steady was a chance for them both to discover those unknown sides. She finally admitted that her real reluctance was because she was worried about what would happen if she ended up liking what she discovered and he didn't, which was a very real possibility, considering who and what he was.

If she said yes, she'd be taking a risk, and she'd never been a risk taker. But, she reminded herself, she was supposed to be changing her life. If she didn't take risks, she'd fall back into the same dull pattern of getting up every morning, going to work, and coming home to bed. Alone. She'd acted impetuously when she'd made love with Shane at the cabin, and now he was asking her to do something impetuous again. What was the worst that could possibly happen? Her heart could be broken.

She thought of the line "'Tis better to have loved and lost than never to have loved at all." She'd loved Carson, lost him, and survived. In some ways, she'd even become a better person for it. However, she had a feeling that if she fell in love with Shane and lost him, it wouldn't be so easy to pick up the pieces. Comparing Carson to Shane was like comparing monophonic and stereophonic.

Shane forced himself to appear relaxed while he watched the emotions move across Charity's face as she worked her way through her thoughts. The tension inside him began to coil tighter and tighter as the minutes passed. The choice of where they went from here was up to her, and the suspense of waiting for her answer was unnerving.

What would he do if she said no? Could he accept her answer gracefully, walk out of her home and never return? Thankfully, he was saved from having to provide an answer to the question.

"I agree that if we are going to continue to see each other, we need to make some kind of commitment," Charity said, her brow furrowed. "If you want to call it going steady, fine. But it isn't going to be easy, Shane. Our lives are too diverse." Her gaze drifted down to his T-shirt, and she smiled ruefully. "You're the sun, and I'm the moon. Everything about us is different."

He wasn't certain what her analogy was supposed to mean, but he knew he desperately needed the reality of her world, and he had a feeling she needed the fantasy of his just as desperately.

"It won't be easy, but the best things in life rarely are. I suggest we take it one step at a time and keep our lines of communication open. That's the best weapon we have against failure. Talking brings about solutions to problems."

"Or proves that there is no solution," she warned.

"For every problem there is a solution," he countered. "Sometimes it's just not the solution we want." Then his expression brightened. "How are we going to seal this agreement?"

She couldn't help but smile. "Doesn't a handshake hold up in court?"

"Sure, but a kiss carries even more weight."

He rose from the chair and began walking toward her with that swaggering grace that always took her breath away. By the time he reached her, Charity was more than willing to seal their agreement with a kiss.

Chapter Seven

Charity and Shane laughed and teased each other through the remainder of the evening. When Shane found in her bookcase an old photo album that Charity's mother had given her, he made her sit beside him, insisting that she give him the history of every person in every picture. She'd found herself reliving happy times and sad times. Times of her youth and the time of her marriage. Shane had hurried her through that part, as if it was a part of her life he didn't want to know existed. But Carson had existed, and she couldn't dismiss him.

She closed the photo album, laid it aside, and leaned back against Shane. Memories were still hovering around her, and she knew there were parts of her life that she had to reveal to him. Parts he most likely didn't want to hear.

With her head resting against his shoulder, she caught his hand and laced their fingers together. "Shane, I'd like to talk to you about my marriage."

He stiffened against her. "There's no need to. It's over. It all happened before I knew you."

"I think you should know about it. I think I should explain what happened. It might help us."

He tightened his fingers against hers and then relaxed. He didn't want to talk about her ex-husband. He hated the fact that she had belonged to another man. But, then again, being forewarned might work to his advantage. If he knew what the man had done wrong, he might be able to avoid the same mistakes.

He nuzzled his chin against her hair and hugged her to him. "All right. If you want to talk about it, I'll listen."

Quietly and without bitterness Charity told the story. She told him how good the first year had been. Then she explained how everything had come apart.

"It wasn't Carson's fault," she concluded. "He'd just worked so hard all his life, Shane. He'd come from nothing and was becoming something. Our careers simply got in the way."

Shane caught some strands of her hair between his free hand and threaded his fingers through it, not quite ready to analyze the story. It was too close to his own, and deep inside he knew that somewhere along the line there existed a real possibility that a career conflict could arise between him and Charity. However, he'd learned to face each obstacle in life as it surfaced, and not before. Fighting shadows didn't get you anywhere.

"This is terrible to say, but I'm glad your marriage failed," he said huskily. "If it hadn't, I wouldn't be sitting here right now. I shudder to think what I would have missed."

"And what would you have missed?" she questioned, tilting her head back so she could see his face.

"Knowing the most wonderful woman doctor in the world."

She reached up and skimmed her fingers along his cheek in the lightest of touches. "And I would have missed knowing the sexiest rock star in the world."

He grinned. "You think I'm sexy?"

"Me, and no doubt half of America's female population."

He ran his finger along her bottom lip. "You sound jealous."

"I am jealous. In fact, I'm so jealous, I hate your T-shirt."

Shane glanced down at his shirt in surprise. "You hate it? Why? I thought it was rather eloquent. For a T-shirt, that is."

"What did your ardent female fan who made it look like?" she asked, shifting so she was snuggled up against him.

"I have no idea. She didn't send a picture with the package."

"You didn't meet her?"

"Good heavens, no." He moved so that she was half lying between his thighs. "How long before bedtime?"

"Mmm. I don't know. What time is it?"

"It has to be after nine. Don't you have to get up early in the morning?"

"Terribly early."

"You should have a good night's sleep so you look good for your first day on the job."

"I probably should," she murmured as she slid a hand beneath his T-shirt and rubbed it against his flat stomach.

He retaliated by doing the same. Slowly he lowered his head and kissed her deeply. When he let her come up for air, she was flushed and breathing shallowly. He let his fingers stray even farther upward, and with a groan, Charity rolled into his hand when it settled around her breast.

"If you keep that up, we won't make it to the bedroom," she murmured breathlessly.

He laughed softly as he brushed his fingers across her nipple, bringing it into a hard peak and causing her to shiver. "This sofa is terribly comfortable, but I guess we really should go to bed. You'll probably sleep better there."

"I do need my rest."

"Mmm," he agreed as he stood and lifted her off the couch. He nuzzled his nose against her neck as he carried her toward the bedroom. "You know what I like best about you?"

"No. What?"

"I can pack you around as easily as a favorite teddy bear."

Charity laughed. "Are you trying to tell me I'm cuddly?"

"Among other things," he answered as he walked into the bedroom and laid her down on the bed.

Slowly and tenderly, he began to remove her clothing, pausing to press a kiss to some particularly tantalizing spot he revealed, or to caress another one. After he finally had her disrobed Charity performed the same act for him. They exchanged smiles, touches and kisses until they were finally tangled in each other's arms.

Whenever they'd been in bed together before, it had been with a fury—as if each time would be the last—but this time their lovemaking was leisurely and ultimately far more satisfying. It was as if they'd stepped up to a higher plane, and both knew it was because they were now binding themselves to each other. They'd made a commitment, however tenuous it might be, and each was determined to show the other just how committed they were.

Afterward they lay contentedly in each other's arms, caressing, kissing and talking. Shane gave Charity a short synopsis of his life, promising to give her more details when they had more time. For now, she was content with what he was giving her, and she lay entwined in his arms, listening to his voice and marveling at how melodious it was.

Eventually their soothing caresses became more ardent, and they made love once more before finally falling into the most restful slumber either of them had had during the past twenty-three days.

Charity shot up in bed at the sound of the alarm clock, and a large male hand boldly fondled her breast before pushing her gently back against the pillows. Shane leaned across her to shut off the alarm and then buried his face against her neck.

"Is it six o'clock already?" Charity yawned widely, then ran her hands over the familiar muscles of Shane's back.

"Nope. It's five," he murmured as he left a trail of tiny kisses around one breast, easing toward its peak, and finally capturing her nipple between his lips.

"Five?" Charity gasped as the flame of desire flickered and then surged to life. "I asked you to set the alarm for six."

"I know," he answered as he moved to her other breast to treat it to the same delights. "But I wanted to make love to you at sunrise."

"Sunrise isn't for another hour," she whispered, arching against him wantonly. "What are we going to do until then?"

"My libido is slow in the morning," he whispered back. "We'll be able to make good use of that hour."

Oh, God, how I'm going to miss this man, Charity thought as she ran her hands over his raspy beard and tangled her fingers in the rich silkiness of his hair. Tears sprang to her eyes, and she blinked them back impatiently. She'd lived without him for twenty-three days. Nine weeks would pass quickly. But, she realized morosely, he hadn't even left and she missed him already.

She pushed at his chest, and when he raised his head to stare at her in confusion, she gave him a provocative smile. "If your libido is that slow, then I'd better get busy."

He gave her a leering grin as he fell back onto the bed and opened his arms wide. "I'm all yours, sweetheart."

"Are you?" she questioned wistfully, but didn't wait for his reply. Instead, she kissed him deeply, unknowingly communicating all her doubts and her need for reassurance.

With eyes tightly closed, she let her hands and lips explore every curve and plane of his face, imprinting on her mind by touch each tiny detail, right down to the small dimple in his left cheek and the arrogant cleft in his chin. His neck came next, and then his arms. She paused at each of his long fingers and traced the outline of each neatly cut nail with her tongue. His wide chest was like a wilderness, and she felt she knew each curling hair intimately by the time she was finished. Shane groaned when she flicked her tongue at his nipples, and again when she teased his abdomen, but he remained still beneath her ardent exploration. She continued to love him and tease him and memorize him until not one inch of his flesh remained untouched.

She trailed her hand lovingly over the velvety softness of his arousal as the first rays of the sun, as if on cue, burst through the sliding glass doors.

Shane let out a ragged gasp, unsure whether it had been caused by her touch or the lovely picture she presented with her hair tumbling about her face in beautiful disarray and the sun turning her alabaster skin a soft gold. He curved his hands urgently around her upper arms, and he pulled her over him and entered her in one smooth motion.

Her eyes gleamed more brilliantly than the sky that served as her background, and he began to murmur her name over and over, wondering how he would survive without having her near him.

He gripped her head and pulled her lips down to his, and then rolled, pulling her under him. They were a living sculpture of love as their arms and legs entwined, and they moved in perfect harmony toward the brink of desire.

"I have never wanted anything more in the world than I want you," he said hoarsely. "Tell me you're going to be mine."

"If it's meant to be," she answered.

"It's meant to be," he whispered, and, with one final stroke, made her his at sunrise.

As much as he and Charity both wanted time to wane, the hands on the clock continued to move forward. Finally, Shane rose on his elbow and said, "You have to get up."

"I know," Charity sighed reluctantly. "I wish I didn't."

"So do I," he murmured as he dropped a quick kiss to her lips. Then he raised his head and gazed deeply into her eyes. "Are you all right? You're not worried about starting at the clinic, are you?"

"Not really," Charity lied.

His knowing smile made her blush guiltily. "Do you want to talk about it?"

She shrugged and pulled the sheet tighter around her. "I'm not worried, actually. I'm…uncertain. What if I can't do it, Shane?"

"You can do it."

"I wish I felt as convinced as you sound."

"If you did, you wouldn't need to talk about it." He brushed her hair away from her face and smiled. "Charity, I haven't known you very long, but I feel as if I know you better than I've known anyone. If you want to do this, you'll do it." He chucked her affectionately under the chin. "You're beautiful, brilliant and filled with determination. Nothing is going to defeat you."

"Except the emergency room," she whispered, her brow furrowing. "I love the emergency room, Shane, but—"

"Give yourself some time," he interrupted as he began to massage her shoulder in an effort to make her relax. "You just need some time."

"And if time doesn't help?" she questioned tremulously.

"Then you'll fall back to plan B."

"I don't have a plan B."

"You will. In fact, if you need to, you'll end up with a plan C or D. You'll work it out."

She wrapped her arms around his neck and sighed. "I wish..."

"Wish what?" he prompted her.

"Nothing." She knew she didn't dare tell him she wished he were staying. "I'm just going to miss you."

He slid his arms beneath her and hugged her close. "And I'll miss you. Would you like to hear a confession?"

"Sure."

"I've been performing for eighteen years, but before every concert, I'm overcome by butterflies. I'm nauseated, my knees shake, and I promise myself that I'll never set foot on stage again. Then, after the first song is over and the crowd begins to applaud my butterflies disappear." He threaded his fingers into her hair and stared into her eyes. "Once you set foot in that clinic, your butterflies will be gone."

"You promise?"

"You bet."

She nodded and almost asked him if he couldn't delay leaving for one more day, but she caught herself before she could ask. He had responsibilities and commitments. He couldn't turn his back on them any more than she could turn her back on hers.

She smoothed her fingers along his eyebrow, and then touched his lashes as he closed his eyes. "Do I get a good-morning kiss?" she asked huskily.

"You get two," he said, then settled his lips over hers.

Despite Shane's pep talk, Charity was nervous about working at the clinic, and she stood outside the small building, staring at it warily. She wondered if she'd find it easier to walk inside if she knew Shane would be waiting for her at the end of the day. But Shane wouldn't be waiting. He'd been on the phone, changing his plane reservation, when she'd walked out the door. In a few hours he'd be in Miami, and she wouldn't see him again for nine weeks.

Nine weeks. It sounded like a lifetime, and it would feel like one, too, if she didn't find a way to occupy her time. And the answer to that problem lay right inside the door in front of her.

She drew in a determined breath and strode briskly into the clinic. The next half hour was like being in the center of a whirlwind. She was whisked from one room to another, introduced to the staff, shown where everything was, given a white coat and a key to the drug box and provided with her first patient.

She didn't have time to be nervous, or even think, for that matter. The patients came through the door one right after the other. She treated a head cold, stitched up a finger, gave a complete physical for a job application, examined and gave prescription refills to three hypertension patients, and spent an hour with Mrs. Andrews, the clinic's infamous hypochondriac, who was positive she had contracted some deadly mutant virus that didn't even have a name.

By noon Charity's feet hurt, her back ached, and she was certain she'd never worked so hard in her life. She sighed in relief when the nurse cheerfully informed her the next wave of patients wouldn't be arriving for more than an hour. When the woman left the office, Charity collapsed behind her temporary desk and closed her eyes, thankful for a moment's solitude.

But her solitude was interrupted by a quick rap on the door. She called out for entrance and smiled wearily when Don Patterson, the clinic's senior physician and an old friend of her father's, entered. He'd heard about her problems and, despite them, had offered her this job. She'd be eternally grateful for that.

"How's it going?" he asked.

"You should provide roller skates with this job," she answered with a yawn.

He chuckled and settled himself in the chair in front of her desk. "The patient load wasn't *that* heavy this morning."

"Then our idea of heavy is different. By the way, speaking of heavy, sticking me with Mrs. Andrews the first day on the job was a dirty, not to say despicable, trick. How can you put up with her?"

Don shrugged. "In her own way she is sick, Charity."

He'd said the words congenially, but Charity felt properly chastised. "I'm not being very professional, am I?"

"Mrs. Andrews would have tested the patience of Hippocrates himself," he replied gallantly. "How did the rest of the morning go?"

"Fine," she said, inwardly admitting that her only really gratifying moment had been when she'd sutured the cut finger. Private practice was a far cry from emergency medicine, but it might be her only alternative. She couldn't dismiss its potential after one morning. "But it's different from what I'm used to."

"I know it's a hard adjustment for you, Charity, but you are going to have to learn to shift your priorities," Don told her with an understanding smile. "In the emergency room, everything is a 'right now' decision. It's fixing what needs to be fixed. Family practice is designed to promote health. To try to keep people well. We want to arrest their illnesses before they end up in the emergency room."

"You're right," she said as she pushed herself out of her chair. "So before we see this afternoon's crowd, we might as well get some lunch. Would you like to join me?"

She was surprised when Don's ruddy face became even redder. "I, uh, already have plans for lunch. And that's one of the reasons I came in here. I wanted to ask a favor."

"Okay."

"Could you possibly take call for me tonight? Something unexpected came up for this evening, and, well . . ."

"I'd be glad to take call," Charity stated, fighting the grin that pulled at her lips. She knew what Don's "unexpected" something for the evening was. Her name was Susan, and she was the administrator at the hospital where Charity normally worked. Don had been a widower for two years, and Susan a widow for five. The rumor mill gave them another three months before they were married. Charity hoped that for once the rumor mills were right. They made a perfect couple.

Not like her and Shane, she thought, startled to realize it was the first time she'd thought about him since she'd walked into the clinic. Was that a good sign or a bad one? If she was "involved" with him, shouldn't he be in her thoughts constantly?

Deciding that trying to find an answer to the question would only make her headache worse, she chose to ignore it. She wouldn't be seeing him for nine weeks anyway. She'd have plenty of time to explore just what this "commitment" she'd made to him meant.

Shane ambled off the plane in Miami and was met by his disgruntled manager. Falling into step beside him, Roger gave an irritated shake of his graying brown head. They were immediately surrounded by six security guards, and Shane wondered why. For once there was no mob. Maybe arriving unexpectedly was something he should do more often.

"I hope you don't plan on pulling any more irresponsible tricks like this in the future," Roger grumbled. "Did you even stop to think about what would have happened if you'd gotten snowed in in Denver and couldn't make it here in time for the concert?"

"No," Shane answered honestly. "But I suppose you'd have done what you always do if we're caught in a storm. Cancel the concert and reschedule it."

He knew Roger was looking for a fight, and Shane wasn't in the mood to give him one. He was too busy worrying about Charity. She'd looked so scared this morning. Like a little girl being sent alone to her first day of school. She'd be all right. She was a professional. But she was scared. He should have been waiting for her when she came home tonight. He should have delayed flying into Miami until tomorrow morning. He should have . . .

He had to stop thinking like that. Having a relationship with Charity was going to be difficult enough without drowning himself in unwarranted guilt. There was no way they could be together on a full-time basis. They were going to have to work out an acceptable part-time arrangement. An arrangement that would fulfill them both.

But was that possible? He'd only spent last night with her, and it hadn't been enough. Already he missed her. Twice on the plane, he'd thought of something he'd wanted to say to her, and both times he'd automatically turned to the empty seat beside him, to be shocked that she hadn't been sitting there.

He pushed his hand through his hair. Was he going crazy? People would certainly say so if he started talking to empty airplane seats. Rock stars were allowed their idiosyncrasies, but that was pushing it a bit too far.

"You didn't hear a word I said, did you?" Roger snapped at him.

"No," Shane said, "and I'm not going to apologize for it. You're getting into something that's out of the realm of manager, Roger. If you want to keep peace, then keep your opinions to yourself. I'm aware of my responsibilities, or I wouldn't be here. And by the way, I'd like a copy of the schedule for the rest of our tour."

Roger released a resigned sigh. "Derek said you would. It's waiting for you at the hotel."

Shane said, "Thanks. I appreciate that."

When Charity unlocked the front door to her house that night, she could barely move. She hadn't really worked that much harder at the clinic than she did in the emergency room, but it was a different kind of work.

She slipped her shoes off and left them beside the front door. It was an unusual action for her, and one that only emphasized her fatigue. Normally, she functioned under the precept that everything had its place and was put in it. Shoes did not belong beside the front door, but for tonight she'd break the rule.

Mister came racing from the back of the house and greeted her with a combination of whines, yaps and tail wagging. She rewarded him with a hug and a "How was your day, boy?"

He yapped again and raced away. He needed to go out, she knew, so she followed him, thinking she really should put in a pet door to the fenced-in backyard so he could come and go as he pleased and not have to conform to her unpredictable schedule.

After she let him out, she opened the refrigerator door to get his food. Her hand froze halfway into the refrigerator. Inside was a huge bowl of stew and a note from Shane that read: "Knew you'd be bushed. Thought I'd make the evening easier. All my love, Shane."

Tears filled her eyes at his thoughtfulness, and it took several blinks to hold them back. He had to have been rushed, but somehow he'd found the time to leave a piece of himself behind for her.

She took out the dog food and the stew. After fixing Mister's dinner and letting him back in, she put the stew into the microwave oven. It was heaven, she decided, when she removed it and sniffed the aroma that rose from the bowl when she lifted the lid. Carson had never known how to cook, and probably wouldn't have cooked if he had. Either he'd waited for her to come home and fix dinner or he'd made a quick trip out for fast food.

She carried her meal out to the sun porch and sat down at the table, staring out at the mountains and watching a full moon rise above their peaks. *"No day can pass without Moon and Sun."*

The words from Shane's T-shirt had come from nowhere, and Charity realized they were true. Every day was marked with the passage of the sun and the moon. But twice during each day—just before sunrise and sunset—the two met, caressed each other and moved on.

She and Shane were like that, she thought. He was a bright spot in her life that filtered through, caressed her and then moved on. Would it always be like this? Would he always be there for a moment and then disappear, taking his light and smiles with him? Probably. As long as he was so actively involved in his career, he'd spread the majority of his sunlight to others.

And she was a part of the night, she admitted. She was wrapped up in the illness and pain of others. Her career faced the dark side of life.

She and Shane were opposites in every way. In coloring, personality and what they did for a living. The old saying that opposites attract came to mind, and she was certain there was more truth than fiction to the saying. People were drawn to the qualities of others that they envied. Qualities they wished they had. But what qualities could she possibly have that Shane would want? In her mind, he had everything. Everything that was bright and beautiful.

She reached for the telephone when it rang.

"Hello, gorgeous. How was your day?"

"Exhausting," she said through a laugh, delighted to hear Shane's voice on the other end, "and surprising. Thanks for leaving dinner in the refrigerator."

"Mmm. Anytime," he murmured.

"How was your flight?" she asked.

"Bumpy for the first few hundred miles, and then it leveled off. Have you got a paper and pencil handy? I want to give you my concert schedule."

"The entire schedule?"

"You bet. That way if you need to reach me, you can."

"Can you hold a minute?"

"I can hold an hour. Take your time."

Charity laid the phone down on the table and raced out into the other room to get paper and pencil. When she returned she said, "I'm ready. Give me your schedule."

She jotted down the days, the towns and the hotels he'd be staying in. When he was finished, he ordered her, "Read it back to me. I want to make sure you've got everything right."

She reread the schedule, then said, "Thanks for doing that for me. It will make the time pass faster if I know where you are."

"I'm glad. Now tell me about your first day at the clinic. Was it as bad as you thought it would be?"

"Yes and no," she answered. "Don says I have to shift priorities. I have to—"

"Wait a minute. Who's Don?" Shane interrupted abruptly.

Did he sound jealous? Some malicious feminine part of her hoped so. "He's the senior doctor at the clinic. He said I have to shift my priorities. Emergency medicine deals with a crisis situation. Family practice is supposed to prevent a crisis situation. So instead of patching up what's wrong, I'm supposed to arrest what's wrong before it needs a patch. Does that make sense?"

"Perfect sense. How old is this Don?"

She grinned. He did sound jealous. "Nearly old enough to be my father. Why?"

"Do you happen to like older men?"

"I suppose that depends on how old they are. You're older than I am."

"Yeah. Charity?"

"Yes?"

She could hear his sigh. "I miss you."

"I miss you, too. So does Mister."

"Does he really?"

She smiled at the childish glee in his voice. "Yes. I'm not as good a roughhouser as you are."

"Put him on the phone."

Charity decided it was crazy, but she lowered the phone to the dog's ear. "You take care of your mistress for me. Do you hear?" she heard Shane say.

Mister whined and looked expectantly at Charity. She laughed and brought the phone back to her ear. "I think your orders were received loud and clear."

"Good. Now, I'd like to talk about me for a minute. I thought of a couple of things I'd like to tell you, and—"

"Shane," Charity said regretfully, "I'm sorry, but I just got a call-waiting beep. I'm on call this evening, and it's probably the answering service. Can I call you back?"

"You're on call the first day on the job?" he asked in surprise.

"It's a special favor for Don. He had something come up unexpectedly, and since I didn't have any plans, I agreed to take his call. I'll call you back as soon as I can if you'll just give me your number."

Reluctantly, he gave it to her, and she told him goodbye and hung up. She had had every intention of calling him back, but by the time she'd handled the patients who seemed to be calling the answering service in a nonstop stream, it was after midnight, which was two in the morning his time. He had a concert to give the next night, and she decided it was best not to disturb him. She'd call him in the morning before she left for the clinic.

Shane, however, was pacing the floor of his suite and waiting for her call. He'd tried her number four times, and all four times it was busy. He told himself that she hadn't forgotten him. She was on call. People got sick.

He stopped at the window and gazed out at the glistening full moon, which was low on the horizon. It reminded him of Charity. She had its same gentle glow and gossamer touch. She also had its ability to disappear.

He leaned his head back and sighed wearily. It was close to dawn, and he had to get some sleep. A performance didn't come easy these days. He was older. He needed his sleep. But he couldn't dismiss the fact that Charity had broken her promise that she would call.

He didn't doubt that she was busy with patients, but he couldn't help the frustration that arose at the reminder that those people were more important to her than he was. Not in a literal sense, of course. It was her job. It was what she had to do. But he had so little time to talk, and he resented having to share that time with others.

He was a fool to have tried to develop a relationship with her. It wasn't going to get easier. If he had any common sense, he'd call it off now. In fact, that's exactly what he was going to do, he decided as he threw himself down on the bed and closed his eyes. He'd been through this once. A man couldn't fight a woman's career, and if he wanted to escape the pain, he would just have to give up now. Diane had hurt him, but Charity had the potential to cripple him.

He wouldn't talk to her again. He wouldn't see her again. It was over. It had to be over. If he didn't let it be over, he'd lose his sanity.

He opened his eyes and looked at the moon. Then he released a harsh bark of laughter. He was behaving like a spoiled child. She had her responsibilities, just as he did, and she hadn't protested when he'd left this morning. She'd wanted him to stay. He'd sensed that. But she hadn't complicated his departure by saying so. He owed her the same kind of understanding. It just would have been easier if she'd called.

He'd been the one to tell her they had to keep the lines of communication open, and when he spoke with her tomorrow, he'd tell her how he felt. He closed his eyes again, and beneath the gentle light of the moon, he finally fell into a restless slumber.

Chapter Eight

Charity awoke long before her alarm clock went off. The first thing she did when she opened her eyes was calculate the time difference between Colorado and Miami. Realizing Shane might still be asleep, she decided to perform a quick morning toilette before calling him. Then she'd have a little more time to talk.

She let Mister out and entered the bath. She completed her routine in record time, let Mister back in and fed him. Then she settled down on the sofa in the living room and called Shane.

Since it was the first time she'd called him, she wasn't prepared for the screening process the hotel went through. By the time she'd talked to three operators and been put on hold so they could check the list of "approved" callers, she was beginning to wonder just what she had gotten herself into. She decided she would have had an easier time talking to the President of the United States.

She was ready to hang up by the time the operator came back on the line, stated she could be put through, and rang Shane's number. Shane's gruff "hello" on the other end didn't improve her disposition.

"You didn't tell me it would take an hour to reach you when I called the hotel," she grumbled.

Shane dropped onto the sofa, his hand clenching the telephone receiver at the sound of her voice. "Charity?"

"Yes. Are all the hotels going to give me a hard time when I call?"

"What do you mean? I told them to put you right through. You're on the list."

She sighed and gave a disgruntled shake of her head. "So I found out. But only one operator has control of the list, and she has to check it. I—"

Shane's temper flared. "I told them to put you right through. If they can't follow simple instructions, then we'll find another hotel the next time we're in Miami!"

His rise in temper only made Charity's temper cool. "They were following your instructions, Shane, but you can't expect them to memorize every name of every person authorized to call. I'm sorry I didn't get back to you last night, but by the time I was through handling patients, it was after midnight here. I decided you were probably asleep."

"I wasn't," he said, forcing himself to ease his grip on the phone. "I was pacing the floor, waiting for your call and angry because you hadn't made it. I forced myself to calm down and accept the fact that you were busy, but, Charity, in the future, if you say you'll call me back, please call me back. I wanted to talk to you, even if it was only for a few more minutes."

Now Charity was clenching the telephone. Just what had she gotten herself into? "I made a judgment call," she stated stiffly. "I'm sorry if it was the wrong one. I simply thought you needed your sleep, since you're performing tonight."

Shane released a resigned sigh. He'd hurt her feelings, and he hadn't meant to. "I'm sorry. I know it sounds childish, but I wanted to talk to you, and I resented the fact that I had to share you."

"You'll always have to share me, Shane."

"I realize that," he said, pushing his hand through his hair in agitation. "I don't mind being interrupted by your patients if I know you'll get back to me. I'm just trying to tell you how I feel. I'm trying to keep the lines of communication open so there won't be any misunderstandings."

Charity eased her grip. "Okay. I understand what you're saying, and in the future, if I say I'll call you back, I'll call you back, regardless of the hour."

"And you really understand?" he questioned.

"Yes."

"Good, because now I'm the one that's going to have to call you back. We have to go over to the concert hall for a rehearsal. Everyone's waiting for me."

Charity sighed. "I wonder if we'll ever get off this merry-go-round we've gotten ourselves onto."

"If we work at it, we will. Is it all right if I call you at the clinic?"

"You can try, but if I'm with a patient, I won't be able to talk."

Shane released a sigh of his own. "I'll call you after the concert, but it will be midnight or later your time."

"I'll be waiting."

"You're sure it won't be too late?"

She now understood how he'd felt last night. Talking with him was what was important. "It won't be."

"All right. I'll talk to you tonight, sweetheart."

She barely had time to say goodbye before he hung up.

The complications of a relationship between them were already surfacing. She wondered if they wouldn't be better off just to say goodbye and never see each other again. But the thought of not seeing Shane in the future was more frightening than trying to deal with the complications.

They'd work it out. And if they didn't? She didn't have an answer.

The remainder of Charity's day did pass quickly, and she arrived home even more exhausted than the day before. And a little more unsatisfied. It wasn't that she minded caring for the patients who came to the clinic; they simply weren't what she was used to. She felt stifled. It was as if all the skills she'd developed over the years were being put into deep freeze, and she couldn't help but wonder if they'd ever be used again.

She'd had lunch with her psychiatrist friend, Mary Rutherford, who'd suggested that she try visiting another emergency room—one where she hadn't been held hostage—and see how she reacted to it. Mary had assured her if it was only *the* emergency room where she'd been held hostage that affected her, then the obvious course of action would be to work at another hospital. However, if it was the environment, then she did have a problem. One that would probably have to be handled by counseling if she was determined to go back into emergency medicine.

Confused and forlorn, Charity wandered through the house, wishing Shane were there to talk to. It would be nice to have someone to tell her problems to. To have a shoulder to lean on. To receive a comforting word and a hug. But Shane wasn't there and wouldn't be for nine weeks. She tried to hold back the wave of frustration at that admission, but it was hopeless.

With a sigh, she walked into the kitchen to fix something for dinner. While she sliced fresh mushrooms for spaghetti sauce, she began to analyze what she wanted out of a relationship with a man. Maybe if she could identify her needs, she could focus on how to deal with Shane.

She needed love, companionship, understanding and respect. Shane had already given her two out of the four—understanding and respect. Companionship was not something he'd be able to give her. He was constantly traveling, and her profession didn't allow her to accompany him. So companionship with him would be limited unless he was able and willing to make some changes in his life. He hinted that he'd like to make those changes, but would he be able to? For eighteen years he'd been living like this, and change might be more difficult than he thought.

And love? Well, love was something down the road. What they had right now was physical attraction, but physical attraction was the first seed of love. One had to tend it carefully, and with a bit of luck, it turned out right.

She shook her head as she dumped the mushrooms into the sauce bubbling on the stove. She hadn't reached any answers. All she'd done was outline what she needed and what Shane was capable of giving her. The next logical question would be, What did he want from *her*? But she didn't know him well enough to outline that. Relationships took time. Eventually she'd understand him more and be able to evaluate his needs. Right now she was walking in unknown territory. She hoped it wasn't territory filled with land mines.

She ate out on the sun porch again, then rinsed her dishes and put them into the dishwasher. After that she yawned and settled down in front of the television set to await Shane's call. Public television was showing an old Bogart and Bacall movie, and she flipped it on. But within fifteen minutes she'd fallen asleep.

Shane paced around his dressing room, unable to ease his tension. He was always nervous before a performance, but tonight it seemed magnified, and he knew it was because he wanted Charity there. If she were there to cheer him on, he'd be able to walk out on that stage with no problems.

He consoled himself with the fact that once he was on stage and had sung the first song, all the butterflies would disappear. They always did. When the crowd went wild, he responded with an inner calm. It was the applause. Always had been and always would be. He loved the applause.

He sneezed and glanced around the room, wondering what had prompted the sneeze. Deciding it was probably dust, he dismissed it, his mind moving back to Charity. Last night he'd been angry with her because she hadn't called. But this morning she had called, and then he'd been the one who'd had to halt their conversation. It didn't seem fair. Being separated was bad enough. They should at least have enough time to talk on the telephone.

But time was the one thing they didn't have. He'd known it from the beginning. He pushed his hand through his hair, then frowned when he sneezed again.

"You aren't catching a cold, are you?" Derek asked in concern from the doorway.

"Of course not," Shane said. "Either it's dust or there's something in the room I'm allergic to."

"We'll be ready to go on in about fifteen minutes. Roger's decided we should leave for New Orleans right after the show," Derek informed him.

"After the show?" Shane questioned. "We can't leave right after the show. I have a call to make."

"To Ms. Infatuation?"

"Yes. I'm not leaving until I talk to her. Besides, we're not due in New Orleans until late tomorrow."

"The weather's changing. There's a hurricane warning. Roger wants to make sure we get to New Orleans before it hits."

"Good old Roger," Shane growled. "No matter what, the show must go on."

"We're where we are today because of Roger," Derek stated. "You know that as well as I do."

"And what has it gotten us?" Shane asked derisively. "You're paying three alimony checks a month, and I'm alone."

Derek sat down on the chair in front of the dressing-room mirror and frowned. "Shane, fame has its failings. When we started in this business, Roger told us we'd be giving up a lot. If you remember correctly, he warned that our personal lives would suffer."

Shane nodded and stuffed his hands into the pockets of the skintight black leather pants he would be wearing through the first half of the show. "When you're eighteen, all that matters is fame. But when you're thirty-six . . ."

Derek didn't try to finish Shane's sentence. He merely nodded in agreement. "If it's any help, Roger's personal life has been as rotten as ours."

"It doesn't help."

"Why don't you call this woman and ask her to join us in New Orleans?"

"Because she's a doctor. She can't just pick up and take off whenever she wants."

Derek let out a low whistle. "Boy, you really know how to pick them, don't you? After Diane, I would have thought—"

"Keep your thoughts to yourself, okay?"

"Okay," Derek agreed easily. "Would you mind telling me her name?"

"Charity. Charity Wells."

"Well," Derek said as he glanced at his watch, "we've got ten more minutes before we have to go on stage. Why don't you call your Charity Wells and tell her you'll be on your way to New Orleans tonight and will call her first thing tomorrow?"

Shane stopped in his pacing long enough to give Derek a rueful smile. "I feel like the flip side of a record. Usually it's me trying to calm you down."

Derek grinned. "You've been through three marriages with me. I've been through only one bad relationship with you. I figure I owe you a couple." He glanced at his watch again. "You have nine minutes. Are you going to make that call?"

Shane didn't answer. He turned and lifted the telephone off its hook.

* * *

And the calls during those first two days were to set the tone for Shane's and Charity's conversations over the next two weeks. There were nights when they were able to relax and talk to their hearts' content, but more often than not they were limited to brief conversations that were barely more than a "hello" and a "how are you?"

But oddly enough, they found that even those short conversations were gratifying, and when they did have more time, they talked about everything from themselves and their dreams to politics, religion and their favorite movies. No topic was left untouched, and even though they frequently found themselves disagreeing over many issues, since Charity was as conservative as they came and Shane was just as liberal, they also discovered they liked many of the same things.

It wasn't an ideal courtship, yet Charity felt it might be the perfect one for them. When they were together, they spent more time making love than talking. Unable to touch, they were spending their time getting to know each other. She felt that in two weeks she'd learned more about Shane than she'd known about Carson, and she'd lived with Carson for two years. She also knew that with each conversation, she was coming closer to falling in love.

Shane had endearing qualities. He wasn't afraid to confess his fears, nor was he afraid to boast of his successes. He was a perfect mixture of humility and ego, a fact that she found astounding. Some nights he'd call her after a concert, riding high on adrenaline and raving about the performance, but it was never an "I" performed well; it was always a "we." The next night he would call her, tired and apologetic, sure he'd sounded like a fool the night before, and she'd always assure him he hadn't.

Like Charity, Shane was filled with wonder at how well they were clicking. It wasn't the perfect courtship. He was a physical man, and he missed the physical side of their relationship, but he was finding himself nearly as content having a simple conversation with her as he would be if they'd made love. At first she was more hesitant to reveal her private side than he was. He sensed it was shyness and took the time to draw her out.

Soon she'd become the pivotal point of his day. She'd normally call him before she left for the clinic, and he'd call her in the evenings or after a performance. Each conversation drew him closer to her, and he admitted that if he hadn't yet fallen in love, he was precariously close to it. He wanted to tell her how he felt, but he refrained. They needed more time—time together instead of apart—and he began to carefully review the personal appearances and recording sessions Roger was scheduling them for after the tour. As Charity had told him at her home, he needed to determine which were obligations and which weren't.

Derek was accepting his changes with good-natured equanimity, but Roger was becoming sullen and withdrawn. Shane shrugged off the guilt his manager was subtly inflicting. He'd given Roger half his life. The remainder of his life belonged to him—and, with any luck, to Charity.

Although Charity's conversations with Shane were uplifting, her dissatisfaction at the clinic was growing. As she'd determined when she'd first started working there, it wasn't that she resented treating the patients; it was simply that they weren't the same challenge she was accustomed to. She missed emergency medicine.

Mary Rutherford met her frequently for lunch, and every time, she encouraged Charity to visit another emergency room. The problem was, Charity feared that visit. If it was the environment, she could continue in private practice. She functioned well in the setting, and even if it wasn't as satisfying as the emergency room, it was better than not practicing medicine at all.

She was still struggling with her decision, thinking it would be easier if Shane could be with her. But Shane couldn't be with her, and she wasn't certain he should be.

He'd become a stable rock in her world, even if it was only by telephone, and she might find it easier to lean against him than to fight her fear.

She would have to do it herself, she realized. She just didn't know when she was going to do it. But it had to be soon. She'd agreed to work at the clinic for three months, and already half of one month was gone. It took time to process applications and verify credentials when one applied to a hospital for staff privileges. If she didn't do it soon, she'd be out of a job.

She was still worrying about her future when she walked into the clinic on a bright Monday morning. Don and the clinic's head nurse were standing in the waiting room, looking irritated and harassed.

"What's wrong?" Charity asked as she dropped her purse onto a red vinyl chair and shrugged out of her black woolen jacket.

"A city water line broke," Don informed her. "We're going to have to close down the clinic for a week."

"You're kidding," Charity said in disbelief. "They can't fix it any faster than that?"

"They say they'll be pushing it to get it done by then." Don sighed and shook his head. "We're just going to have to close the clinic and reschedule our patients. I've arranged to see those who are really urgent at the hospital. Susan—Ms. Ames," he corrected himself quickly, "has agreed to give me some temporary space there."

"Do you want me to handle part of the load?" Charity questioned.

Don shook his head. "No. Most of our patients can be rescheduled after the water line is fixed. Why don't you take a few days off? You can rest and relax and be ready to take on the crowd when we're able to reopen the doors."

"How many days did you say it would take them to fix the water line?" Charity asked.

"At least a week. I'm sure you can find something to entertain yourself between now and then."

Charity wasn't so sure but she nodded. She offered to help the nursing staff make the cancellation calls. Unlike Don, they were eager to accept her volunteering. After she'd made the last call on her list, she leaned back in her chair and wondered just what she could do to entertain herself for the next week.

Her gaze lowered to her calendar where she'd listed Shane's schedule. He'd be in Kansas City tomorrow morning. His concert was scheduled for Wednesday night, and then he'd be giving one in St. Louis the following evening. Kansas City wasn't far from Denver. Did she dare fly out and surprise him?

Her first inclination was no, but as she thought about it, she decided, why not? After all, he'd flown in and surprised her, and he was constantly saying that seeing her would be the greatest gift he could receive.

Did she dare? She picked up the telephone and called the travel agency. She could fly out late tonight and be in Kansas City long before Shane arrived. The flight would depart after Shane would normally call, and she could tell him she was on call and couldn't talk. He'd cut their conversation short and ask her to call him in the morning. When she called, she'd be in his hotel, and . . .

The idea definitely had value, and she went ahead and booked herself on the last flight. Then she called the hotel where he'd be staying. They were having a conference but there'd been a last-minute cancellation. She took the available room. After she hung up she called her sister-in-law, Chris, and arranged for her and Jim to take care of Mister for the next few days.

All she had left to do was pack, and she decided to spend the rest of the day shopping. It wasn't every day that she got to pay a surprise visit to the man she was close to falling in love with, and she decided that she'd do it up right.

Shane sneezed and then sneezed again. He frowned when Derek and Roger looked at him in concern.

"Your cold's getting worse," Derek stated.

"I don't have a cold; it's an allergy."

"Whatever it is, you're getting hoarse," Roger announced.

"I've been singing my lungs out for two weeks. Of course I'm getting hoarse."

"I think we should delay the Kansas City and St. Louis concerts by a day or two," Roger said.

"No way," Shane replied. "I have plans in Denver at the end of this tour, and I'm going to complete it on time."

"We can still complete it on time," Derek insisted. "We'll just have to double up on a couple of concerts. Let's take a day or two off when we get to Kansas City."

Shane gave a vehement shake of his head, sneezed and asked, "Do we really have to appear on the Johnny Carson show in June?"

The concert tour ended in the middle of April. Roger had already scheduled him for two appearances right after that that he couldn't back out of, but he'd managed to free up the majority of May. In June he and Derek had to record an album for release in early December. The rest of June was fairly solidly booked, but Shane was determined to salvage at least one full week out of the month to spend with Charity. July, he'd already determined, was hopeless, but August still had some potential.

Roger leaned back in his chair and looked at Shane with a critical eye. "I'll cancel Johnny Carson if you'll take two days off in Kansas City. That's my offer, Shane. Take it or leave it."

Shane opened his mouth to object but looked down at the calendar in front of him before he spoke. He might be two or three days late ending the concert tour, but canceling out Johnny Carson would give him that one full week in June. He nodded.

"All right, it's a deal. I think I'm going to get some rest. If Charity calls . . ."

"We'll wake you," Derek assured him. "Just get some rest. We need you functioning at your peak for tonight's performance."

Shane nodded but knew he wouldn't be functioning at his peak. He never got sick, but this allergy-cold he'd picked up in Miami was hanging on. So far he'd been able to hide it from Charity, telling her his slight hoarseness was a result of his constant performing. He wondered what she'd do if she knew he was sick.

He took two aspirins, threw himself down on the bed and tried to get some rest. He did manage to fall into a half slumber that was haunted by dreams of Charity. If only he could see her, he thought as he drifted in and out of sleep. If only...

Charity's plan had worked. When Shane had called that evening, she'd told him she was on call and would phone him in the morning after he'd arrived in Kansas City. He'd sounded disappointed but hadn't objected, which had made her feel slightly guilty. Maybe she should have told him she was coming, she thought as she checked her luggage at the airport and moved down the concourse.

Deciding she should have something to read, she stopped at a small gift shop that traded primarily in books and magazines. Flying was not her favorite pastime, and she knew she wouldn't sleep while she was in the air. In fact, she doubted she'd sleep much at all tonight. She was too keyed up with the anticipation of seeing Shane.

After choosing a new murder mystery and a best-selling romance novel, she walked toward the checkout stand. But she stopped as she walked past the magazine rack and turned to look at the image that had caught her eye. At first she couldn't believe it was Shane, and wouldn't have believed it if the headline hadn't read: "Moon and Sun Take the Country by Storm."

It was him, but the rakish man on the cover dressed in black leather wasn't the Shane she'd come to know. Her hand shook slightly as she picked up a copy of the magazine and added it to her pile. The article promised pictures and details of ten concerts and an in-depth interview with two of America's favorite rock stars and most eligible bachelors.

The young woman at the checkout counter sighed as she lifted the magazine to ring it up. She looked up at Charity with admiring eyes and said, "Aren't these the two sexiest guys in the entire world?"

Charity gave the woman a weak smile and nodded. "They are attractive."

The woman arched a brow at Charity's understatement but didn't say anything more. Charity carried her package to her departure gate and refrained from looking at the magazine, deciding she'd have more time when she was in the air. Besides, she told herself, most of the article would be publicity hype. It was probably filled with more fiction than fact.

But that didn't stop her from pulling out the magazine as soon as her plane was airborne. She looked at each photograph in detail, frowning at the suggestive costumes Shane and Derek had worn during various concerts. They both blatantly displayed their well-cared-for bodies, and her frown deepened. She didn't like the fact that half of America's female population was fawning over Shane's physique. She didn't like it at all. Particularly when she ran across one picture where Shane wore nothing but black pants with white suspenders and a matching black hat with a white band. His bare chest was gleaming with perspiration beneath the stage lights, and he'd pulled down one suspender as if he was preparing to strip. Charity slammed the magazine shut and closed her eyes.

He was an entertainer. This was what he did for a living. Her firm statements didn't help. She let the magazine lie on her lap as she opened her eyes and gazed out the airplane window, watching the moon, which was no more than a slice of light against the sky. Soon it would disappear completely and then begin to appear again, a slice at a time, until it was full. Its light was given and taken away by the sun as they both moved through their cycles. She had a feeling she was beginning to move into a new cycle with Shane, and she wondered if his light was taken away, she'd feel as cold as the dark, sunless side of the moon.

With a heavy sigh, she closed her eyes. She toyed with the edges of the magazine but refused to read the article. It was more fiction than fact, she reminded herself. But even though she was intelligent enough to realize that, she also knew she wasn't emotionally equipped to pick out the facts and ignore the fiction. It was the first time she'd been faced with proof that Shane was a famous personality, and she needed time to adjust.

When her plane landed she moved through the routine of arrival without conscious thought. After she'd checked into the hotel and arrived at her room, she realized she'd left the magazine on the plane. It was just as well, she told herself. If she'd kept it, she might be tempted to read it, and if she read it, she might find her feelings for Shane affected. It was more important than ever that she see him, and she was thankful that she'd once again performed an impetuous act where he was concerned. She needed to be reassured that he was the man she'd come to know and not the one spread across the pages of the magazine.

When Charity awoke the next morning she was surprised at the late hour. She'd been sure she wouldn't be able to sleep, but she had, and she felt rested and less uncertain about Shane. She showered and dressed and then placed a call to the hotel switchboard, asking if Shane had arrived.

As usual, the operators treated her warily, but after they'd determined that she was on the approved list of callers and had verified that she was registered at the hotel, they put her through.

She was surprised when Shane didn't answer. When she asked for him, she received a hesitant "May I ask who this is?"

"Charity. Charity Wells."

The man on the other end said, "He's here, but he's resting. Could he call you back?"

Charity was almost overwhelmed by disappointment, but it was short-lived when the man said something that was muffled and then Shane came on the line.

"Hi, sweetheart," he said. "Sorry about that, but Derek is being a little protective of me lately. How are you?"

"Fine," she answered, too excited to spring her surprise on him to be aware of his raspy voice. "In fact, I'm better than fine. You'll never guess where I am."

He chuckled. "Probably not, so why don't you save my weary mind the effort and tell me."

"I'm in room two-twelve. Exactly four floors below you."

There was dead silence on Shane's end, and Charity's heart began to beat a little faster. Had she made a mistake in coming?

"Would you repeat that?" Shane asked, sure his mind was playing cruel tricks on him.

"I said I'm in room two-twelve, four floors below you."

"You're in the hotel?"

"Yes. I had a few unexpected days off and decided to fly out and surprise you." She hesitated and clenched the phone tightly. "It is all right, isn't it, Shane?"

"You're damn right!" he exclaimed, bursting into laughter and then cursing when he began to cough. "Sorry, sweetheart. I've caught a small cold. Get on the elevator and come right up. No, you won't be able to do that. Give me five minutes. I have to inform security that you're cleared to come up. I'll be waiting for you."

Charity felt the first resurgence of yesterday's doubt. Having difficulty reaching him by telephone was one thing. Having to be "cleared through security" was another. She hung up, checked her hair and stared at the clock, counting down the minutes. She was just walking toward her door when there was a knock. It was loud and impatient, and she knew who it was. She raced to the door and threw it open. She'd been right. Shane was standing on the other side.

He laughed, caught her in his arms and swung her around. Then he placed her down on her feet and turned toward the two security guards who were standing in the hallway behind him, their faces impassive masks.

"Give us a couple of minutes," Shane said as he closed the door. He leaned back against it and let his gaze rove over Charity hungrily. Then he grinned and shook his head. "Good heavens, you're a sight for lonely eyes. When did you arrive?"

"Last night," she answered as she made her own hungry tour. When she glanced back at his face, she frowned. "You don't look well, Shane."

He threaded his fingers through his hair. "I've caught some kind of damn cold and can't shake it."

She immediately moved toward him and placed her hand against one of his flushed cheeks. Then she gave a knowing nod. "You have a fever. Have you seen a doctor?"

"Everyone knows a doctor can't cure a cold. Besides, I'm seeing one right now, and I must say I like what I see." He wrapped his arms around her and hugged her close, stopping her from any further examination. Resting his chin against the top of her head, he said, "I want to kiss you, but I don't want to make you sick. I guess I'll just have to be satisfied with holding you. How long can you stay?"

"Today and tomorrow. Maybe a day after that, but you'll be leaving before then, won't you?"

"No. Roger's delaying both the Kansas City and St. Louis concerts to give me a chance to kick my cold." He urged her back so he could look into her face, absorbing every detail. He gently touched the corner of one of her exotically tilted eyes. "I'm afraid this might delay the end of the concert tour."

Charity, understanding his meaning, smiled to reassure him. "It's more important that you get well. I can survive a couple of extra days at the end."

"You're sure?"

"I'm positive."

"Good. Let's pack up your bags, and I'll have Roger check you out. You're staying upstairs with me."

She blushed and glanced shyly toward the floor. "I'd hoped you'd say that. I've already packed." Then she raised her gaze to his face and hesitantly asked, "What will Derek and Roger say?"

"Once they see you, they'll say I'm the luckiest man in the world. Let's collect your luggage and get out of here."

Since Charity's luggage consisted only of one medium-sized suitcase and her ever-present doctor's bag, it took them a mere heartbeat to gather her things. Shane opened the door, winked at the security guards and moved toward the elevator. The first elevator that arrived had four people on it, and the security guards refused to let Charity and Shane enter it. They had to wait through two more elevators before an empty one arrived, and Charity was once again wondering what she'd gotten herself into.

She glanced up at Shane's face, and her doubts were immediately replaced by concern. His complexion was sallow compared to his normal healthy radiance, and he sneezed three times in rapid succession, giving her an apologetic smile as he pulled his handkerchief from his back pocket to blow his nose. By the time they'd reached his floor, Charity was determined that before she did anything else, she was going to give him a good examination.

But her examination was delayed as she was introduced to Derek and Roger. Derek grinned as he gallantly accepted her hand and brought it to his lips in European fashion.

"I can see why this old dog is misbehaving. If I had you waiting on the other end, I'd be growling constantly, too."

Charity blushed and laughed self-consciously.

Roger wasn't as gallant. He accepted her hand, gave it a brisk shake and dropped it. "We were hoping Shane would get some rest over the next couple of days. He has a cold."

She was offended by Roger's undercurrent of disapproval but dismissed it when Shane stiffened beside her. Knowing he was ready to jump to her defense, she gave Roger her friendliest smile and said, "So I found out, and since I'm a doctor, I'll make sure he has the best of care. In fact, he should be in bed right now, so if you'll both excuse us, I'm going to make sure he gets there."

Roger scowled and Derek laughed as he placed an arm around his manager's shoulders and lowered his head to the older man's ear. In a dramatic stage whisper he said, "Why do I have the feeling her idea of putting him to bed and his are different?"

"Why don't you two go play in the elevator shaft?" Shane grumbled. "But before you do it, Roger, would you mind checking Charity out of her room? She'll be staying up here."

Roger gave a stiff nod and obediently walked to the telephone. Charity wondered if the man really disliked her or if he was simply concerned about Shane's health. She had a feeling that it was a little of both, and she shifted uncomfortably from one foot to the other.

Shane wrapped his arm around her shoulders, picked up her suitcase and led her toward his bedroom. Once they were inside with the door closed behind them, he said, "I apologize for Roger. I'm afraid he's a little like a jealous mother hen. He's been in control of our lives for so long that he finds it difficult to let go. It's nothing personal, Charity."

"I'm sure it's not," she answered, but that didn't ease her uneasiness toward the older man. She was a threat to his hold on Shane, and she wondered if he'd ever be able to accept her or any woman.

But now was not the time to worry about Roger. "Sit down on the bed and take off your shirt," she ordered

Shane as she set her doctor's bag on the foot of the bed and opened it.

"Is this some new seduction technique?" he asked as he stripped off his shirt and sat on the edge of the bed. "If it is, I think I like it."

Charity didn't answer. She walked over to the windows and opened the curtains. Satisfied with the light that filled the room, she walked to the bed, extended a tongue depressor, and said, "Open your mouth, stick out your tongue and say *ah*."

"You're joking," Shane said with an uneasy laugh. "You aren't really going to examine me!"

"I most certainly am," she said as she gave him her most firm doctor's look. "You are working under a hectic schedule, Shane. A simple cold could easily turn into bronchitis or pneumonia. Not only that, but if you continue to sing before you get this under control, you could damage your voice. Now, open your mouth and stick out your tongue."

Shane didn't like it, but he did what he was told, grumbling beneath his breath when she removed the tongue depressor and murmured a noncommittal "Hmm."

"So what did you find down there?" he asked when she began to palpate his neck, searching for swollen lymph nodes. "Were my tonsils doing something illicit?"

She arched a brow, stuck a thermometer into his mouth and said, "Shh. I'm working."

He scowled but maintained his silence. She checked his nose and ears and eyes, continuing to give that noncommittal "Hmm." It was driving him crazy.

She removed the thermometer from his mouth and shook her head at his high temperature. When she pulled out her stethoscope, Shane's scowl deepened. But he didn't object when she listened to his chest, poking and prodding and ordering him to cough and to breathe. But when she pulled out the blood-pressure cuff, he did object.

"I have a cold, not high blood pressure."

"We'll take it anyway."

"Charity—"

"Shane, when you get your medical degree, you can tell me what to do. I don't tell you how to sing, so don't tell me how to practice medicine, okay?"

He mumbled a curse but extended his arm. When she was done, she didn't say a word. She just began to reload the doctor's bag. Shane watched her warily when she removed a small vial of medicine and then a syringe.

"What is that?" he asked.

"An antibiotic. Are you allergic to any drugs?"

"No, but I am allergic to shots. Unless you want to see a grown man cry, you'll put that thing away."

She smiled indulgently. "You won't even feel it."

"That's what they all say, and I have yet not to feel it."

"Drop your pants and lie on your stomach."

"You're going to give me a shot in my...? The hell you are!" he exclaimed, blushing furiously.

Her indulgent smile turned into a grin. "Why are you so shy? It's not as if I'll see anything I haven't seen before."

He glared at her. "In this case it's different. If you have to give me a shot, give it to me in the arm."

"No. It will hurt less and work faster if I give it to you in your buttock. Drop your pants and lie down, Shane."

"And if I don't?"

"Then I'll call Derek and Roger in for assistance."

"You wouldn't dare," he said, but unable to read her expression, he wasn't quite convinced she wouldn't. Finally, he let out a resigned sigh, released the zipper on his pants, and lay down on the bed, deciding he liked Charity the woman and the lover a hundred more times than Charity the doctor as she lowered his pants, exposing his hip. In fact, he wasn't certain he liked this aspect of her personality at all.

He grimaced when he felt her swab his hip, and when she pinched a portion of his flesh, he buried his face in the pillow, muttering, "Hurry up and get it over with so I can weep in private."

She chuckled, gave a fond swat to his exposed bottom and said, "It's already over, and you didn't feel a thing, did you?"

"You didn't really give me a shot," he said as he raised his head and glanced over his shoulder.

"Sure I did," she replied as she destroyed the needle and disposed of the syringe. "Now, I want you to put on your pajamas and climb into bed while I order you a good supply of orange juice from room service."

"Why is it I get the feeling this visit of yours isn't going to be a romantic interlude?"

He sneezed half a dozen times and coughed for a good thirty seconds. When he was finished, she shook her head. She, too, had planned on a romantic interlude, and if he could see the inside of her suitcase, he'd know it. She'd spent a fortune on lingerie. It was a good thing she'd automatically tucked in a flannel nightgown, since their only romantic romps were going to be having her drown him in orange juice.

"Get into your pajamas, Shane."

He gave her a mischievous grin. "I don't own a pair of pajamas. I sleep *au naturel*."

Charity's gaze dropped to his chest and then moved lower. The blush that colored her cheeks was due to the remembrance of how he looked in his most natural state.

"Then I guess I'd better order some extra blankets, too," she said.

She turned toward the phone, but Shane wrapped his arm around her waist before she could lift the receiver. He pulled her back onto his lap and rubbed his cheek against her hair.

"We aren't really going to spend the next two days playing doctor and patient, are we?" he asked huskily.

Charity had to fight against the urge to squirm as his warm, muscular thighs pressed against her bottom. Desire began to erupt, but she quickly capped it. He wasn't in any physical condition to play lover. Normally, a cold wasn't that serious, but with his hectic schedule, interrupted sleep and constant changes in environment, it could prove to be very serious. She had to make her professional side take control.

She leaned her head back against his chest and said, "We'll have plenty of time in the future for romantic interludes, Shane. It's more important that you get well. If you won't do as I say, then I'm going to go home."

His arms tightened around her. "You wouldn't really leave me in my hour of need, would you?"

She chuckled in defeat. "No, I won't leave you, but you are going to do exactly what I tell you to do. If you don't, you'll end up in the hospital with pneumonia."

Oddly enough, Shane found himself liking her concern. He knew she wanted him. He could feel it in the tension of her muscles. She wanted him, but she wanted to nurse him more. He decided that playing doctor and patient might not be so bad after all, and if he played his cards right, he still might be able to slip in a romantic interlude.

He lifted her off his lap and rose to his feet, smiling secretly to himself as he watched her eyes dilate when he dropped his pants to the floor and stepped out of them. Yes, he just might be able to slip in a romantic interlude.

He left his briefs on, deciding it would be easier on them both if she didn't see how nothing more than her gaze could affect him. By the time he slid between the sheets, she had turned her back on him and was on the telephone, calling room service.

Chapter Nine

Charity did nothing more than nurse Shane for the rest of the morning, but it was one of the most satisfying mornings she'd ever spent. Whenever he would doze, she would sit beside the bed and study his face. When he was in repose, the lines of weariness faded, making him look even more handsome, and she had to fight the impulse to crawl into bed with him.

Around noon, he was able to fall more deeply asleep, and she wandered out into the living room he shared with Derek. Derek was reclining on the sofa, eating pizza and watching a soap opera. He glanced toward her with a welcoming smile.

"I love the soaps. They have so much tragedy they make my own life look inconsequential and boring. How's my other half doing?"

"He's sleeping. How long has he had this cold?"

"He caught it in Miami, but it's only gotten bad over the last few days. It isn't really serious, is it?" he asked in concern as he sat up.

Charity sank onto the overstuffed chair that faced the television set. "No, but it could have been if he'd continued performing. I'm glad you decided to take a couple of days off."

"You can thank Roger for that. That's one of the reasons he's such a good manager. He always puts our health before the show. Want some pizza?"

She accepted a piece of pepperoni pizza and nibbled at it absently while she stared unseeingly at the television screen. Her thoughts were still with Shane, and she wondered if fate had broken the water pipe that serviced the clinic so she could be here to look after him. She had to shake her head to bring herself out of her reverie when she realized Derek was talking and she hadn't heard a word he said.

"I'm sorry. What did you say?"

"Shane said you saved his life, but he never gave me any of the details. Would you care to fill me in?"

Charity blushed at the memory of the night she'd found Shane in the woods and had to undress him. "I think Shane should tell you. He's a better storyteller than I am."

"A polite way of telling me to mind my own business." He chuckled and shook his head in defeat. "I'll probably go to my grave never knowing the story."

"You might," she agreed with a grin. "How are you feeling? You aren't catching Shane's cold, are you?"

"Naw. I haven't been physically ill in years. My illnesses lie more in the mental arena. Shane says I'm crazy. Roger says I'm eccentric. Frankly, I'm probably a little of both."

Charity laughed. "I think most people are."

"I don't suppose you'll be able to finish the tour with us."

"No. I'll have to return to Denver in a few days."

He sighed and rested his elbows on his knees. Then he laced his fingers together and began to swing his hands between his legs. When he glanced up at her, Charity knew he wanted to tell her something; she could also tell he wasn't sure he should do so.

"What is it, Derek?"

"There's nothing worse in the world than an interfering friend."

She regarded him thoughtfully. "I suppose that depends on what kind of interference the friend is running."

He glanced back down at his hands. It was several long moments before he heaved a resolved sigh and said, "There's a war brewing between Shane and Roger. I've managed to keep it under control so far, but I don't know how much longer I'll be able to do it. Especially after seeing Shane's eyes when he looks at you."

"Are you saying I'm causing trouble between them?" When he nodded, she asked, "How?"

"You're making Shane reassess his life. I don't have any problems with that. I'd like to do a little reassessing myself, and I'm willing to roll in whatever direction Shane decides to roll. But Roger..."

He picked up the remote control and turned off the television set. Then he leaned back against the sofa and stared at the ceiling. "Roger discovered us when we were eighteen-year-old kids. He's worked hard to bring us to the top and keep us there, and he isn't going to let go easily. I'm not defending him; I'm merely stating a fact."

"I sensed he thought I was an interloper when I met him."

Derek gave a dismissive shrug. "He was the same way with all three of my wives, but he got over it."

"You were married three times?" Charity questioned in disbelief.

He laughed ruefully. "Almost four, but Roger talked me out of the last one. Thank heavens he did. It would have been my worst marriage yet." He paused and drew in a deep breath. "One of the reasons we've lasted as long as we have is because we're not only a group, we're a family, and right now Shane is rocking the foundation of the family.

"Like I said, I don't mind Shane reassessing his life, and I'll support him in any decision he makes, but if you don't see yourself as a part of Shane's future, please walk away from him now. Don't let him possibly destroy a good friendship for no reason."

She glanced away from him and stared out the window. The sky was overcast and gave the day a touch of gloom. Like Denver, Kansas City was prone to violent spring snowstorms. She hoped one wouldn't hit before she left.

Then she closed her eyes and made herself face what Derek had said. Roger and Shane were disagreeing, and she was the cause. If Derek was right, there could be a serious rift in a friendship that had lasted eighteen years, and that rift might not be repairable.

Did she see herself in Shane's future? When she was with him, she did. But when she was alone with her thoughts, she wasn't certain. They were so very different, and even though they were handling those differences now, they were still new to each other. As the weeks and months passed, the newness would wear off. Would they be able to handle the differences then? Or, as it had with Carson, would it all begin to unravel?

"Here I was, expecting round-the-clock medical care, and the first thing I know, I fall asleep and you're out here flirting with Derek."

Charity's eyes flew open, and she smiled as she spied Shane leaning against the door frame leading into his bedroom, his jeans riding low on his hips. He was barefoot and bare-chested. His hair was wildly tousled, his cheeks and jaw were beard-stubbled, and there were dark circles beneath his eyes, but he looked like a beautiful ray of sunshine to her.

"You must be feeling better. You're beginning to grumble," she said.

Derek burst into laughter, and Shane scowled at him as he responded with "I think I'm about to suffer a relapse, and I'm going to definitely need more medical care." His gaze lowered to the coffee table. "Did I read somewhere that pizza is good for a cold?"

"It's all yours," Derek said, pushing the plate with the remainder of the pizza in Shane's direction, "but whether or not it's on your diet is up to your doctor."

Shane's eyes lifted to meet Charity's, and she felt his gaze right down to her toes. It told her he was hungry for more than pizza; however, she knew she was only going to let him appease one appetite.

She forced her racing pulse to slow and said, "Actually, pizza is good for a cold. It's full of protein. So if you'll crawl back into bed, I'll bring it in to you."

He nodded and went back into the bedroom. She rose and reached for the pizza but stopped when Derek touched her hand.

"I really do hope it works out, Charity. I'll continue to intervene between him and Roger."

Charity smiled her thanks. "I think they're both lucky to have a friend like you, and as far as seeing myself in Shane's future, I guess only time will tell."

"Good old father time." Derek sighed heavily, leaned back against the sofa and hit the remote control switch, turning the television back on.

Charity paused to heat the pizza in the small microwave oven in the suite and then entered Shane's bedroom. He'd crawled back into bed and piled the pillows behind his head; now he gave her a grateful smile when she handed him the plate.

He polished the food off without a word, set the plate aside and reached for her. Charity, anticipating his move, quickly stepped out of his reach.

"You need your rest, Shane."

"So do you. Lie down and take a nap with me. I promise I won't breathe on you."

"It's not your breathing I'm worried about."

He gave her a rakish grin. "Yeah? What are you worried about?"

She chuckled and sat down on the chair next to the window. "Let's talk."

"Sure, but with you sitting way over there, I'll have to yell, and that won't be good for my voice. In fact, I really shouldn't be talking above a whisper," he said, forcing a cough and looking at her woefully.

She laughed. "You missed your calling. You should have gone on the stage."

"Aren't you going to take pity on me?"

"I am taking pity on you. That's why I'm staying on the chair."

He rolled to his side, placed his head in his hand and let his eyes move over her languorously. Charity knew he was trying to arouse her, and he was doing a good job of it. She resisted the urge to shift on the chair and pretended a calmness she definitely didn't feel.

"Boy, this doctor-patient business isn't what I expected," he drawled. "I expected you to sit beside me and rest your cool hand against my fevered brow."

She chuckled. "When your brow is fevered again, I'll rest my cool hand against it."

"How long do you plan on staying away from me?"

She shrugged. "As long as it takes."

He released a resigned sigh and decided to change the subject. "How's work at the clinic going?"

"It's not going at all right now. We had a water-pipe break and had to close the doors for a few days while the city repairs it. That's how I was able to play hooky and come here to see you."

He didn't miss the look of relief that flickered across her face. He also knew she'd never tell him what she was thinking unless she was pressed. Charity was a master at keeping her emotions in check, and he'd already discovered she had to be pushed to open up. Didn't she realize that you had to talk out your problems before they could be resolved?

"You still miss the emergency room."

She closed her eyes and nodded. He had the uncanny ability to voice her innermost feelings when she least expected it. Unbidden tears began to burn her eyes, and she closed them more tightly. She wasn't going to cry over her frustration. She just wasn't going to do it.

"Oh, babe, I didn't mean to upset you," Shane said as he crawled out of bed and went to her.

She tried to protest when he slipped her shoes off her feet, lifted her off the chair and carried her back to the bed, but she couldn't get the words past the tears clogging her throat. After he'd tucked her under the covers and crawled in beside her, he wrapped his arms around her to bring her close.

Tenderly he smoothed her hair away from her face. "Why don't you cry it out? You'll feel better if you do."

She shook her head in denial, wrapped her arms around his neck and pressed her face against his shoulder. He rubbed her back and massaged her neck, trying to make her relax.

When it didn't work, he pulled her even more closely against him, deciding that after living with his body for thirty-six years, he really didn't know it. A minute ago he had been ready to ravish her. Now all he wanted to do was hold her and comfort her. Was that love? It sure felt like it.

"You're never going to find your answers until you release that dam you're holding inside," he stated quietly. "Shed your tears, Charity. Once they're gone, you'll think more clearly."

"I cried for two weeks, and all it did was make everything more cloudy."

"But you were reacting to a situation then. Now you're searching for answers. Let the tears fall, babe. I'll be here to get you through them."

She shook her head again. "I look awful when I cry. My eyes get red and swollen, and my nose gets stuffy."

"Well, with my cold, that will only help us talk with the same accent, and my eyes are all blurry. I won't see how bad you look."

"But I don't want to cry!" she exclaimed impatiently, cursing when the first tear leaked out.

Shane tangled his hand in her hair and forced her to look up at him. His gaze followed the path the tear had taken. She had to get the tears out, and he knew that as surely as he knew the sun would rise tomorrow. The problem was getting her to accept that fact.

"Well, we got one out. Give me one out of the other eye."

"No." She sniffed, cursing again when a second tear obediently leaked from the other eye.

"Now do it again."

"I don't want to cry!" she reiterated, hating it when her lower lip trembled.

"I know you don't, but you're going to do it anyway. Give me a couple more tears. Let's get rid of that dam so you can take control of your life. Come on. Let's get one from each eye at the same time. Once we get the faucet running, we'll be in business."

She tried, really tried, to hold back the tears, but they began to fall beneath his quiet encouragement, and when they started, she couldn't make them stop. Shane pulled her head back down to his shoulder and held her, rubbing her back and crooning soothing words in her ear.

Charity had no idea how long she cried, but when it was over, she was exhausted, and as much as she hated to admit it, she did feel better. Shane continued to hold her, and she was grateful that he didn't try to make her look at him. She really did look awful when she cried, and she didn't want him to see her like this.

"Let's take a nap," he whispered, tightening his hold around her reassuringly. "We'll both feel better when we wake up."

She nodded and snuggled close to him, feeling secure and safe and more at peace with herself than she had since the day she'd been taken hostage.

After her breathing deepened, Shane shifted so he could look down into her sleeping face. He smiled and gently brushed the back of a finger against a tear-stained cheek.

"Even red-eyed and stuffy-nosed, you're the most beautiful woman I've ever seen," he murmured before pressing a butterfly kiss to her forehead.

Then he settled down beside her, heaved a contented sigh, and fell asleep.

When Charity awoke, it took an effort to open her eyes. They were swollen from crying, and she was thankful that Shane still slept.

She untangled herself from his embrace and slipped out of bed, hurrying to the bath. The damage she surveyed in the mirror was even worse than she'd thought. She wet a washcloth with cold water and pressed it to her eyes, chiding herself for succumbing to tears and determined to remove most of the swelling. It was a long process, but she finally felt she'd pulled herself together enough to be presentable.

When she walked back into the bedroom, Shane was awake and sitting up in bed. With a show of sensitivity, he avoided studying her face and didn't mention her crying jag. Instead, he yawned and informed her he was starving.

Charity smiled wryly. Their relationship seemed to revolve around bed and food; if they weren't in the one, they were eating the other. She busied herself by calling room service.

While they waited for dinner, Shane pulled a large calendar from the drawer of the bedside stand and began to show her his schedule after the tour. Despite his claims that it was a light schedule compared to what he was used to, she thought it was extremely demanding.

She frowned as he pointed out which weeks he would be available to spend with her and hinted that he'd like her to arrange for a few days off.

It wasn't that she didn't want to give him the time but that she knew it wouldn't always be possible for her to do so, particularly if she stayed in private practice. If she ventured out on her own and opened a new practice, she'd be tied down to her patients. If she joined a group of physicians, she'd be the junior staff member and the last on the list when it came to time off. But Shane was so excited by what he'd accomplished that she didn't have the heart to express her doubts. She'd take it a day at a time and see what happened. Besides, she really wouldn't know how her schedule meshed with his until she had decided what to do with her career.

Shane put the calendar back into the drawer when Derek knocked, stuck his head inside and informed them their dinner had arrived. He wheeled it in with a flourish, gave them an exaggerated bow and left. Charity chuckled at his antics, and Shane grumbled something about having to put up with a clown.

While they ate, Shane began to rave about what a good doctor she was, claiming he already felt ninety-nine percent better. Knowing that he felt better because of the shot she'd given him and that he wouldn't be feeling as well once the antibiotic began to wear off, she leaned back in her chair and studied him thoughtfully, trying to decide what course of treatment she should give him.

Shane paused in the middle of cutting off a piece of his steak and eyed her warily. "Just what's going on in that gorgeous mind of yours?" he asked.

"I'm trying to decide whether you'll remember to take your pills if I give them to you, or whether I should give you another shot in the morning."

"Another shot!" he yelped, and gave a vehement shake of his head. "There's no way you're going to give me another shot."

She grinned. "Tell the truth, Shane. You didn't even feel that shot this morning."

He gingerly rubbed his cotton-covered buttock. "I didn't feel it then, but I sure feel it now. I'm going to have six inches of scar tissue."

Her grin widened. "Well, if we give you a shot on the other side, you'll have a matching set."

"I can do without a matching set. Just give me the pills, even though I don't need them. I am feeling better, Charity."

"You won't once the shot wears off."

"Then the pills it is," he said as he put the piece of steak in his mouth and waved his fork at her. "If you don't trust me to take them, give them to Roger. I can assure you he'll make sure I take them."

Charity frowned at the derision in his voice and immediately recalled Derek's words.

"Are you and Roger quarreling?" she asked.

He refused to look at her, centering his attention on his plate. "Of course not."

"As far as I know, you've never lied to me, Shane. Don't start now."

He clenched his steak knife. "Derek has a big mouth. I never should have fallen asleep."

"What makes you think Derek said anything?"

"Because I know him. He's a busybody. A well-meaning one, but a busybody just the same." He heaved a resigned sigh. "Don't take everything he says to heart. Roger and I have squabbled before and survived. I'm sure we'll make it through this."

"But you've never squabbled over me before, and I don't understand why you're doing it."

"Because he doesn't want to give me any time!" Shane exclaimed impatiently. He looked at her and gave a disgusted shake of his head. "All I want is some time to spend with you, Charity. I'm doing what you suggested. I'm evaluating my obligations and deciding which ones are important and which aren't. I'm still stuck with a few appearances that I don't feel are important, but since Roger had already scheduled them, I agreed to keep them. Considering that fact, I don't see why he feels he has the right to complain."

Charity gnawed on her bottom lip as she thought through what she wanted to say. "I'm glad you're evaluating your schedule. You deserve some time, Shane, but you should be making those changes for you, not for me. If things don't work out between us—"

"Don't say that!" he interrupted her harshly. Then he closed his eyes and drew in a deep breath. "I'm sorry. I shouldn't have raised my voice, but don't say that, Charity. Don't even think it. If you do, it might come true."

"We have to face facts, Shane, and the facts are that what we have going is working right now, but it's only been working for two weeks."

He opened his eyes as he corrected her with "Two-and-a-half weeks."

She smiled indulgently. "All right, two-and-a-half weeks."

"And don't forget the time at the cabin."

"I'll never forget the time at the cabin, but I don't think we can really include that time as a part of our relationship. It was something that just . . . happened," she said.

"Just like my falling in love with you 'just happened'?"

Charity collapsed against the back of her chair, feeling as if he'd struck her. "You're not in love with me."

He sighed and raked his fingers through his hair. "If I'm not, I'm pretty damn close to it."

She rose to her feet and stuffed her hands deep into the pockets of her jeans. She walked to the window and stared out into the night. The moon was even smaller. By the time she was ready to leave, it would probably be gone, and she had the strangest feeling that when it disappeared, everything in her life was going to go wrong.

"Charity," Shane stated wearily, "in the past two-and-a-half weeks I've told you more about myself than I've ever told anyone, and I think you've done the same with me.

And you know something? We're not only good lovers; we've become good friends. If that's not love, what is it?''

She shrugged. She didn't have the answers and was terribly afraid that if they weren't in love, they were awfully close. So close it was frightening. Could it happen that fast? Her grandmother had claimed that she'd fallen in love with her grandfather on sight, and her parents had married exactly nine weeks from the day they'd met. Both marriages had endured. Her grandparents had been married fifty-three years before her grandfather died, and her parents would soon celebrate their thirty-eighth anniversary. But neither couple had faced the challenges she and Shane faced. The next obvious question was, If it was love, could it endure?

Shane knew he'd spoken too soon, and he wanted to grab the words back. She hadn't been ready for his confession, and if he was truly honest with himself, he had to admit he wasn't certain he'd been ready to make it. But the words had been spoken, and he and Charity were going to have to face them.

He set his plate aside, rose from the bed and pulled on his jeans. Then he went to Charity, put his hands on her shoulders and drew her back against him. Resting his chin on the top of her head, he, too, stared at the moon.

When it disappeared behind a cloud, he said, "I wrote a song for you the other night. It was after one of those calls where we couldn't talk because I had a flight to catch. I felt bad, because I sensed you needed to talk. I guess I compensated by convincing myself that the song would make the difference. I'm a little hoarse, and my guitar's in the other room, but if you'll overlook those little details, I'd like to sing it for you. Would you like to hear it?''

Charity nodded, too overwhelmed by the fact that he'd written her a song to speak.

He hummed softly for a moment, then began to sing.

If you need someone there to comfort you,
Think of me. I'm always close.

The sun itself is my smile.
Each ray of light, my prayers for you.
Each rising dawn is my morning kiss.
Each setting sun is my good-night hug.
So never feel you are alone
When every day is made of me.
I'll comfort you and stand by you.
Just reach for the sky and call my name.

"Oh, Shane," Charity whispered as she turned in his arms and buried her head against his chest.

"Does that mean you like the song?" he asked huskily as he wrapped his arms securely around her.

"More than you can ever know. You couldn't have given me a more precious gift."

"I'm glad, because the words are the truth, Charity. I may not always be with you in person, but I'm always with you in spirit. Promise me that no matter what happens, you'll remember that."

She leaned her head back, her eyes glistening with unshed tears. "I'll always remember."

He chucked her affectionately under the chin, once again longing to kiss her but still fearful she'd catch his cold. "Good. Now, what would you say about our spending some time having fun?"

"Shane, you really do need your rest."

"Ah, lady, you have a one-track mind," he teased, brushing his thumbs over her blushing cheeks. "As much as I'd like to have that kind of fun, I agree that I need to take it easy. I thought we'd spend some time with Derek and Roger. That way you can get to know them and they can get to know you. Who knows? The three of you might end up liking each other."

"Who knows? We just might."

"That's my girl," he said as he wrapped his arm around her shoulders and led her out into the living room.

* * *

Charity did enjoy her evening with Derek and Roger. Since she and Derek had already struck up a tentative friendship, he was relaxed, trading teasing banter with Shane that was so reminiscent of sibling rivalry that Charity couldn't help but laugh.

For the first hour Roger was withdrawn, barely looking at her, but as time passed, he seemed to accept her presence and also relaxed.

When Derek expressed a longing for popcorn, Roger miraculously came up with a huge supply of freshly popped theater popcorn, and as they sat around and munched on it, Shane and Derek began reminiscing about the days when they'd first begun singing. Even Roger warmed to the topic, and Charity sat curled up against Shane, listening to the often hilarious but frequently sad stories.

The three men had shared more in eighteen years than most families shared in a lifetime. Trained to observe people and read between the lines, Charity found herself automatically doing that with each of them.

Shane had told her that Derek was moody, and he was right. Derek's moods shifted within the blink of an eye. However, they weren't manic mood changes, and Charity knew the man's claim to being crazy wasn't true. But as she listened to him talk about his marriages, she realized that like Shane, Derek was terribly lonely. He was also an incurable romantic. He was in love with love, rushed into his relationships, and by the time he learned they weren't what he'd expected, he was already married.

Roger was a little more difficult to understand at first. It was evident that he adored Shane and Derek with a fervor that bordered on obsession. She was surprised to learn Roger was only ten years older than the singers; he looked fifteen to twenty years older. Later, after Roger had retired for the night, Shane told her his story, and Charity's innate compassion went out to him.

He'd been a young man himself when he'd discovered Shane and Derek, and certain they were going to rise to the top, he'd devoted himself to them to the exclusion of all else—that "all else" had included his wife and young son. He'd convinced himself that once Moon and Sun was on top, he'd have all the time in the world, but when his five-year-old son had fallen into the swimming pool at home and drowned, his wife had left him.

"He blamed himself," Shane informed her, his eyes dark with painful memory. "His wife never wanted the swimming pool, and he'd insisted on putting it in."

"How terribly sad," she whispered.

But despite the compassion she felt for Roger, she knew Shane had to make some changes in his life. As she listened to him talk, she was given a greater amount of insight into what motivated him. Roger worked hard for the group because it was all he had. Derek worked hard because being a rock star was all he'd ever wanted to be. Shane worked hard because music was his life. But unlike the other two, Shane was torn between two worlds—his world with Moon and Sun and the world he'd shared with his parents. A world of family, stability and love.

In order to be fulfilled, Shane would have to bridge those worlds, and Charity wondered if she was the right one to help him build that bridge.

Like him, she wanted the best of both worlds, but he was settled in his career and hers had been blown apart. She'd have to come to grips with the working part of her life before she could even begin to think about the personal part.

Her conscience told her she should walk away from him now. Her heart begged her to stay. When she glanced up at him and he smiled down at her, she knew her heart was going to win.

Shane smiled inwardly when Charity stepped out of the bath, clad in a sedate flannel nightgown that covered her from her chin to her ankles. He knew she'd donned the nightgown in order to cool his ardor, and he wondered what she'd say if he told her the outfit only heightened it. She looked small, fragile and definitely in need of protection. He would have wanted her less if she'd been dressed in a lacy nothing that revealed everything. Well, maybe not less, he corrected himself as his mind conjured up the image of her in a lacy nothing, but definitely in a different way.

He lifted the covers on the bed invitingly. She eyed the bed warily.

"I still think I should sleep on the sofa, Shane. You really do need your rest."

"I do," he agreed, "and I'll rest more easily if you're in my arms. I miss you when you aren't with me."

"I miss you, too, but—"

"Come to bed, Charity. If you don't want to make love, we won't make love."

"It's not that I don't want to," she explained, nervously fingering the lace at the cuff of her gown. "It's just that you really do need your rest."

"Then come to bed so I can get it," he ordered her.

Charity moved hesitantly toward the bed, still uncertain about whether or not she should be sharing it with him. She wasn't worried about catching his cold. But she wanted him to take advantage of the short time he had to recuperate, and she had a feeling he wouldn't do much recuperating with her in his bed.

But any thoughts of turning away from him were dismissed when he extended his hand and regarded her steadily. The gesture symbolized more than an invitation into his bed. It was a symbol of trust. She took his hand and crawled in beside him.

He sighed in relief as he wrapped his arms around her and rested his cheek against her hair. Holding her was more important than making love to her, he admitted. He still wanted her and didn't dare deny it. His body would give ample proof that it was a lie. But he'd gladly ignore his desire just to have her beside him.

Even though Shane carefully refrained from molding himself to her, Charity knew he was aroused. She could feel it in the tension of his muscles and hear it in his shallow breathing. She was tempted to roll against him to feel the physical proof of his need, but she closed her eyes and forced herself to lie still.

"Why can't we make love?" he asked after several minutes.

"You can't afford to get overheated. You might get chilled afterward, and it could make your cold worse."

"It'd be worth it," he murmured as he rested his hand against the gentle curve of her waist and gave it a loving squeeze.

"Not if you ended up with laryngitis and couldn't sing. Roger isn't too fond of me as it is."

"I don't care about Roger," he said, his body tensing with more than desire.

She sat up and stared at him in frustration. "Roger is one of the best friends you'll ever have."

"You're right," he said, wrapping his arm around her shoulder and bringing her back down to the mattress. After tucking the covers securely around her shoulders, he said, "I know Roger is my friend, but he can't give me the same satisfaction you can, Charity. If it comes to a choice, I'll choose you."

"Why?"

"Why? That's a silly question."

"Answer it anyway."

"Ever since I met you, you've filled gaps in my life. Gaps that could never be filled by Roger."

"You're talking about sex?"

"No!" he stated emphatically, his blue eyes darkening with impatience. "We have never experienced *sex*, Charity. We have experienced lovemaking."

"It's the same thing."

"No, it's not, and if you were more experienced, you'd know that."

"And how do you know I'm not more experienced?"

He tightened his arms around her. "Because if you were, you never would have made that statement. Sex is uninvolved, Charity. When you have sex, you don't care about talking afterward. You don't need to touch or to kiss or to assure each other it was good."

"I'll go along with that," she said with a sigh, "but I also think you're making too much out of what we have. We spend more time in bed than anywhere else. There's more to a relationship than physical gratification."

"Are you intimating that we don't have anything outside the covers?"

"Are you intimating that we do?"

"Yes."

She closed her eyes in defeat. "Then tell me what we have, Shane."

"Friendship, understanding and respect. We can talk, Charity. Really talk. And we've proven that a few dozen times over the telephone."

"But if we didn't have the telephone between us, would we have done that talking?"

"You bet. Now, if you really want me to get my rest, I suggest you stop agitating me and let me go to sleep."

She nodded and laid her head against his chest, but his roving hand didn't make sleep her first priority. "Shane..." she began to object.

"Shhh," he whispered. "I promise I won't get overheated."

"How can you promise that?"

"Because you're going to do most of the work. Trust me, sweetheart."

"But—"

"Shhh," he whispered again.

He barely moved. Only his hand was in constant action, and what it was doing to her was driving her wild.

"Shane!" she protested as he eased the hem of her nightgown toward her hips.

"Trust me," he repeated, and Charity didn't have a choice. He'd moved her beyond her capacity for reason.

He sat up to slip the nightgown over her head and slide her panties down her hips and legs. Then he removed his briefs. When he lay back down beside her and pulled her close, they both released sighs of relief. He wanted her. She wanted him. The professional in her tried to surface, but the woman inside ignored the warnings when his hand slid to the apex of her thighs and his fingers began to caress her in a manner that she could only describe as magic.

As was his specialty, he stoked the fire and then moved away to let her cool, but before she could completely cool, he was rebuilding the heat until she was in a fever.

When she thought she couldn't stand any more, he pulled her over him and slipped inside her. They gasped in unison, both unable to move at the beautiful sensation of their joining.

Then Shane shifted slightly, encouragingly. At first Charity was overcome by shyness, but when each gentle motion of her hips elicited a low moan from Shane, her shyness was replaced with confidence.

Shane gripped the sheet beneath him as he fought against taking control, and he drew in one deep breath after another. She was moving over him in a rhythmic pattern that he could only describe as music—primitive music—and his heart supplied the beating drums.

When he was certain he couldn't bear any more of her torment, the waves swept over them both, and Shane released his hold on the sheet to wrap his arms around Charity. His hips moved to meet hers, and he groaned as his world exploded in a symphony of feelings.

When she collapsed on his chest, he smiled and pulled the covers over her, protesting when she tried to move. He'd never felt closer to another human being than he did at this moment, and he didn't want the closeness to end.

When he finally rolled so that she was lying at his side, he was convinced he was in love with her, and Charity was not going to persuade him otherwise.

Charity was lost in her own whirlpool of thoughts, and the one that kept surfacing no matter how she denied it was that what she felt for Shane was love. It was still tenuous—so very fragile—but it was love.

Chapter Ten

As usual, Charity awoke before dawn the next morning, but she didn't get out of bed immediately as she normally would have. Instead, she snuggled against Shane and released a luxurious sigh when his arm tightened around her.

"You are the most restless woman I've ever met," he grumbled sleepily when she shifted again a short time later.

"I'm sorry. I didn't mean to wake you," she said, tilting her head so she could see his face and smiling as she met his hooded gaze.

He yawned and rubbed his hand over his morning beard before dropping a quick kiss to her lips. "You're forgiven." Then he glanced toward the clock, frowned and asked, "Do you always get up this early?"

"Yes."

He gave a rueful shake of his head. "I can't believe I'm involved with a morning person."

"You don't like the morning?"

"I work nights, Charity. I'm usually crawling into bed when the sun's coming up."

She regarded him thoughtfully. "We really are opposites, aren't we?"

"Yes, and I like it that way."

She smiled and rested her hand against his forehead. "Your fever's gone. How do you feel?"

"With my hands," he replied as he made a playful foray of her body beneath the covers. "I can't get over how soft you are."

She chuckled. "I'm supposed to be soft. I'm a woman."

"And I'm a man," he said huskily as he wrapped a leg over her hip and rolled against her. "Now that I've convinced you that I'm feeling just fine, are you going to teach me how to make good use of my mornings?"

"Are you sure you're up to it?" she teased.

He grinned wickedly. "I'm about as up as I'm going to get."

She laughed, wrapped her arms around his neck and began his lessons.

The next few days were a wonderful time of discovery. In the mornings, Charity would go with Shane and Derek to the deserted hotel cocktail lounge, where she sat at the piano bar, enthralled, as she watched them work on a song they were composing. Shane devoted the afternoons to her exclusively, and they sat and talked just as they had over the telephone. Only now it was more rewarding, because they could watch each other's faces and add emphasis to their words by reaching out to touch a cheek or entwine fingers or share a brief kiss.

She didn't realize that Shane had carefully orchestrated the pace of each day. When she'd expressed concern that all they shared was a physical relationship, he'd sensed she was uncomfortable with her passion, and knowing she was trying to analyze and categorize it, he decided it was time to court her intellectually.

He soon saw the results of his efforts. Where Charity had been tense and rarely laughed before, she now was relaxed and laughed frequently. He recognized that they still had a good number of problems to solve—as any new relationship would—but he felt that they were establishing a solid foundation upon which to begin building a future. And more than anything, he wanted that future.

Charity represented everything he'd lost so many years ago. When he was around her, hazy memories clicked through his mind—memories that recalled the rare and loving relationship his parents had shared. He knew in his heart that that kind of love was a viable reality between him and Charity, and that with a little time, a lot of patience and a small piece of luck, he'd finally be able to recapture that part of the world he missed so badly.

Shane's cold was fast disappearing, but when the four band members wandered into his suite every evening to practice, Charity still forbade him to sing, explaining the importance of giving his vocal cords a rest. Shane accepted her orders good-naturedly, despite the razzing he received from the band. They were a fun-loving group of men and had her laughing constantly, and she was amazed by their camaraderie, particularly considering the fact that they'd been on tour for more than four months and were constantly in one another's company.

She soon learned that the major reason for the high morale was the fact that every few weeks, the band members' families were flown in at Shane's and Derek's expense—a benefit that was a part of their contracts. When Charity questioned Shane about the rationale for such a clause, he shrugged and said, "It's hard to keep a good band together, and even harder if they're having family problems, which is inevitable with long separations. This way the men don't get as restless, since they know they'll see the wife and kids every few weeks, and the wives don't feel so abandoned. It isn't a perfect solution, but it's a good compromise."

She liked his explanation, and as she studied the smiling faces in the room, she knew the psychology was working. The expenses of flying the families in had to be staggering, but Shane and Derek put more emphasis on the personal needs of the band than on their wallets, and she loved Shane even more for it.

On Friday Charity let Shane sing during practice, since his concert was scheduled for Saturday night, but she insisted that the practice be short so he didn't put unnecessary strain on his voice. She watched the performance critically, absorbing the material they were feeding her.

The repartee that Shane and Derek shared was hilarious and would appeal to all ages, she knew. It was also filled with subtle warnings against drugs and alcohol, and when they sang about love, they sang about commitment.

When Charity voiced her discoveries after practice, Shane gave her a wry smile.

"We're heroes to these kids, Charity, and it's our responsibility to ensure that we're providing them with a good role model. Somewhere along the line, the guys in the white hats got confused with the guys in the black hats. We're only trying to help them see the difference."

That night Roger and Derek disappeared, and she and Shane shared an intimate candlelight dinner in the room with slow, romantic music playing in the background.

Mellowed by champagne, good food and Shane's companionship, Charity melted into his arms when he urged her to her feet and pulled her into his arms to dance. She leaned against his shoulder and breathed in the intoxicating scent of him as he gracefully moved them around the room.

When he lowered his head and caught her lips with his, she responded ardently, knowing that time was once again slipping away from them. In less than forty-eight hours, she'd be on her way back to Denver and Shane would remain behind. It would always be like this, she realized with a pang of regret. A short time together and then a long separation. She tightened her grip around his neck and deepened the kiss.

Shane sensed the desperation behind her action, and even though he wondered what was causing it, he didn't pull away to find out. They had so little time left, and he wanted to fill that time with loving, happy memories. They would face the problems when the tour was over and they had time to really talk. And that was exactly what he planned on doing when he joined her in Denver. It was essential that they bring their differences to the surface and confront and solve them, because by the end of the summer, Shane wanted Charity to be his wife.

He wasn't sure when marriage had become his ultimate goal. Perhaps it had been her first day here, when she'd fussed over him, doctored him, and then made love to him. Perhaps it was later as he'd watched her befriend Derek and the members of the band and even earn a grudging respect from Roger. All he knew was that she belonged in his world. She balanced it and made him complete, and when she left on Sunday, she'd be taking his heart with her.

As the last strains of music died away on the tape deck, he lifted her in his arms, carried her into the bedroom, and gently laid her on the bed. With loving reverence, he removed her clothes and proceeded to make love to her with every ounce of love inside him.

Saturday proved to be hectic. Roger scurried in and out of the room, firing nonstop instructions, and finally hauled Shane and Derek away for a rehearsal at the concert hall where they'd be performing.

Left to her own devices, Charity wandered through downtown Kansas City, stopping at an exclusive boutique to buy a sinfully expensive dress for Shane's concert.

Shane still hadn't returned when she arrived back at the hotel, so she made arrangements to have her dress pressed. Then she piled her hair on top of her head and crawled into a hot bath overflowing with bubbles. That's where Shane found her.

"I thought scenes like this only took place in the movies," he drawled as he leaned against the door frame and eyed her with interest.

"Want to join me?" she asked coquettishly.

He sniffed the air and shook his head. "Derek and the band would never let me live it down if I arrived at the concert smelling like jasmine. That is jasmine, isn't it?"

"It is," she replied as she stretched a leg upward and squeezed a full sponge of water over it, smiling to herself when Shane's eyes dilated as he watched the action.

Seductively, she repeated the action with the other leg as she said, "I bought a new dress today."

"Mmm," he said absently, watching her squeeze water over her shoulder and following the trail of droplets as they slid down her slender back. "You went shopping?"

"Yes."

He entered the room and sat on the toilet, his eyes never leaving her as she continued to bathe. "That must have been fun for the guards. Which one went with you?"

"None. Would you wash my back for me?"

"You went shopping alone?" Shane questioned sharply.

"Of course," Charity said, glancing up in surprise at his tone of voice. "Why wouldn't I?"

Shane's brows drew together in a concerned frown. "Charity, don't ever leave the hotel alone again."

"Why?" she asked in confusion.

"Because you're with me." He sighed at her bewildered expression and explained, "I'm famous, Charity, and with that fame comes an element of danger. You're involved with me, so I'm afraid a certain amount of that danger transfers to you."

"Don't be ridiculous. No one knows me."

"That's only because the press hasn't discovered you, and I have every intention of making sure they don't for a good while to come."

He knelt beside the tub, took the sponge from her hand and leaned her forward so he could wash her back. She pulled away from him and shifted so she could see his face. He looked so grim that she shivered. A thousand questions rose to the surface—questions she wasn't certain she wanted the answers to but knew she had to ask. But before she could part her lips, Shane eased her around in the tub and began to wash her back in long, languorous strokes.

"You have the most beautiful neck in the world. Did you know that?" he asked as he began to nibble a tantalizing path along the back of her neck that made her bones feel like liquid. "What the hell," he finally whispered hoarsely. "Jasmine doesn't smell that bad, right?"

"Right," Charity agreed with a smile when he began to strip off his clothes. All her questions had disappeared by the time he joined her in the tub.

Charity's cheeks were still flushed from the afternoon's bout of lovemaking as she finished dressing for the concert that night. Uncontrolled, fiery passion had exploded between her and Shane, and she wondered how they'd managed to keep the bath water from boiling. When they'd both reached a fevered pitch, Shane had lifted her out of the tub and carried her to the bed, where they'd united urgently, heedless of their wet bodies, which had soaked the sheets.

Although the memory was one she would always treasure, it also frightened her. She'd never considered herself a particularly passionate woman, and she was uncomfortable with the fact that Shane was able to draw out parts of her she'd never known existed. Until now she'd been able to clinically slot her response to his lovemaking; her medical books were filled with all the explanations. But this afternoon she and Shane had transcended the medical books. They hadn't made love with their bodies; they'd made love with their souls, and the medical books couldn't explain that.

Somehow Shane was changing her, and she didn't know if she liked the changes or could even live with them. Would she be able to continue to measure up to the passion he demanded from her with every kiss, every touch?

The change she was undergoing became even more apparent as she slid her dress over her head and regarded her image in the mirror. Before Shane, she never would have considered buying this black silk dress, which plunged daringly in the front and clung seductively to her soft curves, nor would she have let her hair fall straight and sleek down to her shoulders. In fact, the woman staring back at her was a total stranger, and Charity took an involuntary step backward in alarm.

"Hey, watch the toes," Shane said as he suddenly appeared behind her. He arched a brow as he regarded her image in the mirror and let out a low wolf whistle. "You are gorgeous. Absolutely, unequivocally gorgeous."

She smiled weakly. "I think I'm overdressed, or maybe I should say underdressed," she said, self-consciously adjusting the low neckline.

Shane chuckled, placed his hands on her hips and pulled her back against him. Resting his chin on the top of her head, he once again eyed her image in the mirror.

"Nope. I think you're dressed just right. You are missing something, though."

"I am? What?"

"This," he replied as he slipped a necklace from his jacket pocket and dangled it in front of her.

"Oh, Shane, it's beautiful!" Charity exclaimed as she lifted the small gold heart dangling from the end. Then she frowned and shook her head as a circlet of diamonds in the center caught the overhead light. "I can't accept this. It's much too expensive."

"Of course you can accept it."

"No I can't. I—"

"Looks stunning with this dress, doesn't it?" he interrupted her as he draped the necklace around her neck and reached over her shoulder to position the heart between her breasts. "But it does look a little lonely, so I guess you'll have to put on the earrings that go with it."

"Shane, no!" Charity insisted as she caught the heart in her hand and spun around to face him. "I can't accept this."

"You are going to accept it, Charity," he said with a stubborn lift of his chin. "I want to give you something, and you aren't going to take that pleasure away from me."

"Then give me something inexpensive." She opened her hand and extended the heart. "This is too much."

He stuffed his hands into the pockets of his slacks. "Why don't you turn it over and read the inscription?"

Automatically, Charity's gaze dropped to the heart, and she had a sinking feeling in the pit of her stomach as she turned it over. It read: "Charity. Forever, Shane."

"Oh, damn you," she whispered as she closed her fingers around it and brought them to her lips. "Oh, damn you anyway, Shane Burke."

Shane wasn't offended by her words, because he saw the sentimental tears glistening in her eyes. He smiled and said, "A simple thank-you would have been sufficient, Charity."

She scowled at him. "I should still make you take this back."

"Probably, but you won't." He reached into his pocket and withdrew the earrings, which were tiny hearts with a diamond in the center of each. "Put on your jewels, babe, while I get dressed. You can thank me properly after the concert tonight," he said with a lascivious wink.

Before Charity could think of an appropriate comeback, he disappeared into the bath, closing the door behind him. With a sigh she studied the necklace. She knew the gift was his way of telling her he was entrusting her with his heart, and the realization overwhelmed her.

For a moment—a short moment—she nearly laid the necklace aside, but when she gazed down at the circle of blinking diamonds, she knew she couldn't.

Her hands shook as she fastened it around her neck. The heart fell into place between her breasts and was warmed by the heat of her skin. Tears filled her eyes once again as she gently touched it with the tips of her fingers. *Forever,* he'd had inscribed. She feared that forever wouldn't come true, especially when he learned just how ordinary a woman she really was.

Shane was worried as he dressed for the concert. He knew that Charity was confused and concerned about the depth of her feelings for him. He'd seen it in her eyes after they'd made love this afternoon, and it scared the hell out of him. Tomorrow she'd be leaving. In the days to come she'd have too much time to sit and fret, and he wouldn't be there to combat her worries.

That was why he'd given her the necklace. It was meant to be a bond, and he could only pray that it was a strong enough bond to hold her through the days that lay ahead.

He finished donning the black leather costume that had become his trademark, drew in a deep breath, and went looking for Charity. He found her sitting in the living room, chatting with Derek.

"Ah, my other half has finally arrived," Derek drawled as he lifted his feet to the coffee table. "Tell me the truth, Charity. Don't you think I've out-sexied Shane a hundred times over?"

Charity's gaze drifted over Derek, who wore skintight white leather. A white panama hat with a black hatband sat rakishly on his head. A flash of the black suspenders he wore beneath the jacket were a dramatic, eye-catching contrast to his costume. Then she studied Shane, who was dressed identically, except in black leather, with a white hatband and white suspenders. The pictures she'd seen in the magazine on the airplane came back with perfect clarity, and she shifted uneasily on her chair. The Shane she knew wore jeans and T-shirts or simple casual clothes. He was a "regular" guy. The striking man standing in front of her could be called anything but "regular."

"Is 'out-sexied' a word?" she asked, struggling with the fact that she was about to face the professional side of Shane's world and wasn't certain she wanted to do so.

"She's got you there, Derek," Shane said as he pushed the brim of his hat backward and winked at her. "But I think Charity has out-sexied both of us, don't you?"

"Indubitably," Derek replied with an affected English accent that was so bad Charity had to laugh. "Now I understand why you're insisting that she go to the concert hall with Roger and the band. She'd steal all our thunder."

"I'm going with Roger and the band?" Charity questioned in surprise. "Why?"

"Because I don't want the press photographing you."

"Are you ashamed to be seen with me?" she asked, the teasing tone she'd strived for failing miserably as she fought to control her uncertainty. *Her* Shane would take her any way, wouldn't care who saw her, but evidently this Shane did care, and she couldn't help but feel that the reason was that she didn't measure up.

Caught off guard by her question, Shane could only give her a startled stare. It took him a moment to realize she'd actually been serious. He glanced toward Derek as if seeking help, but Derek shrugged, looking as dumbfounded by her question as Shane felt.

"Of course I'm not ashamed to be seen with you," Shane said as he took her hands and pulled her to her feet and into his arms. Then he caught her chin in his hand and tilted her head upward so he could look into her eyes. "I want to protect you, sweetheart, and the only way I can do that is to make sure no one can identify you."

"I don't know a soul in Kansas City. No one could identify me."

"It's not that simple, Charity. I'm afraid the gossip rags are sold all over the country. If your picture hits the front page, someone will step forward to tell who you are if for no other reason than to have a moment of fame. Then you'll have reporters camped on your doorstep and in your office waiting room. You won't have a moment's peace, and I won't be there to run them off.''

When she still looked unconvinced, he said, ''Very soon I'll have to share you with the world, but I'm afraid I'm feeling selfish, and for now I want to keep you to myself, okay?''

''Okay,'' she agreed, knowing that when he was looking at her with his blue eyes filled with warmth and love, she couldn't deny him anything.

''I just love it when you're obedient,'' he teased her. He dropped a quick kiss on her lips before saying, ''Go get your coat. Roger will be here any minute, and nothing makes him grumpier than having to wait.''

After she'd walked out of the room, Shane glanced at Derek and arched a brow at his friend's frowning countenance. ''What's wrong with you?''

''I'm trying to figure out what you hope to accomplish by shielding her from your world. She has to face it sometime, Shane, and the sooner the better.''

Shane shook his head in denial of Derek's words. ''I haven't had enough time to prepare her for what it will be like when the world learns about us.''

''Then you'd better start preparing her, because she won't remain a secret for long. Half the hotel staff knows about her, and you know as well as I do that the moment we're gone, they're going to talk. The longer you wait, the harder it's going to be, particularly if some sharp reporter starts doing a little digging and discovers Charity on his own.''

Shane knew Derek was right. He also knew that Charity was a very private person, and he feared that unless he had her bound irrevocably to him, he'd lose her when she was thrust into the public eye. All he needed was just a little more time so he could make certain she was his—all his. He needed enough time to get her to say she loved him, and once she had committed herself that far, he knew that not even the press would be able to chase her away.

Chapter Eleven

Even though Charity would have preferred being with Shane, she did enjoy the ride to the concert hall. The band members teased her and laughed with her, and even Roger seemed friendlier than usual, insisting that she sit beside him while he boasted of how he'd wangled her a front-row seat since she'd never seen Shane perform.

That's why she was so surprised when Roger cursed, quietly but violently, a short time later when the limousine eased out of traffic and he gazed out the window.

"What's wrong?" she asked, leaning forward so she could see what had upset him. "My God, what's going on?" she whispered, staring in disbelief at a massive crowd of people being held back by a line of security guards.

"I told Shane it wasn't cold enough to keep them away," Roger mumbled as if to himself. "Drive to the other stage entrance," he ordered the chauffeur.

The man nodded, hit the gas and pulled back out into traffic.

Since it was evident Roger wasn't going to explain the crowd, Charity turned toward the drummer, who sat on her other side. "Mac?" Charity whispered questioningly.

"Those are fans who couldn't get tickets."

"Fans?" Charity repeated as she turned to peer out the back window disbelievingly. "There must be two or three hundred people out there!"

"Easily," Roger agreed, turning to face her with a worried frown. "I have a feeling it's going to be the same at the other entrance, but at least we'll be closer to the door." He nervously tugged at the knot in his tie. "Charity, the crowd won't realize at first that we aren't Derek and Shane, and I'm afraid we're going to have to make a dash for the stage entrance. All you have to do is stay in the middle of all of us, and you'll be safe."

She didn't have time to voice the questions that were on the tip of her tongue. The limousine came to a screeching stop, Mac grabbed her arm, and Roger pushed her from behind.

Guards immediately moved around the car door and surrounded the group the moment they exited. As she was hauled out of the car, Charity stumbled and would have fallen if Roger hadn't grabbed her around the waist. She was still trying to regain her balance as flashbulbs began to explode around her. The roar of the crowd was deafening, and she stood frozen in place, blinking blindly, until Roger forced her to move forward.

Even though there were ropes holding back the crowd on either side of them, and security guards between those ropes, people still managed to slip hands through, and Charity let out a scream of alarm when someone managed to grasp the back of her coat. She spun around to escape the hold, only to scream in pure terror when one of the guards went down on his knees and three kids came swarming right over him.

"Run!" Roger screamed in her ear as he grabbed one of her arms and Mac grabbed the other, lifting her off her feet as they raced toward the stage door, which stood open and waiting. It was the longest, most terrifying twenty-five feet Charity had ever crossed in her life.

Unknowingly, she had gripped Roger's hand and was squeezing it unmercifully as she concentrated on shutting out the faces of the screaming fans who were swarming around them. She was reminded of a cattle stampede she'd witnessed as a child. Certain they'd never make it to the stage door alive, she was trembling violently by the time they arrived.

"Are you all right?" Roger asked the moment they were inside with the door closed securely behind them.

"No," she whispered as she collapsed against the wall, covering her mouth with her hand in an effort to hold back a sob. "How will Shane and Derek get in?"

"They'll be fine," Roger assured her. "They won't be here for another hour, and by the time they arrive, there will be twice as many guards, and as cold as it is, a lot of those people will go home."

Charity knew he was lying about the people going home. If anything, there'd probably be more. She could only pray he wasn't lying about the guards.

Mac wrapped an arm around her shoulders, and she gratefully leaned against him as he led her toward a door with a gaudily painted gold star on it.

Once they were in the dressing room, he settled her on a small sofa and asked, "How about a shot of brandy?"

"I think that sounds very... medicinal," she answered, forcing a smile that she knew looked more like a grimace.

When Roger handed her a glass with an inch of brandy, she took a healthy swig and immediately choked.

"Hey, take it easy," Mac ordered, pounding her on the back.

She glanced up and blushed as she found the three other band members staring at her in concern. "I'm all right, guys. Really." They all nodded, but she could tell by their expressions that they knew she was lying. She turned toward Roger. "Is it always like this?"

"To a certain extent, but the crowd isn't always this large."

She took another sip of brandy, admitting that the total dimension of Shane was something she hadn't been prepared for. She loved him with all her heart, but after what she'd just encountered outside, she wasn't sure love was enough.

"Don't you think you should show me to my seat?" she asked Roger.

"Don't you want to wait for Shane?"

She shook her head. There was no way she could stand by, watching him fight his way through the crowd outside, and not be afraid for his life. She also knew he'd be disappointed in her if she couldn't handle it. This was what he did for a living. She felt sick to her stomach. "He'll be busy getting ready for the show. I don't want to be in his way."

Roger appeared reluctant, but he escorted Charity to her seat, and she curiously eyed the people around her. She'd imagined a young crowd, and even though many were young, there was a good mix of an older, more conservative group.

Ten minutes before the show was scheduled to begin, the crowd began to clap their hands and stomp their feet while calling out for Moon and Sun in a nonstop litany that, despite her doubts, sent a rush of adrenaline flowing through her. They wanted to see Shane—her Shane. It made her feel proud, and oddly humble.

And then the lights dimmed and darkness temporarily prevailed. The crowd quieted and then burst into a wild roar of approval as spotlights hit the stage and Shane and Derek burst into a medley of songs.

By the time they'd begun their third song, Charity could only stare at the stage in disbelief, certain that somewhere between the hotel and the concert hall Shane had been snatched away and replaced with a man more talented, more handsome—and more sexual.

His eyes were such a pure, clear blue—bluer than she remembered. His tanned body was larger and moved more gracefully. His blond hair was longer, shaggier, more appealing, and his smile was a thousand times more rakish. It couldn't be Shane, and yet the voice was the same melodious baritone she'd heard in the shower and on the tape deck. And the song he and Derek were singing was the same one she'd watched them compose in the dark and deserted hotel cocktail lounge.

When he sang a solo, the room became deathly quiet. She risked a glance around her and was shocked by the expressions that adorned the faces of the women and girls. They looked as if he were making love to them, and as she returned her gaze to the stage, she knew he was doing just that. His voice was low, husky and intimate. His eyes were dark and luminescent. His hands strummed the guitar with the gentle touch of a lover that moved down every vertebra of her spine. When he rose off the stool he was sitting on and moved toward the front of the stage in that unconscious swagger, which was exaggerated in the skintight leather, Charity caught her breath. His hips were rotating seductively when he came to a stop, and when he thrust them forward, she felt him pressed against her as intimately as if they were in bed.

Her hand shook as she tugged nervously at a lock of hair that rested against her shoulder. The man on the stage was the one she'd come to know—and yet he wasn't—and she would have been blind not to see how much he loved what he did. He'd never be complete without the performing side of his life. She also knew she'd never be comfortable sharing him with his adoring public, knowing that every woman in the room wanted to ravish him—wanted him to touch them as he had touched her. Make love to them as he'd made love to her.

When intermission came, the crowd once again began its incessant chanting. Charity glanced up at Roger in relief when he arrived at her seat. He had to lean close to hear her request to leave. With a frown he took her arm and escorted her backstage.

"Don't tell Shane I'm leaving," she entreated as Roger called for a taxi.

He opened his mouth as if to object, then closed it and nodded. An uneasy silence existed between them until the taxi arrived. Roger helped her into it and then turned and walked away without looking back. Charity closed her eyes and leaned back against the seat after giving the driver the hotel's address, knowing that whatever measure of acceptance she'd gained from Roger had just been lost.

When she was back in the suite, she stripped off her dress and donned her jeans and a white cashmere sweater. Then she settled down in the living room and waited for Shane.

She relived each moment she'd spent with him since the night Mister had found him in the woods. She'd fallen deeply in love with Shane the man, and tonight as she'd watched him perform, she'd also fallen hopelessly in love with Shane the entertainer. But that part of him was foreign, and she was certain she could never measure up to the man on stage. In order to hold on to him, she would have to compete with every young woman who threw herself at him and somehow ensure that she was the one and only woman he wanted.

It would be an impossible task because of her career, which would demand long separations. He could periodically fly her in just as he did the band's family members, but she knew in her heart it would never be enough—at least not for her. She needed the companionship that came with marriage. She needed the shoulder to lean on when times were bad and the pat on the back when she'd done something well. She needed a man who could share her day-to-day world. She needed the "regular" guy she'd come to believe Shane was.

There was only one answer to their relationship. When he returned, she'd say goodbye and never see him again.

Charity sat bolt upright on the couch when the door to the suite opened three hours later. Derek entered first, gave her a hesitant smile, and announced that he was tired and would be retiring for the night.

Only when Derek had entered his bedroom and closed the door behind him did Shane step from the shadows to confront her. She wasn't sure what she'd expected. Anger? Disappointment? Disapproval? She hadn't expected the weary resignation that etched his face.

He leaned against the wall, crossed his arms over his chest and stared at her. His continued silence was unnerving, and she finally drew in a deep breath and said, "You're really something up on that stage." It was the closest she'd ever come to admitting to him how he'd affected her along with his mob of adoring fans.

"Yeah," he replied. "Are you all right?"

"Of course. I just...had a headache and decided to come back to the room." It wasn't a lie. Her head had been throbbing unmercifully.

"Did you take something for it?"

"Yes."

"Then you're feeling better."

"Yes," she whispered, clasping her hands in her lap and praying for the courage to tell him what she had to say.

He glanced past her and out the balcony doors, which looked over the lights of the city. Tonight he'd given the best performance of his life, and he'd done it just for her. Ironically, after it was all over he'd learned that she'd stayed for only half of it, and that hurt. Really hurt. "I must admit I was surprised to find you here," he finally said.

"Why?"

"Because I was sure you'd run away." He stepped away from the wall and spread his arms out from his sides as if searching for words he couldn't find. "Charity, I know wading through that crowd of fans upset you, but you have to put it into perspective.''

"How do you put something like that into perspective?'' she asked as she impatiently pushed herself to her feet and began to pace around the room, refusing to correct him. The crowd had upset her, but it was his performance that had scared her to death. However, she could never tell him that. She could never give him that kind of leverage. If he ever used that stage charisma against her, she'd be lost. She clung to the excuse he'd just unknowingly given her. "What I witnessed tonight was violence.''

"No. You witnessed adulation.''

"Adulation?'' she repeated as she turned to stare at him. "Those people wanted to tear you apart!''

"No, they wanted to touch me, Charity. For one brief moment they wanted to be a part of the fame. Can't you see that?''

"No,'' she answered belligerently, "and nothing you can say could convince me it was anything more than what it was. I lived through violence once, Shane. But that thirty-two hours when I was held at knife point was nothing compared to what I faced tonight. At least in the emergency room I was dealing with a kid on a one-to-one basis. I could talk to him. There's no way you can talk to a fanatically screaming crowd.''

"Charity,'' he said, the low tone of his voice an indication of his rising anger, "the majority of people in this world are nothing more than the average Joe. They get up in the morning, drag themselves to work and then drag themselves home again at night. They eat the same meals and they watch the same programs on television. They laugh, they cry, and they make love, but their lives are nothing more than the same repetitive pattern. I'm a break in that pattern. They have no intention of hurting me and would be horrified if they did.''

"But they would hurt you even if it was unknowingly!'' she exclaimed, more upset to realize that the average Joe he'd just described was her and he didn't even see it. "And you can't deny that."

"I won't deny it," he stated calmly. "I have been hurt by the crowds, but I'm not going to stop living because of 'what might happen.' I've learned to accept this part of my life. If I can learn to do that, then you can, too."

"No," Charity answered with a firm shake of her head. "I could never learn to accept what I went through tonight, and I don't see how you can."

"I can because it's my chosen career, just like medicine is yours." She started to respond but let him continue when he raised a hand. "As a doctor, you often face violence. It may not be as blatant as that screaming crowd tonight, but you face it whenever you have a patient come in with a knife or gunshot wound, and I'm sure that in a city as big as Denver you've seen a lot of those. You also see it in accident victims, and if you were truly honest with yourself, you'd admit that even a heart attack is an act of violence. The difference between us is that I'm willing to accept my world for what it is and learn to live with it."

"That's not fair, Shane. You're trying to compare two incomparable situations. What you do for a living incites violence. I'm the person who picks up the pieces when you're through!"

"Dammit, Charity, that's not true!" he roared angrily. Then he closed his eyes and drew in a deep breath, realizing that bellowing at her was not going to get him anywhere. Calmly he said, "Did you see anyone get hurt tonight?" He opened his jacket to expose his chest. "Am I hurt?"

"No," she admitted, thinking about the security guard who had gone down but had quickly regained his feet, "but the potential for injury was there."

"Yes, it was there, but nothing happened. In eighteen years Derek and I have sustained minor injuries twice. As far as I know, none of our fans has been hurt. That doesn't mean it won't happen, but I think our record is pretty damn impressive."

He sighed, raked his hand through his hair and said, "And you're being unfair to me. You were held at knife point, but when it was all over, you didn't give up medicine. You're still a doctor, and you still see patients. Don't ask of me what you won't ask of yourself."

Charity turned away from him, rested her forehead against the cool pane of the window that looked out over the city and sighed. "I can't handle what I saw tonight, Shane." It was the truth, even if she didn't explain that it was his stage presence she couldn't handle.

He walked up behind her but refrained from touching her. He wanted to win this war with words. "Is it the crowd that upset you, or is it your memories of the emergency room?"

"It's the crowd!" she exclaimed much too ardently, snapping her head away from the window.

"Then prove it," he challenged her. "Go with me to an emergency room here in Kansas City. Show me that it's my situation that has frightened you, and not your own past."

She raised her hands to her temples and massaged them. "You're trying to confuse me!"

"I'm not trying to confuse you. I'm trying to understand what's wrong. You're running, Charity. You're running so fast I can't catch up with you. Stop running and tell me what's really bothering you. Explain to me why you're so upset."

"I can't," she whispered on a hiccup of a sob.

He released a long, resigned sigh and reached out to touch her, but her posture was so unapproachable that he let his hands drop back to his sides.

"I love you, Charity. I want to marry you. But you have to accept my life, just as I'm attempting to accept yours. Do you think it's easy competing with ill patients? Do you think I like having my conversations cut short or knowing that in the future my lovemaking will be interrupted? Hell no, I don't like it, but I accept it because you're important to me. I want you to accept the fact that I'm going to stand beside you for better or for worse and that I'm not going to turn

my back and walk away at the first sign of trouble. In return, I'm asking you to give me that same consideration."

She heard what he was saying but shook her head. "I'm
not walking away at the first sign of trouble. It's just
that...you're different, Shane. Tonight you were not the
man I'd grown to love. You were—are—a star, a rising
comet, and I can't hold on to the tail of that comet. You
were different!"

Shane almost doubled over as the impact of her words hit
home. It wasn't the crowd but the man on the stage she was
fighting. He clenched and unclenched his hands at his sides,
wanting to grab her and shake her and rail at her. It was
Diane all over again, and he wasn't going to let it happen.

"No!" he exclaimed angrily. Grasping her shoulders, he
spun her around to face him. "I wasn't different. *You* were
different! I didn't change when I walked up on that stage. I
was still the man who talked to you and worried about you.
I was still the man who crawled into the bathtub and made
love to you this afternoon. I didn't change, Charity. You
did!"

"I did not!" she denied, tears welling up in her eyes.

He released her and ran his fingers through his hair. "Yes,
Charity, you did change," he stated quietly, his anger suddenly gone as his heart filled with sadness.

She watched him turn away from her, pace around the
room and finally stop several feet away. His eyes were blaz-
ing blue flames of unidentifiable emotions when they met
hers.

"When I look at you I see a woman. A beautiful woman
I'm desperately in love with. But do you know what I see
when I think of what you do for a living?"

She shook her head, wondering what he could possibly be
driving at and what it had to do with tonight's performance.

"I see a god, Charity. You are a *god*!"

"I am not!" she said with a vehement shake of her head.
"I'm a doctor!"

"You're wrong." He walked to her, put his hand beneath her chin and lifted her head. "Every person you treat reveres you, worships you. You have the power over life and death."

"I do not!" she cried, tears brimming in her eyes and spilling down her cheeks as he struck a chord she'd been trying to ignore ever since she'd hung up the diploma that declared her to be a physician. She knew her patients often elevated her above the level of human, and they were wrong. "I can help, but I can't make a difference!"

"Can't you?" he whispered as he brought his face close. "With all your science, drugs and training, can you really claim that you don't make a difference? Come on, Charity, tell me the truth."

"Maybe sometimes," she whispered as she pulled away from his grasp and swiped at her cheeks. "But I am *not* a god! I'm nothing more than a woman."

"And I am nothing more than a man," he said, reaching out to tenderly wipe from her cheek a tear she'd missed. "I write and sing songs. People love me for that, and I'm grateful they do, but I'm just as human as you or my fans.

"I laugh and I cry," he continued. "I love and I hurt. I catch colds and the flu. Don't change on me. Don't look at me as if I'm something sacrosanct. I am the man you've come to know and the man I hope you've grown to love."

"Oh, God, I'm so confused!" She raised her hand to her mouth as she sobbed again.

"Oh, babe," he said as he pulled her into his arms. "All I want is your love. Look beyond the stage lights. Look for the man, Charity. Please look for—and see—the man."

She began to cry, and he held her close.

"I love you," he whispered into her hair. "Please love me back."

Chapter Twelve

Shane didn't try to make love to Charity that night or the next morning, and she was thankful he didn't. She needed some distance—some time to analyze and sort through her tangled feelings.

Sensing her wariness, Shane allowed her some space. He had only to look into her eyes to see that she was struggling to understand what he'd said last night, and he couldn't afford to push her. In just a matter of hours she would board a plane, and it would be another five weeks before he saw her again. He couldn't have been more frightened if he'd just been told he had five weeks to live. And, he admitted, if Charity rejected him, it would be the same sentence. Life without her would be unbearable.

When he tried to talk to her she answered with polite one-syllable answers, until he finally gave up and sat on the bed, watching her pack and wondering if she understood that she was placing an insurmountable barrier between them by shutting him out. Didn't she realize that part of loving was sharing the good times and the bad? Didn't she know that it was being the crutch the other needed to help write the last verse to an unfinished song?

But how could she, he realized as he watched her carefully fold the black silk dress she'd worn last night, slip it into her suitcase and close the lid. The one time she'd needed that kind of support her ex-husband had walked away, and Shane was paying for his mistakes. With a heaviness of spirit, he lifted her suitcase from the bed and carried it into the living room.

Roger arrived a short time later and announced that he would escort Charity to the airport.

"I'm going, too," Shane stated.

"No!" Charity and Roger exclaimed in unison.

Before Shane could respond, Roger said, "It's much too dangerous, Shane. We haven't arranged for security."

"Yes," Charity agreed quickly, unable to bear another moment in his silent, brooding presence. "It's much too dangerous."

"I don't care!" Shane said so quietly it could have been a shout, tilting his chin defiantly. "I'm going to the airport!"

Despite Shane's adamant insistence, it was Roger and only Roger who accompanied Charity to the airport. She managed to convince Shane to stay behind by telling him she'd be worried sick the entire time he was with her. She hated the emotional blackmail, but she wasn't ready to face a replay of last night's mob scene and feared that was exactly what would happen, even though Shane had insisted that his fail-safe disguise had never failed.

When the limousine arrived at the airport, she assured Roger that he didn't need to wait until her flight left. Though he appeared reluctant to leave her alone, he finally nodded and hung around just long enough to help her check her bags.

Once he was gone, she walked down the concourse, trying to imagine what it would be like if she were on Shane's arm.

The images her mind conjured up weren't pleasant, and not ready to face them, she pushed them away as she arrived at her gate, sat down and forced herself to begin reading the murder mystery she'd bought at the beginning of the trip.

As the week passed, Charity found no solutions to her problems with Shane, so she threw herself into her work, welcoming the bone-weary fatigue at the end of each day. Shane still called her daily, but he was usually rushed, since they were trying to make up the concerts they'd delayed so they could meet the remainder of their contracts on time. She was grateful for his hectic schedule. Only twice had he had enough time to tentatively approach her about the night of the concert, and both times she'd quickly changed the subject. She loved him and would always love him, but she simply could not see herself as a part of his professional life. She wasn't ready to say goodbye yet, either, and she had a feeling that when they finally confronted each other, that's exactly what she would have to do.

On Saturday morning she got out of bed, completed her morning routine and climbed into the car to run errands. One of those was to arrange to have a pet door installed for Mister. More and more frequently she was delayed at the clinic, and she felt guilty about leaving the dog locked inside the house.

She visited a pet shop, picked out the type of door she wanted and let the shop owner handle the details for the installation. She wandered through the mall, stopping to gaze in windows at new fashions, not really certain any of them suited her. Everything seemed to be either too long or too short, and she was still partial to the conservative, middle-of-the-knee hemline.

Finally she returned to her car and started toward home. Halfway there, she was forced to pull to the curb as an ambulance, siren blaring, came sailing up behind her.

A sense of excitement rushed through her as she watched the ambulance turn into the emergency entrance of a small neighborhood hospital, and she followed it. She came to a stop a good football-field length behind it, watching as the paramedics jumped out the back, pulled out a stretcher and hurriedly wheeled it through the wide double doors.

Without any conscious thought, she climbed out of her car and followed the entourage. Once inside the doors, she paused to let her eyes adjust to the dimness of the interior. It looked like any other emergency room, she decided as her gaze roamed around her surroundings. Patients sat in lobby chairs, appearing ill and put-upon over their wait. Some of their faces had hardened into sick resolve as they looked at the stretcher, knowing that their one- or two-hour wait could now stretch into three or four.

A nurse behind the reception desk gave her a pleasant smile. "May I help you?"

Charity said, "I'm a doctor, and I saw the ambulance. I thought I might be of assistance."

"Our staff has everything under control."

"I'm sure they do. Is it all right if I take a quick look around?" she asked as she removed her medical identification from her purse and handed it to the nurse. "I've never been in your hospital."

The nurse handed back Charity's credentials and nodded. "I don't see why not. Just stay away from examining room three."

"Of course. I'll only be a few minutes."

"Take your time, and if you have any questions, I'll be glad to answer them. In fact, if you're interested in staff privileges, our medical-staff office is at the end of the hall. Last door on the right."

"Thank you. I just might pay the office a visit."

The nurse's attention was drawn away when someone else entered. Charity walked down the hallway toward a sign that read: Examining Room One. The corridor walls were the same uncluttered off-white she was accustomed to. The floor was the same shiny linoleum, even if the pattern was slightly different than the one she'd traversed day after day.

She stopped at the entrance to the examining room. The door was open, and as she gazed inside, all the equipment that made an emergency room what it was rested within her line of vision.

There was the crisply sheeted bed with a tray of instruments standing nearby, and a small EKG monitor rested in a corner. She spied an intravenous stand, as well as a stack of hospital gowns. Her gaze moved over other various familiar pieces of equipment, and she was drawn forward, moving into the room, her hands thrust deeply into the pockets of her jacket.

At the bed she stopped and idly fingered one of the restraining straps that lay alongside the mattress, remembering how she'd lifted a strap just like it to confine the madly struggling young boy that long-ago fateful night. She still didn't know how he'd managed to break away from the two brawny police officers. One minute she'd been beside the bed with the strap in her hand, and the next minute she'd been in front of him, unable to breathe as his arm squeezed her throat while the deadly tip of a gleaming knife flashed before her eyes.

She glanced nervously around her, her eyes wide. He wasn't here with her, but she could feel his presence, feel the anger and rage seeping through him. He had been filled with hatred, and she would never know why he'd chosen her to be the object of that hatred.

Her breathing began to change and her heart began to race wildly as she took several steps back from the bed and stared at it as if it had just come to life. All the fear she'd experienced during those thirty-two hours of terror began to course through her in one crippling wave after another, and she wrapped her arms around her middle as she fought against the nausea churning in her stomach. She couldn't stay there, but she felt frozen in time as that night began to replay in her head like a videotape in fast forward. She was so lost in the past that she let out a startled scream when a hand touched her arm.

"Are you all right?" the nurse from the reception desk asked in concern.

Charity couldn't find her voice, but when the woman's eyes narrowed, she managed to whisper, "Of course." But it was a lie, and she knew that if she didn't get out of there and back into the sunshine, she was going to collapse.

"You're sure you're all right?"

Charity nodded and began to back away from the nurse. "I'm fine. Thank you for letting me..."

She couldn't finish the sentence, and even though she knew the nurse was regarding her suspiciously, she turned and ran out of the emergency room, gasping in great gulps of air as she blinked against the blinding sunshine. She didn't stop running until she reached her car. She threw herself inside, closed her eyes and let the tears fall. It was the environment. She'd never be able to work in an emergency room again.

She wanted to lay her head down on the steering wheel and sob until there were no more tears, but she forced herself to dry her eyes and start her car. The tears could come once she was back in the privacy of her own home. There she could cry, wail, scream and curse and no one would hear her. And when it was over, she could begin to glue the pieces back together and decide where she went from there.

The crowd was screaming, clapping and stomping their feet. They would only calm down when they were given what they wanted: the presence of Shane Burke and Derek Halston on stage.

Roger strode angrily toward the dressing room and pounded on the door for the fifth time. When Shane didn't respond, he threw open the door and entered uninvited.

Shane waved at him impatiently, the telephone receiver pressed against his ear. "Be quiet. It's ringing."

"Shane, you were supposed to be on stage fifteen minutes ago."

"It'll have to wait."

"It can't wait!" Roger bellowed at him.

Shane bristled. "I've been trying to reach Charity for two hours, and she's not answering."

"Maybe she had an emergency," Roger stated. "Get the performance over with, and then you can try again."

"She couldn't be involved with an emergency. She isn't on call today. She said she was going to do some shopping and then hang around the house and relax. She works too hard, Roger. She's at the hospital before seven in the morning to make rounds. Then she's in the clinic until six or seven o'clock at night. Then she's back at the hospital to see her patients again. By the time she gets home she's put in four-teen or fifteen hours. But no matter how hard she's work-ing, she never misses my calls. If nothing else, she has the answering service pick up. That's what's got me worried. The answering service isn't picking up."

"Maybe the lines are out of order. You go on stage, and I'll call the operator and have it checked out," Roger said. "If the lines aren't out, I'll keep calling her."

Shane's attention was drawn toward the open door and the reverberating sound of the screaming crowd. He had to go on stage, but he couldn't calm the feeling of desperation that was clutching his stomach. If Charity said she'd be there when he called, she was always there. He knew some-thing was wrong, but he was five hundred miles away, with a restless audience that demanded his presence. He didn't like it, but his only option was to hand the telephone re-ceiver to Roger, and he did so, vowing that once this tour was over, he was going to make some drastic changes in his life.

"If you haven't reached her by intermission, charter me a plane to Denver," he ordered, striding out of the room without a backward glance.

It was nearly dawn when Shane slowed the rental car as he approached Charity's house. To the average person, the dark windows would seem normal, but Shane knew

Charity's habits. By now she would be up and wandering through the house, feeding Mister and making coffee, switching on lights as she went.

She was up late last night and decided to sleep in, he told himself, but he wasn't convinced. She was a morning person who lived with an internal alarm that went off despite the hour she retired the night before.

He pulled into the driveway, only to stare in disbelief at her car. It was parked drunkenly in the driveway with the right front tire resting in the flower bed.

He began to tremble as a jolt of fear shot through him, and he jumped from the car, ran toward the house, and punched the doorbell before his feet even came to a stop. He could hear the chimes pealing as he leaned on the bell, and when it continued to go unanswered, he cursed, pulled open the screen, and banged on the door.

The door swung open the moment his fist connected, and his heart slammed against his rib cage so violently it hurt. The door hadn't been latched, and the very last thing Charity did before going to bed was to make sure her door was locked.

He should call the police, he realized as he stared into her dark living room. The thought jolted him back to reality. If Charity was hurt, each second might count, and he fairly leaped through the door, heedless of any danger that could be lurking inside.

The house was so silent that he jumped in surprise when the furnace kicked on. Should he call out for her? If there was an intruder in the house, would Shane's presence endanger Charity?

He tilted his head to the side and listened for any suspicious noise. While his eyes adjusted to the darkness of his surroundings, he forced himself to recall the layout of furniture. Cautiously, he moved through the living room, and then wavered when he reached the hallway leading to the bedrooms. If nothing was wrong and she was asleep, his sudden appearance would frighten her.

Uncertainty overwhelmed him. Should he continue creeping through the house or call out for her? Mister suddenly appeared at his feet and whined. Shane let out a sigh of relief and bent down to pat the dog's head. Mister didn't seem overly excited, so Charity must be all right.

"Where's your mistress, boy?"

Mister headed for the kitchen, and Shane followed. The dog moved swiftly ahead of him, and Shane almost missed the small flash of black and white that entered the sun porch as he stopped to switch on a light.

He immediately headed for the sun porch and stopped in the doorway to stare at the room in disbelief. Enough light filtered in from the kitchen for him to see that every plant lay shattered on the floor, and Charity sat in the middle of the ravaged plants and shards of pottery, her clothes and face filthy and her hair in a wild tangle.

She looked up at him through dull and glazed eyes and let out a brittle laugh. "I've made a mess, haven't I?"

"You sure have," he answered, taking an uncertain step into the room. Once again he surveyed the damage, and a shiver crawled up his spine. She had loved these plants. Every leaf, stem and blossom. What could have possibly happened that she'd destroy them like this? His answer came to him from out of nowhere. "You visited an emergency room, and you can't handle the environment," he said.

"Yes." Her voice was nothing more than a hiss of breath, and her body seemed to close in on itself as she wrapped her hands around her knees and drew them to her chest.

She looked so fragile, so lost, that tears filled Shane's eyes. He wanted to grab her off the floor, carry her from the house and never let her come back. Instead, he knelt in front of her and gently brushed his hand over the back of her bent head. "Do you want to tell me about it?"

"There's nothing to tell."

"You don't destroy every plant you own over nothing," he chided her softly. "What happened?"

"I don't want to talk about it."

Her words lanced through him. She was still shutting him out, and all his worry and fear of the past several hours began to coalesce into simmering anger. He reached out to grab her and shake her, determined to force her to let him in. But when he touched her frail shoulders, he automatically curled his hands around them comfortingly and his anger disappeared. She was hurting desperately, and though he knew she'd never admit it, she needed him.

"We'll talk later," he said, rising to his feet and lifting her into his arms. He carried her through her bedroom and into the master bath, where he seated her on the toilet.

He placed his hand beneath her chin and tilted her head up, shaking his own head as he stared into her tear-ravaged face. He pulled his handkerchief from his pocket and began to wipe away the dirt and the tears.

"What we're going to do is give you a hot bath, wash your hair and put you into bed. You'll feel better after you've had some sleep."

"I'll never feel better again," she replied morosely, and wiped childishly at the new tears that began to roll down her cheeks.

"Well, you're going to get some sleep anyway," he answered as he knelt down in front of her and began to unbutton her blouse.

With the same care he'd give a child, he undressed her, bathed her and washed her hair. Then he dried her, wrapped a dry towel around her and led her into the bedroom, where he seated her on the bed. Her eyes were heavy-lidded with fatigue as he found a clean flannel nightgown and helped her into it. Then he tucked her under the covers, kissed her forehead and said, "I'm going to lock up the house, and I'll be right back. Okay?"

She nodded, curled into a ball in the center of the bed and closed her eyes. Shane knew that by the time he returned, she'd be fast asleep.

"Damn," he muttered as he went through the house, locking the front door and switching off lights. Mister was in the kitchen, standing in front of the refrigerator, and Shane fed him before returning to the sun porch. "Why the plants?" he asked aloud as he hit the switch to turn on the light so he could look more closely at the room. The destruction was so much harsher under the glare of the overhead light that he immediately switched it off. "It just doesn't make sense."

He threaded his fingers through his hair and returned to the bedroom, where he crawled into bed with her and held her in his arms.

But unlike Charity, he couldn't fall asleep. He stared at the ceiling, thinking. What she'd done to her plants was so uncharacteristic of her gentle nature that he knew he had to understand her motivation. He put himself into her place. How would he feel if he suddenly discovered he'd never be able to sing or perform again? The exercise worked so well that for the first time since his parents' death, Shane cried.

Charity struggled against waking when sunlight streamed across her face. Her head and body ached, and she felt weak and ill. But the sun wouldn't go away, and she finally cracked open an eye to peer groggily at the alarm clock.

She let out a gasp and sat straight up in bed. It was two in the afternoon! She'd never slept so late in her life.

"It's about time you woke up," Shane murmured, and she glanced at him in disbelief. He wore nothing but his familiar blue jeans and was reclining beside her on the bed with the Sunday paper open to the variety page. Vague images of him bathing her and talking to her teased at her brain, but she couldn't bring them into focus.

"What are you doing here?" she asked.

"I'm reading the paper," he answered, a grin playing at his lips as he rustled the paper and raised it in front of his face.

Shane saw that although her face bore all the traces of yesterday's emotional upheaval, her eyes were clear and bright. It was more than he'd hoped for, but he should have known she'd be back on her feet after a few hours' sleep. Charity was a survivor. It was one of the things he loved about her. "There's freshly squeezed orange juice in the refrigerator, and I just put on a pot of coffee. If you want anything else, you'll have to fix it yourself. I close the kitchen at noon."

Charity reached out and pulled the top of the paper down so she could see him. "Shane, what are you doing here?"

He studied her for a long time as if trying to decide whether or not to answer the question. Finally he said, "Do you want the truth?"

"Of course I want the truth!" she exclaimed impatiently.

"All right. I'm here because I love you."

"Oh," she said, not certain how else to respond.

He was still studying her as she pushed her hair away from her eyes. Uncomfortable with his scrutiny, she glanced around the room.

"I tried to call you, and when you didn't answer, I got worried," he informed her.

"I'm sorry you were worried," she whispered as she nervously toyed with the edge of the sheet, refusing to meet his eyes. "I unplugged all the telephones."

"I know. They're still unplugged."

"I'd better plug them back in," she said, throwing back the sheet and climbing from the bed.

Shane almost reached out to stop her, but decided against it. He was determined to find out exactly what had happened yesterday; however, she wasn't ready to be pushed yet.

After she'd plugged in the bedroom telephone, she headed for the hallway. Shane rose from the bed and followed, watching her reconnect the telephones in the living room and kitchen. Then she opened the cupboard, pulled out a mug and filled it with coffee.

"You missed one," Shane stated quietly as he leaned against the door frame, his hands stuffed into the back pockets of his jeans.

"One what?" Charity asked, centering her gaze on his bare chest as a guilty blush rose to her cheeks. She realized he was talking about the phone on the sun porch.

"One telephone," he answered. "You forgot the one on the sun porch."

"I'll get it later," she murmured, flashing him a quick smile that immediately disappeared when he shook his head.

"Plug it in now, Charity."

She glanced over his shoulder. "I'm not ready to go out there."

"All right, you can plug it in after you finish your coffee."

"I'm famished. I think I'll have some eggs. Interested?"

"No."

He'd issued the word so flatly that she intuitively knew it was not a refusal for breakfast. She raised her head, her eyes flashing with anger. "I'm not going out on the sun porch until I'm ready to do so."

"All right." He crossed his arms over his chest. "Instead of going out there, you can tell me exactly what happened yesterday, and you are not to leave out one tiny detail."

She bristled at his arrogantly issued order. "Who died and made you boss?"

"One board-certified emergency room physician by the name of Charity Wells," he answered.

The coffee mug in her hand slipped through her fingers and hit the floor.

Shane cursed violently as he rushed to her, grabbed the hem of her nightgown and stripped it over her head before the hot coffee could burn its way through the fabric.

Charity backed away from him, her hands ineffectually trying to cover herself as his eyes raked over her naked body.

"Are you all right?" he questioned. His voice was too husky for him to be considered merely concerned.

"I'm fine," she whispered, trying to slip past him, but he caught her arm and spun her around and into his arms.

"Stop running away from me!" he exclaimed angrily. "Dammit, Charity, I love you. When are you going to realize that?"

"If you love me, then let me go!" she demanded, her voice quivering with a sob.

"I will never let you go," he enunciated carefully as he crushed her against him. He caught her chin, lifted her head and forced her to meet his eyes. "Look at me. Look at me carefully. I am Shane Burke, not Carson Montgomery. I love you, and I'm going to stand by you no matter how rough life gets. Nothing you can do is going to change that, babe, so you might as well accept it and stop shutting me out."

"You'll stand by me?" she repeated with a laugh that bordered on hysteria. "For how long, Shane?"

"Forever."

"That's what you say now, but will you say that five years from now, when I've put on twenty pounds, my hair is starting to turn gray, and you have a thousand young women hovering in the wings?"

"Charity—"

She pulled away from him and strode to the center of the kitchen. Then she turned to face him, her naked body held stiff and proud.

"You want to know what happened yesterday, so I'll tell you. I walked into a strange emergency room, and everything came back. I'm affected by the environment. I was angry and afraid, and I came home and destroyed every plant on the sun porch. I was having a temper tantrum, Shane. One hell of a temper tantrum."

"But why the plants?" he asked, perplexed. "Why did you take it out on the plants?"

"Because every one of those plants was a gift from an emergency-room patient," she answered, turning around and burying her head in her hands.

His heart ached as he watched her shoulders shake, though he knew she wasn't crying. He walked to her, turned her around and held her against him. Tenderly he stroked her back and the gentle curve of her hip.

She buried her head against his shoulder and said, "Until I straighten out this part of my life, I have to stay away from you."

"Why?" he rasped harshly as he caught her chin and raised her head.

"Because I can't lean on you," she answered honestly, her eyes brimming with tears. "You're here today, but you'll be gone tomorrow."

"No," he said with a firm shake of his head. "The remainder of my concerts are scheduled within two or three hours' flying time of Denver. I've already told Roger that I'll fly in just before the concert and will be flying back here when it's over. I'm not going to leave you alone, sweetheart," he murmured as he dropped a gentle kiss to her lips. "From now on I'm going to be here to lean on."

Charity sniffed and nodded, wanting desperately to believe that what he was saying was true. Right now she needed him and his strength more than air.

He smiled, eased her away from him and slipped her nightgown back over her head. Then he took her hand and said, "I want you to see the sun porch."

She didn't hesitate when he tugged on her hand. When she stepped out into the room, tears once again filled her eyes. Shane had cleaned it and replaced each and every plant.

"I love you!" she cried as she threw herself into his arms.

Shane's heart soared, and he bent his head to capture her lips in a sweet kiss while whispering, "Say it again, Charity. I need to hear the words again."

Chapter Thirteen

Shane was true to his word. He flew in and out of Denver daily, but Charity soon began to worry about him. He usually came in the door just as she was getting up and left before she was home. The soft hollows beneath his eyes were bruised, and the lines of fatigue that etched his face became heavier with each passing day.

He would manage to stay awake long enough to share breakfast with her, and then he'd give her a quick kiss, fall into bed and be sound asleep before she left for work.

Whenever she expressed concern over his appearance, he'd dismiss her words, kiss her breathless and only let her go when she told him she loved him.

Charity was becoming frustrated with the situation and wasn't sure how to handle it. One of the most wonderful parts of their relationship had been their conversations, and now she and Shane rarely talked. They also rarely made love.

Shane was also becoming frustrated, although not for the same reasons. He hated arriving home as Charity was leaving and then leaving before she was home. He also hated the pressure he was getting from Roger. Twice his plane had been late, and in one instance a concert had been delayed for nearly an hour.

"It's not professional," Roger had stated angrily. "Somewhere along the line you're going to have to decide which is more important—your career or Charity."

Shane had laughed bitterly at Roger's words. Both were essential to him, and to choose one over the other would be impossible. He appeased Roger by agreeing that he'd fly in even earlier for each concert. He then began to count down the days when the tour would finally be over.

But he had yet to find a way to lessen the pressure with Charity. She was becoming more restless each time he saw her. Instead of greeting him in the morning with a smile, she was staring at him in concern.

"You're killing yourself," she'd told him only today. "You can't keep up this kind of pace."

"I'm always exhausted toward the end of a tour." It hadn't been a total lie. "After tonight's concert, I'll have two days off, and I plan to sleep in. We'll also do something special."

"Shane—"

He'd cut her off by yawning, bussing her on the cheek and falling across the bed. He would spend the next two days making up for all the time they'd lost.

He smiled at the thought as he lifted his guitar and readied himself to walk on stage. It seemed like forever since they'd made love, and he promised himself that by this time tomorrow night, that fact would be remedied.

At that very moment, Charity was sitting across the kitchen table from her brother Jim and pouring out her troubles. When she finally finished, Jim said, "What do you want me to say?"

"I want you to tell me what to do!"

He regarded her over the rim of his coffee cup. "I can't do that. You're the only one who can make that kind of decision."

"You're right." She rose from her chair, rinsed out her cup and placed it into the dishwasher. Then she turned and leaned against the counter. "I was crazy to get involved with him in the first place. We're as different as two people can be."

When Jim didn't answer, she sighed and shook her head. "He's a free, soaring spirit, Jim, and I'm firmly earthbound. When I'm around him, he makes me feel as if I can fly, but in my heart I know I can't. So why am I in love with him?"

"When you solve that mystery, I want to be the first to know."

"You're such a helpful older brother. It's nice to know I can turn to you and get sage advice."

He chuckled at her sarcasm. "I remember making that same accusation about a little sister a few years ago when Chris and I were having some problems. Do you happen to recall your advice?"

Charity did remember what she'd said, and as the words came tumbling from her memory, she drew in a deep breath and let it out slowly. "I told you to treat one problem at a time instead of trying to doctor all your problems at once."

"I think you've just hit on your own solution." He glanced at his watch. "I've really got to run. I've got a big case starting tomorrow, and I need to review some notes."

After Jim was gone, Charity still didn't have any answers, but she knew she'd wait until after Shane's concert in Denver before confronting him. Her mind told her the situation was hopeless. Balancing personalities would be difficult enough, but as this past week had proved, balancing their careers would be impossible.

Shane groaned when the alarm clock went off the following afternoon, but he forced himself out of bed. He had two days to woo Charity back into complacency, and the first step in the plan was a gourmet meal. A quick search of her cupboards this morning had proved that he had to make a trip to the grocery store, and he had to get moving. He yawned, rubbed his stubbled jaw and stumbled toward the bath. A hot shower and a shave should do the trick.

An hour later he wandered into the neighborhood grocery store, wearing worn blue jeans, a faded T-shirt, running shoes and a battered Stetson. The lenses of the glasses that rested on his nose changed with the light, so he didn't have to remove them.

Confident with his disguise, which had always worked, he grabbed a cart and strolled down the aisles, agreeing with a matronly woman in the produce department that tomatoes just weren't what they used to be. In the cereal aisle, he swept up a toddler who was giggling as he tried to make his great escape and returned him to his harried but grateful mother.

By the time Shane approached the checkout stand, he was whistling softly and smiling to himself. After nodding pleasantly to the woman in front of him, he let his gaze settle on the rack of gossip magazines, wondering who this week's victim was.

He chuckled as he read a glaring headline that reported an inevitable marriage breakup for a famous movie star. The actor was a friend, and Shane knew the only way the man would leave his wife was if he'd been beaten unconscious and dragged away. Another headline boasted the "inside" scoop on the season's opening show for a nighttime soap, and he chuckled again. He knew the director and was certain that if the magazine was right, the man would change the script.

But when he read the headline of the third magazine, he frowned and reached for it. Plastered across the front page was a hazy but recognizable picture of Charity that had been taken in Kansas City. Roger and Mac were holding on to

her, and a screaming mob was in the background. The
headline read: A New Moon and Sun heartthrob! A Re-
ward Is Offered to Anyone Who Can Tell Us Who She Is
and Which Member of the Group is Smitten.

The curse Shane released caused both the woman in front
of him and the checkout clerk to gasp. He dug into his
pocket, pulled out a handful of bills and tossed them toward the cashier. Tucking the magazine beneath his arm, he
began to run toward the store's entrance, leaving his basket
standing in line. Why now? he railed inwardly. Why did they
have to start in when he and Charity were in such a turmoil?

Outside, he hesitated, not sure what to do. He glanced at
his watch, knew Charity would still be at the clinic, and tried
to decide whether or not he should call her. He should
probably wait until tonight, he thought, glancing back down
at the picture. The glamorous woman didn't really look like
the doctor most people would be accustomed to seeing. Tonight he could feed her, lull her, and then spring this damn
surprise on her. Going public was the only answer, but she
was having so many personal problems; going public was the
last thing she needed at this point.

Damn! He jammed the Stetson down further on his head,
stared at the rental car and knew that it couldn't wait until
tonight. If one of her patients recognized her and called the
magazine, all hell would break loose. It was up to him to
solve this blasted mess, and even though Charity would be
furious with him, he knew exactly what he had to do.

With long, purposeful strides, he crossed to the car,
climbed inside and turned the ignition. Thank God he had
another day to soothe her ruffled feathers, and there was no
question in his mind that Charity was definitely going to be
ruffled.

Charity glanced up in surprise when the door to her office burst open unceremoniously. Her pen hovered over the
chart she was writing in, and she arched an inquisitive brow

at Don, who looked as if he was about to suffer from apoplexy.

"You're needed at the front desk," he stated stiffly.

"What's wrong?"

"That's what I'm waiting to find out!" he exclaimed, his face becoming even redder.

Since Don was renowned for his even temper, Charity immediately rose to her feet, nervously smoothed down her navy-blue skirt, and adjusted her white coat. Without a word she crossed to the door and headed for the front desk, Don at her heels. She stopped so abruptly at the sight that greeted her that Don ran right into her.

Shane was standing in the middle of the waiting room, dressed in his famous black leather, his legs spread apart in an arrogant stance and his thumbs tucked casually in his pockets. Behind him stood at least a dozen reporters and photographers.

"Shane?" Charity whispered in disbelief.

He swept his hat off his head and directed an elaborate bow in Charity's direction as he drawled, "Ladies and gentlemen, meet Dr. Charity Wells, the woman I'm in love with and have every intention of marrying. Take your pictures and ask your questions now, because from this day forward, she is off limits."

Flashbulbs began to explode furiously, and Charity blinked frantically. This couldn't be happening! Why would he pull a stunt like this?

He was suddenly standing in front of her, the smile on his lips not matching the grim look in his eyes.

"You're sexier than hell in that white coat," he murmured as he swept her up into his arms and kissed her so passionately that she didn't need flashbulbs to create the stars in front of her eyes.

It was an exhausting hour later before the press left Charity's office, and she collapsed in her chair and regarded Shane angrily. "How dare you pull something like this!'' she railed at him. ''I'm a doctor! I had patients to see!''

''I'm aware of that,'' he stated, pushing the brim of his hat back and returning her glare unflinchingly.

''Then why?'' she asked, slamming her hand down on her desk.

''Because you were spread across the front page of this.'' He pulled the front page of the magazine from his pocket and tossed it toward her.

With shaking hands, Charity unfolded the paper, frowned at the picture and the headline, and then wearily leaned back in her chair. ''We can't go on like this, Shane.''

''That's exactly why I hauled those reporters in here this afternoon,'' he said. ''Trying to avoid them would have been challenging them. Facing them and giving them the facts was preferable to having them print lies about us. And believe me, Charity, they would have printed bald-faced lies.''

''They probably still will,'' she whispered as she crumpled the sheet of paper and tossed it into the wastepaper basket.

''Yes. But at least we gave them the truth. We did our part, so to speak.''

''We weren't exactly truthful,'' she said, pushing away from the desk and rising to pace around the office. ''You told them we planned to marry.''

He rested a lean hip against the desk and regarded her warily. ''I do plan on marrying you.''

She braced a hand against the windowsill and half turned to face him. ''I don't recall ever saying I would.''

''There are some things in life you take for granted.''

''I'm not one of those things, Shane.''

''And what does that mean?''

She refused to look at him. She stared out the window at the now empty parking lot and ran her hand up and down the painted wood of the window frame.

"Our relationship isn't working. You're at my house every day, but I never see you. We don't talk, and we don't make love. The only way I know you're there is that I see your underwear in the clothes hamper and your shaving cream on the bathroom counter. You also squeeze the toothpaste tube in the middle, which drives me crazy."

"You're going to kick me out over the toothpaste?"

"Stranger things have happened."

"Yes, they have." He walked up behind her and gently touched her hair. "But it isn't the toothpaste that's the problem. It's time, Charity. And until this tour is over, I simply can't give you more time. I promise to make a concerted effort to squeeze the toothpaste properly if you'll promise to wait until the tour is over before you make any decisions regarding us. Give me some time with you. Let me prove to you how much I love you. Let me show you that what we have can work despite our personal and professional problems."

Charity knew in her heart that it wasn't going to work, but she loved him and could never ignore the pleading in his voice. He wanted some time, and she'd give it to him. She nodded.

Chapter Fourteen

The days that followed consisted of an uneasy truce. Charity refrained from voicing her doubts, and Shane made certain that he made each free day something special.

But as the day of his Denver concert grew closer, they both grew more silent and brooding. Charity tried to find the words that would make him see their problems clearly, and Shane sought the words to convince her that no problem was more important than their love.

Finally, the day of the Denver concert arrived. Charity rose early and was surprised when Shane joined her on the sun porch a short time later.

"Good mornin', babe," he greeted her with a quick kiss before settling into a chair across from her.

As he sipped at his coffee, he gazed at the mountains. The snow on the lower elevations had begun to melt. It would be July before the peaks were clear. He both yearned for and dreaded the end of winter. It represented another year past; it also reminded him that his future was uncertain.

"You're up early," Charity stated as she studied him cautiously.

He smiled ruefully. "You know I can't sleep when I know you're in the house and you aren't with me."

Charity dropped her toast to her plate and let out a frustrated sigh. "You always make me feel guilty when you do this. A morning person and a night person just can't live together, Shane! It's impossible."

He shrugged dismissively. "I think we've been doing pretty good so far. Are you going to make rounds this morning?"

"Now you're changing the subject. Why do you keep ignoring everything?"

"I'm not ignoring anything," he answered impatiently. "I told you that when the tour is over we'll talk, and the tour isn't over."

"Tonight's your last concert. I'd say the tour is over."

"It isn't over until the last note is sung, and that won't be until well after midnight."

"Sometimes you're so damn frustrating!"

"Are we going to have our first fight?"

"Our first fight?" she echoed with an incredulous shake of her head. "I'd hardly call it our first one."

"I guess fights are easily misinterpreted. I'd say that up until now, all we've had are some heated disagreements."

"You always underestimate everything!"

"Not everything," he drawled as he rose to his feet and moved around the table. "I've never underestimated this." He dropped to his knees, wrapped his arms around her and treated her to a kiss that nearly melted the soles of her slippers.

"You don't fight fair," she protested breathlessly.

"When I can help it, I don't fight at all." He sat back on his heels, cradled her face between his hands, and said, "We have problems, Charity. Some are big problems, some are small problems, and a lot are of indeterminate size. During this next week, I'll discuss each and every one of them with you, but I will not discuss any of them until this tour is officially over."

"And that last statement is one of our major problems!" Charity exclaimed as she pushed back her chair and moved away from him, determined to state what was on her mind without him physically deterring her. "Time and again you've accused me of holding things inside—not getting my feelings out in the open. Yet when I try to do that, you stop me. It's driving me crazy, Shane. Absolutely, bats-in-the-belfry crazy!"

He raked his fingers through his hair as her accusation hit home. It was true. He was constantly challenging her to express her feelings, and now that she was trying to do it, he was demanding she not do so. When had he begun to make two sets of rules? When those rules had started interfering with what he wanted.

"You're right, and I'm sorry. I do want you to express yourself, and I want to know exactly what you're feeling, but quite frankly, I'm not up to handling that kind of pressure before a concert. It takes all my mental and physical energy to perform, Charity, and if I deplete that energy in a discussion with you this morning, I won't perform worth a damn tonight. Can you understand that?"

"Yes," she responded morosely as she leaned her head against the window and stared out at the mountains. "I just feel as if I'm treading in deep water, and I'm getting tired of trying to stay afloat. Does that make sense?"

"Yes," he answered with a resigned sigh. "I guess the only solution we have at this moment is to compromise. How about if you give me a list of the problems you're worried about. I'll think about them and be prepared to discuss them tomorrow. You aren't on call tomorrow, are you?"

"No," she replied. "I collected on all those calls owed me. I'm yours tomorrow and every night this coming week."

"I appreciate that." He stood, resettled himself in his chair and took a healthy swig of coffee, realizing that it was essential that he be fully awake and hoping the caffeine would accomplish the task. "Okay, you can lay the list on me. Tell me what you think our problems are in this relationship."

"Besides the obvious?"

"Don't assume anything is obvious. Give me a clear-cut, unadulterated list, and I'll sort through it from there."

"I'm a morning person and you're a night person."

"Right."

"You're an optimist and I'm a pragmatist."

"I'll think on that one."

"You're a liberal and I'm so conservative that you can see me coming from a mile away."

"I'll think on that one, too."

"You're talented, Shane," she stated, turning to face him with tears in her eyes. "You have the world by the tail, and I can barely hold on to the tip of that tail."

"I'd say you're holding on pretty well, but we'll discuss that in further detail after we've handled the first three problems."

Charity drew in her breath and rubbed her temples, trying to sort through her scattered thoughts. She couldn't seem to keep any problem in place when he was facing her. Only when he was gone could she see things clearly.

"You confuse me when you're with me," she told him.

He arched a brow at that one. "You confuse me, too."

"I can't get the right words out when you're sitting right in front of me."

"So write them down on paper."

"You also oversimplify everything! You say, 'Charity, cry,' and I'm supposed to cry. 'Charity, talk,' and I'm supposed to talk. 'Charity, ignore the problems until I say it's time to face them,' and I'm supposed to ignore them. Shane, I'm much more complex than that."

"Is that your complete list?"

"No." She turned back to the window and scrawled his name across the fog her breath had made. "Personally we're ill-suited. We have very little in common. Professionally we're even worse. You're a musician who's built himself a kingdom in the stars, and I can't compete with your adulating followers."

"I've never asked you to compete with anyone, Charity. All I've ever asked is that you be what you're capable of being, and I have to disagree when you say we have nothing in common. I say we have a lot in common."

She spun around to face him. "Like what?"

"I love you and you love me. We're good in bed together, and we're even better outside of bed. We balance each other, Charity. You give me the reality that's absent from my life. You make me face all the mundane little chores that make life what it is. And in return I give you the dreams. I take you through the heavens, introduce you to the gods, and I show you the way to the pot of gold at the end of the rainbow. You need my fantasy as much as I need your reality. Together we're an unbeatable team."

"When we can be together," she stated sarcastically.

"And that is the one big problem that we both have to work on. All I ask is that you give us a chance. Don't walk away until we're both convinced that our differences can't be solved. I promise you that if we reach that point, I'll walk away without a complaint, but I'll only make that promise if you'll promise to fight until there is no logical compromise to whatever lies in our path. Will you do that, Charity? Will you give our love that much of a chance?"

"I'll try," she whispered. "I really will try."

"That's all I'm asking of you," he answered.

Charity shifted from one foot to the other as the crowd in the concert hall continued to roar. She frowned as she watched Shane and Derek in consultation with an electrician. Everything had been fine during rehearsal, but now the equipment had developed some kind of electronic glitch, and until it was fixed, the show wouldn't begin.

When Mac, the drummer, laid his hand on her shoulder, she started, surprised. He grinned through his full beard and shook his head. "Why be so jumpy, Charity?"

"I'm not used to all this noise."

"The crowd is a little more rambunctious tonight than normal, but that always happens when a show has to be delayed. They'll calm down as soon as the curtain goes up."

"*If* it goes up," she responded doubtfully.

"It'll go up."

Charity nodded, though she remained doubtful. She couldn't imagine what would happen if they had to cancel the show. She'd watched Shane and Derek fight their way through the crowd tonight, and she was sure that if they had to make their way back out without performing, they'd be in mortal danger.

She closed her eyes and sighed, trying desperately to shut out the noise of the crowd. For one brief moment she saw a flash of her and Shane at the cabin. It was so peaceful there. So quiet. At the cabin all their problems would be nonexistent. They would be nothing more than two people in love. She longed to walk across the stage, grab his arm and drag him away to the cabin. Then she opened her eyes just as Shane rose, smiled and gave her the thumbs-up sign from the darkened stage. The glitch had been fixed.

Shane pulled his guitar strap over his head, positioned himself in the center of the stage and threw her a kiss just as the lights went on. And then he and Derek burst into a song that couldn't possibly have been heard over the crowd's resounding roar, which literally shook the rafters.

By the time Shane and Derek started the second song the crowd had quieted, but as Charity watched them from her position backstage, she realized the fans were still unsettled, and that restlessness didn't decrease as the show progressed.

When Shane rushed off stage during Derek's solo, he grabbed Charity around the waist, gave her a hungry kiss and then released her as he ran toward the dressing room to change.

Charity followed him, ignoring Roger's disapproving frown when she stepped into the room.

"Shane, I'm worried about the crowd," she told him. "They seem so... hyped up."

He glanced up with a smile as he stripped off his shirt and pulled on a glittering sequined silver one that was open almost to his navel and had blouson sleeves. Then he slipped into a black leather vest that matched his pants, and turned up the collar of his shirt. When he was done he looked like an eighteenth-century pirate.

"They worked up a lot of adrenaline during the delay, but they'll get it out of their systems. There's nothing to worry about."

Despite his words, Charity wasn't reassured. He gave her another quick kiss and then raced back toward stage, ready to take over when Derek finished his song.

"Everything is going to be all right, Charity," Roger said as he took her arm and began following Shane. "They've handled this kind of crowd before."

Roger had barely uttered the words when there was a sudden roar from the crowd, and Shane threw his guitar to the floor and rushed out on stage.

"My God, what happened?" Charity exclaimed in alarm as she began running toward the curtain.

She gasped in disbelief at the scene that confronted her. Shane was trying to pull a young girl away from Derek, and all pandemonium had broken loose in the concert hall. The crowd had gone crazy and was moving toward the stage in a massive human wave. The security guards were trying to control them, but outnumbered fifty to one, they didn't have a chance.

The band had joined Shane and helped him free Derek from the girl, and then they formed a human barrier between the two entertainers as they pushed at fans that were beginning to flow up on the stage.

Charity couldn't move as she watched everything happening around her, and she became caught up in the wave of people who flooded up the stairs to the stage, pushing and screaming and fighting. She was slammed against the wall and gasped as her head collided with it. Dazed, she tried to orient herself as she was caught up once again in the moving crowd. She finally managed to break loose to huddle in a corner, trembling in terror.

Then, almost as suddenly as it had begun, the riot ended as police officers poured into the building.

"Are you all right?" one young officer asked her a short time later as he knelt in front of her and hesitantly touched her arm.

All right? Charity repeated silently. No, she wasn't all right, and wasn't sure she ever would be again.

"Here, let me help you," he said as he took her elbow and pulled her to her feet.

Charity was shaky when she first stood, and her head was spinning, but then her vision cleared and she smiled gratefully at the young man who was regarding her in concern.

He led her toward the stairs and out into the auditorium. "The paramedics are on their way. You'd better let them take a look at the bump on your forehead."

"I'll do that," Charity said as she gingerly touched the spot where she'd hit her head.

The officer nodded and moved on. Charity's stomach churned as she let her gaze move around the room, unable to assimilate the number of injured victims. Close by, a young girl sat in a chair, crying and holding her arm. Charity could tell, from the awkward angle, that it was broken. Not far behind her a young man was sitting in the middle of an aisle, his hands over his face and blood covering his shirt. And there were so many others beyond them.

Stunned by the scene, Charity could only stand and stare. It was only when the wail of sirens penetrated her mind that she was snapped into action, and she hurried toward the girl, yelling at the young officer who had helped her, "I'm a doctor. Tell the paramedics to set up a triage area and then call the hospital and alert the emergency room that they need to round up every doctor they can."

The officer nodded and headed toward the entrance, where the ambulances were already arriving.

Shane was frantic with worry over Charity and furious that Roger refused to let him out of the dressing room.

"Roger, get out of my way—right now!"

"Dammit, Shane, you can't go out there! That crowd will rip you to pieces! I'll go find Charity."

"No! Charity is my responsibility, and I'm going to go find her. Now, open the door, Roger, or I assure you that Derek is not going to be the only injured person in this room."

Roger looked as if he still might refuse, and Shane curled his hand into a fist at his side. Friend or no friend, he'd knock Roger's teeth right down his throat if he continued to stand between him and the door.

Thankfully, the tension was removed when there was a solid knock at the door. Roger opened it to find six burly security guards standing on the other side.

He glanced back at Shane and gave a resigned nod. "Go out there and find her, but take four of these guards with you."

"Right," Shane said as he stepped out of the dressing room, motioning for the guards to follow.

What he found when he entered the auditorium both stunned and sickened him. Police officers and paramedics moved through the room, assisting injured people. Nearby, two paramedics were carefully lifting a young girl onto a stretcher.

Automatically, Shane moved toward her. "What's wrong with her?"

One young man glanced up, his eyes widening slightly in recognition. "A possible back injury, Mr. Burke."

. "A serious one?"

The young man shrugged. "We won't know until we get her to the hospital."

The girl's eyes were closed tightly, and she was crying softly. Shane reached out and gently brushed her hair away from her face.

"What's your name, sweetheart?"

The girl's eyes opened, and she gasped in disbelief.

Shane chuckled and tapped his finger against her nose. "If you don't tell me your name, I can't possibly send you flowers, can I?"

"Flowers?" she repeated. "You want to send me flowers?"

"You bet."

"My name's Megan. Megan Jones."

Shane nodded. "A beautiful name for a beautiful girl, and I'll make sure you get the most beautiful bouquet in town. Now, you do whatever these people tell you to do. Got that?"

"Yes," she whispered in an awed voice.

Shane lifted her hand and gave it a fond squeeze before returning his attention to the paramedic. "I'm looking for Dr. Charity Wells. Do you happen to know her?"

"Sure," the paramedic responded. "Every paramedic in town knows Charity." He glanced toward the back of the auditorium, where a large group of people were gathered. "She's up there working triage."

Shane sighed in relief. Thank God she was all right.

He once again motioned for the guards to follow as he made his way toward the back of the auditorium, stopping several times along the way to speak to an injured fan and give an encouraging word. When he finally came close to the group of people, he spotted Charity and released another relieved sigh.

For several minutes he just stood watching her as she examined patient after patient, giving quick, quiet instructions to the paramedics before turning to the next patient. He felt proud of her and in awe of her. She was more than any man could want, and much more than he could have ever hoped to deserve.

When there was a lull in the stream of patients, he stepped forward and touched her shoulder.

She spun toward him in surprise, and he frowned at the lump on her head, which was already turning purple. But when he reached out to gently touch her injury, she flinched.

Not sure what was happening, Shane cleared his throat uncomfortably and asked, "What can I do to help?"

"Help?" she repeated, her eyes flashing angrily. She flung one arm out toward the auditorium, and said, "Look around you. Don't you think you've done enough?"

He opened his mouth to deny her accusation but closed it as his gaze shifted to the paramedics bringing another patient up the aisle on a stretcher. This wasn't his fault, he wanted to say, but indirectly it was. This had happened because of who and what he was, and as she'd said in Kansas City, she was the one picking up the pieces. She was right. He had done enough, and the best thing for both of them would be if he got out of the auditorium and out of her life.

"Take care of your patients," he stated woodenly as he turned on his heel and walked away.

Charity stared after him, wanting to grab the words back and run after him. The hurt that had flared into his eyes at her unjust accusation had lanced through her. Why had she even said those damning words? She hadn't meant them. She supposed they'd been spoken under the pressure of the moment and, if she was truthful with herself, because of the relief of seeing that he was all right.

She took a step forward, determined to catch him and explain that worry and relief had combined and been released in an angry outburst, but she stopped when a paramedic called her name. She was torn between running after Shane and taking care of the patient on the floor in front of her. But as she looked at the young man, who was having difficulty breathing, she knew where her allegiance belonged, and she knelt on the floor to examine his ribs. Her explanation to Shane would have to wait until later.

Chapter Fifteen

Charity didn't know how many hours had passed since the riot started. She also had no recollection of how she'd ended up in the emergency room. But she had, and as she stripped off her stained white coat and tossed it into the laundry bin, she felt exhausted and brilliantly alive.

For one flash of a moment she'd experienced the fear when she'd walked through the doors, but she'd been needed, and she'd ignored it. Her medical instincts were too strong. Nothing could stop her from doing what she was destined to do.

"So, when are you coming back to work?" asked Walter Scott, another member of the emergency-room staff. He threw his coat in with hers, wrapped an arm around her shoulders and led her toward the doctors' lounge.

"I still have a month at the clinic," she answered, gratefully accepting the steaming cup of coffee he handed to her.

"I suppose we can continue to cover for you for another month." He dropped down on the sofa, lifted his feet to the table in front of him and regarded her curiously. "I was afraid you'd never come back."

"Join the club," she murmured, settling into the chair across from him. "In fact, until tonight I was certain I wouldn't."

"Thank God you were at the concert. Surgery will be working around the clock, but a lot of those victims wouldn't have survived if you hadn't been there to determine which people were in immediate danger. By the way, Derek Halston was admitted. He has three broken ribs and a nasty laceration that required plastic surgery. He's in room 420, if you want to look in on him."

Charity immediately rose to her feet. "Thanks. I do want to look in on him."

When she reached the fourth floor, she waved to the nurses on duty and moved toward Derek's room. She stopped as she watched Shane and Roger exit, uncertain how to approach them after what she'd said to Shane in the auditorium.

Roger gave her a hesitant smile. Shane seemed to look through her. She parted her lips to speak, but he turned his back on her, said something quietly to Roger and then walked back into Derek's room.

After he was gone, Roger awkwardly approached her. "Shane said to give you this. He said you wouldn't have to worry about the toothpaste anymore."

Tears welled into Charity's eyes as she accepted the key to her home. It was over—finished. She'd never see him again. She blinked back the tears, tucked the key into her pocket, and turned and walked back to the elevators. Tonight she'd regained her career, and in the process she'd lost the man she loved.

It was for the best, she told herself as she pushed the button that would take her to the lobby floor. So why did it feel as if her heart had just been ripped out of her chest?

Nothing could compare to sunrise in the Rocky Mountains. That's why Charity had loaded Mister into the car and

headed toward Cripple Creek and her cabin in the middle of
the night.

She pulled her car to the edge of the dirt road, climbed out
and stuffed her hands into the pockets of her parka as the
beautiful golden sun eased its way over the far peaks.

Jim had been right to encourage her to come up here before she started back to work at the emergency room. She
didn't relish facing the memories of Shane that would hover
in the cabin, and yet it seemed appropriate that she do so
since she was putting the rest of her life in order.

Her gaze dropped to a small herd of deer that exited the
trees and moved toward the stream that flowed in the gully
below her. She smiled as she watched a fawn enter the
meadow, its legs still weak and wobbly. Winter had been
harsh, but the strong survived, and in the past few months
she'd learned that she was one of the strong.

Mister yapped, insisting that he be released from the car
and she laughed, slid in behind the steering wheel and said
"When we reach the cabin."

Another half hour passed before she pulled up in front of
the cabin. Mister bounded across her lap and out the door
heading for the stand of trees, swaying to wade through the
few snowdrifts that still covered the ground.

Charity chuckled, climbed from the car, and pulled her
suitcase from the trunk. Then she climbed the stairs and
unlocked the front door.

The inside of the cabin was dark in contrast to the brilliant glow of the newly risen sun, and she hesitated for a
moment to let her eyes adjust.

She let out a scream when Shane's voice drawled, "It's
damn cold in here. Unless you were born in a barn, close the
door!"

Her suitcase clattered as it hit the floor, and she took another step inside, whispering, "Shane?" in disbelief.

He was sitting Indian-fashion on the bed, dressed in the
same clothes he'd been wearing when she'd rescued him

three months before. "I'm real, and I'm cold. Close the door, Charity."

She did so, then leaned against the door. "What are you doing here?"

"The same thing you are. I'm taking a vacation."

"In my cabin?"

"Actually, in mine, but I went out for a jog, ended up here and decided to stop in and raid the cupboards," he said, his eyes moving over her hungrily.

"You've lost weight," she whispered, eyeing him just as hungrily.

"So have you, and you don't have any weight to lose."

"Actually, I'm at my ideal weight."

"Actually, I'd like to see you a little over it."

They stared at each other silently, not certain where to go from there. Charity wanted to discover what had happened to him since the night of the concert, but she didn't know how to open the conversation.

Evidently, Shane read her mind. "Derek is still recuperating, so I've been given a couple of months off and have been living up here. Your brother said you're going back to work in the emergency room."

"You've talked to Jim?"

He laughed ruefully. "Why do you think he insisted you come up here?"

"This was a setup?"

He nodded.

She laced her fingers together nervously. "Why?"

He rose from the bed and put his hands into his back pockets. "I'll interpret that to mean why did we set you up." When she nodded, he said, "Because I'm not ready to let you go. You promised me a week, and I didn't get it."

"You didn't get it because you left."

"True," he acknowledged. "I've done a lot of foolish things in my life, and that was one of them."

She drew in a deep breath and let it out slowly. "Nothing's changed. We're still basically incompatible."

He nodded and walked toward the fireplace, staring up at the sand paintings. "If we're incompatible, why do I feel so damn lost?" When she didn't answer, he turned toward her and said, "I've stopped squeezing the toothpaste in the middle."

Tears filled her eyes, and she smiled weakly. "It really is a wasteful habit."

"I love you."

"And I love you," she whispered, "but I just can't see a future for us. It's not the toothpaste, Shane. It's just that we're so different. Maintaining a relationship is hard enough when two people like the same things and believe in the same things. When they don't, it's impossible."

"Just like you and Carson?" he challenged.

"That's not fair. It wasn't incompatibility that came between me and Carson."

"No, it was careers. And that's really what's happening here, isn't it? It's my career. If I were anyone but Shane Burke of Moon and Sun, I'd be worth taking a chance on. You'd overlook a lot of those so-called incompatibilities."

"Yes," Charity admitted. "Who you are does enter into this. I need a husband full-time, Shane. I can't be satisfied being flown in to see you whenever I have a day or two off, nor can you take the physical strain of flying to Denver."

"So we say goodbye?"

"Do you see any other alternative?"

"No, but you're not helping me look for one. A relationship consists of two people, Charity. When they can't blend, they compromise. Can you honestly say that you've ever compromised with me?"

She didn't answer. Instead, she joined him at the fireplace and stared at the sand paintings over the mantel. Lovingly, she moved her gaze over each and every one of them, willing them to talk to her. It was several moments before she realized that they were talking, giving her her answers, and she'd been too wrapped up in her own emotions to listen.

Carefully, she surveyed each picture again. They showed harmony with nature, and more than half contained images of the moon and the sun. In order to reach harmony, one had to let things follow their natural course. She and Shane had to follow their careers, but there was a compromise that would allow them to do so and still have each other—at least on an acceptable part-time basis.

She turned toward him. He was no more than three steps away, and his eyes were filled with a mixture of love, yearning and regret.

"Shane, how much are you willing to compromise?"

He shrugged uneasily. "As much as I can without giving up what I am. I can't give up the performing side of my life, Charity. Not yet. I need it."

"I know that, but as an emergency-room physician, I'll work twelve-hour days, seven days a week. Then I'll have an entire week off."

He looked confused. "And?"

"And I have trouble facing your world, Shane. I can't leap from hotel to hotel and wade through thousands of screaming fans. At least I can't do it on a daily basis. I'm a homebody who loves her privacy. However, if you could adjust your schedule, we might be able to make this work."

His eyes lit with understanding. "I could be on tour, record and make my special appearances the weeks that you're working and be home during the weeks you're off."

"Basically," she agreed. "I realize that there will be times when either we'll have to be separated or I'll have to follow you on the road. I can handle being married to a famous rock star on a part-time basis as long as I know that when he's at home, he's all mine."

For the first time, he touched her. His fingers skimmed along her cheek, and lingered against her jaw. "I'll be yours at home or away, Charity, and I can guarantee that."

She reached up to catch his hand, and she brought his fingers to her lips. "I'm still going to be a morning person, and we're still going to drive each other crazy."

"A little craziness is good for a marriage. It keeps the sparks flying so you can have all that fun making up."

She tilted her head thoughtfully to the side, her lips twitching. "You know, it's funny, but I still don't remember your ever asking me to marry you, and I certainly don't remember agreeing. Since you seem so intent on taking me for granted, you might have to work hard to convince me to say yes."

"Then I guess I'd better start convincing you," he said, grinning as he caught her and swung her up into his arms.

Charity smiled as he carried her to the bed, and when he came down over her, Charity knew that whether her moon was rising or setting, Shane's sun would always be there to welcome her.

* * * * *

Silhouette Intimate Moments

PARRIS AFTON BONDS
The Cowboy and The Lady

Marianna McKenna was used to bright lights, big cities and the glamorous life of a Hollywood star, so it came as quite a shock when she found herself living at the Mescalero Cattle Company, victim of a tragic mistake and a convict sentenced to work on the ranch for the next six months.

Tom Malcolm was a true cowboy, rugged and plainspoken, and he didn't have much use for hothouse flowers like Marianna McKenna. Or so he told himself, at least, though that didn't stop the yearning in his heart—or the fire in his blood.

Look for Tom and Marianna's story in *That McKenna Woman* IM#241, Book One of Parris Afton Bonds's Mescalero Trilogy, available this month only from Silhouette Intimate Moments. Then watch for Book Two, *That Malcolm Girl* (September 1988), and Book Three, *That Mescalero Man* (December 1988), to complete a trilogy as untamed and compelling as the American West itself.

IM241

Silhouette Special Edition

COMING NEXT MONTH

#463 DANCE TO THE PIPER—Nora Roberts
When cheery Maddy O'Hurley (triplet number two of THE O'HURLEYS!)
scattered sunshine and color at cynic Reed Valentine, both were dizzied by the
kaleidoscope of emotions that began to swirl around them.

#464 AMARILLO BY MORNING—Bay Matthews
Chasing shiny city dreams, Amarillo Corbett tried to forget gritty Russ
Wheeler. But rodeo Russ kept bucking Amy's objections, refused to be thrown,
and vowed to hold on—forever.

#465 SILENCE THE SHADOWS—Christine Flynn
Pregnant, widowed and nearly bankrupt, Megan Reese had problems. Financial
wizard David Elliott offered assistance, but could he rightfully offer his heart to
his late best friend's wife?

#466 BORROWED TIME—Janice Kaiser
On the eve of Stephanie Burnham's wedding, tragedy struck, and the medical
profession abandoned hope for her fiancée. She found solace in compassionate
neurosurgeon Peter Canfield—until compassion evolved into something
more....

#467 HURRICANE FORCE—Lisa Jackson
Amid a hurricane and a storm of accusations, Cord Donahue had sailed away.
Heartbroken, Alison banning believed him dead. But now prodigal Cord was
back, accusing *her* of *his* crimes . . . and demanding sweet vengeance.

#468 WHERE ANGELS FEAR—Ginna Gray
When her twin tied the knot, Elise knew marriage was in *her* cards, too. But
could she accept intimidating Sam Lawford's chilly proposal? Find out in this
companion edition to *Fools Rush In* (#416).

AVAILABLE THIS MONTH:

#457 BEGUILING WAYS
Lynda Trent

#458 SUMMER SHADOWS
Pat Warren

#459 A DIFFERENT DRUMMER
Maggi Charles

#460 MOON AND SUN
Allyson Ryan

#461 INTENSIVE CARE
Carole Halston

#462 PROMISES
Mary Alice Kirk

Silhouette Special Edition

THE O'HURLEYS! — MADDY'S STORY

from
Nora Roberts

Dance To The Piper

Available July 1988

The second in an exciting new series about the lives and
loves of triplet sisters—

If *The Last Honest Woman* (SE #451) captured your
heart in May, you're sure to want to read about Maddy
and Chantel, Abby's two sisters.

In *Dance to the Piper* (SE #463), it takes some very
fancy footwork to get reserved recording mogul Reed
Valentine dancing to effervescent Maddy's tune....

Then, in *Skin Deep* (SE #475), find out what kind of
heat it takes to melt the glamorous Chantel's icy heart.
Available in September.

THE O'HURLEYS!

**Join the excitement of
Silhouette Special Editions.**